Mitchell Symons was e[...]
After working at BBC TV as a researcher and director,
he co-wrote early British editions of Trivial Pursuit
before becoming a full-time journalist and writer. He
has a regular column in the *Express* and he has devised
many print and television formats. He has written
twenty-three non-fiction books and one previous novel,
*All In*. He lives with his wife and two sons on the coast
in Sussex.

Praise for *All In*:

'His dialogue is convincing, he has a good sense of how
to structure a story and he writes with zest and panache'
*Daily Telegraph*

'Compelling . . . an edgy switchback ride to the outer
limits of the male psyche. *The Dice Man* goes *Trainspotting* and the hardest drug is adrenaline. A gut-
wrenching climax tops off a stylish debut'
*Daily Express*

'An entertainingly, darkly funny novel that is strangely
moving at the end' *The Times*

'A superb new book . . . often bitingly funny, and writer
Mitchell Symons speaks the punter's language fluently
and with style' *Mirror*

'The novel's diary format keeps the plot ticking along
briskly, and the characters . . . ring remarkably true . . .
if you know your way round a betting slip or the green
baize, *All In* is a must for your bookshelves' *FHM*

*Also by Mitchell Symons*

All In

To Gilly & Jim,
with love glove

*[signature]*

# THE£

# LOT

Mitchell Symons

**headline**

First published in 2002
by HEADLINE BOOK PUBLISHING

A HEADLINE paperback

10 9 8 7 6 5 4 3 2 1

ISBN 0 7472 7390 1

Typeset in Meridian by
Letterpart Limited, Reigate, Surrey

Printed and bound in Great Britain by
Clays Ltd, St Ives plc

HEADLINE BOOK PUBLISHING
A division of Hodder Headline
338 Euston Road
LONDON NW1 3BH

www.headline.co.uk
www.hodderheadline.com

To Penny, Jack and Charlie.
My three favourite people.
No question.

All the characters in this book are made up and any resemblance to anyone living or dead is purely coincidental. In particular, the names of all the Beatles tribute bands are made up – the author having gone to great trouble to check that there are no real bands of the same name. However, there are so many such bands that if, inadvertently, I've replicated a name, then please accept that it was purely an accident and anything said about the band of that name only applies to the band in the book.

In other words, let it be.

# CHAPTER ONE

Until I met Gaby, the longest I ever lived with a woman was forty-eight hours – and that was only because I put my back out. I'm telling you this not to brag about how shallow I am – nor, indeed, to demonstrate just how much Gaby means to me – but because it shows what can happen in one year.

Twelve months ago, I was miserable and skint. Now I've met the mother of my child and I'm a millionaire. And, no, I didn't win the lottery.

This probably reads like one of those ads you see in *Exchange & Mart*: *'I'm David Marriott. I used to be heavily in debt until I discovered WHAT-A-FUCKING-BRILLIANT-SCAM. Now I have two homes and drive a Mercedes. My only problem is whether to holiday in the Bahamas or the Maldives. Send an s.a.e. for full details of how YOU too can have an enviable life like mine.'*

Except I'm not selling anything, and besides, what happened to me is unique – so extraordinary – that it would be impossible to sell it to anyone.

See, it was all down to luck.

Luck is where opportunity meets preparation – I'll give you that one for free. But I can't sell you luck, and even if I could, I wouldn't. At the moment, I need as much of it as possible for myself.

It's never easy to know where to start a story. I could begin on that glorious day in 1985 when I played *Trivial Pursuit* for the first time and realised that the fund of trivial information I'd built up over seventeen years wasn't totally worthless. This led eventually to my first regular newspaper column, the TOTALLY TRIVIAL TRIVIA CHALLENGE in which I shared 'amazing' facts with the readers like . . .

- There are only two words in the English language ending in -gry: *hungry* and *angry*
- John Wayne once won the film star the dog Lassie from its owner in a poker game
- The strongest muscle in the body is the tongue
- Charlton Heston's mother's maiden name was *Charlton*
- French Fries originated in Belgium, not France

Instead, I'll start it just over a year ago when I was sharing a flat in Kilburn, North London, with Peter Franklin and, briefly, a guy named Chris whose surname I now forget. The flat was tiny and horrible – even grottier than the one Peter and I later shared with my mate Ziggy – but it was better than moving back home to my parents house in Wembley. I mean, thirty-three's a bit old to be sharing mealtimes with Mummy and Daddy, though I can't pretend I wasn't tempted – especially after eating beans on toast for the fifth day running. Reason I was so boracic was because my TOTALLY TRIVIAL TRIVIA CHALLENGE had finally been given the heave-ho by Kirsty the Cow, the features editor, on the grounds that 'trivia is so passe'. Yeah, well maybe it was but then so is lipstick lesbianism. Not that I had any proof of KtC's Sapphic inclinations but she'd been an absolute bitch and she'd made it clear that she didn't fancy me so I'd taken that as prima facie evidence.

Fact was, by the late 1990s, trivia had died. Or at least the fashion for it had. To judge from my postbag – although people only ever wrote in to point out mistakes that they thought I had made – the readers were still interested, but that didn't count with KtC, who was so obsessed with being fashionable that she would never agree to a feature idea unless it had previously been road-tested elsewhere. Originality passed her by – whoosh – went right over her head. All that mattered to her was not getting it wrong.

KtC was sussed out in the end – last heard of doing the PR for a handbag company that wasn't Prada, which was ironic since almost every article she had ever commissioned seemed to contain the words '*I'd rather die than live without my Prada bag*', but, by that time, I had long gone.

So there I was, sitting in the grotty kitchen of that wretched flat in Kilburn, working out just how I was going to make some tiny chore like going to the post office to buy a stamp last all day – you do that when you're unemployed: it's the opposite to that saying, 'if you want something done, ask the busiest person in the room' – when Peter walked in.

'Sorry 'bout waking you, man,' he said, employing his customary mode of address which was only – what? – a quarter of a century out of date.

'Don't worry about it. You only got me up three hours earlier than I needed to be.'

'Sorry, man. Just that I had to, like, practise.'

'Yeah, so I heard. What was that noise? It sounded like a cat being anally penetrated.'

'It's a sitar,' he said with boyish pride. 'I'm teaching myself. The idea is for me to be able to play "Within You, Without You".' He began to sing but I interrupted him, not because he's got a bad voice but because 11 a.m. is too early to listen to dirges.

'See, like, at the moment I do "Here Comes the Sun" and I sing "Something" but I want to, like, broaden my repertoire – 'specially as there's a kind of revival thing going for *Pepper* and that.'

I should explain at this point that Peter is the

late, great George Harrison. Well, he isn't, he's
Peter Franklin. But he 'plays' Beatle George in this
tribute band called the Best Beatles – which is a
boast as there are loads of Beatles bands and, as
he's often obliged to explain, has nothing to do
with Pete Best, Ringo's predecessor as the Beatles'
drummer.

'I mean,' he continued, 'I'm a much better
singer than John [who 'is' Paul McCartney which
is *very* confusing] and I play the guitar twice as well
as Roy [John Lennon].'

Something I've noticed about Peter is that, just
like a stutterer will lose his stutter when he's
angry, so too does Peter ditch that 'heavy, man'
accent when he's making a big point. Ah, the
benefits of a Winchester education – although
Peter goes mad when I remind him of it.

Meanwhile, there was something much more
important to let him know. 'If I'd got up at two, as
I'd intended, I could've done without breakfast. As
it is . . .'

'Yeah, well.' He looked down at the newspaper
he was clutching. 'Hey,' he said, 'dig this.' He
passed me the paper, which was open on the
familiar *Creative & Media* pages. I looked for the ad
he wanted me to 'dig' without much enthusiasm
since – as he well knew – I had made upwards of
two hundred applications for jobs advertised there
without even so much as an interview.

Sounds corny, but when I actually saw the ad,

my heart leapt. Even to this day, I can still remember what it said:

Which members of *The Magnificent Seven* made it to freedom in *The Great Escape*?

If I'm stuck in the middle with you, who or what are to the left of us?

How many months of the year have 28 days?

Give us a ring and if you can answer these (and three more) questions correctly, you could be a full-time question writer on a ground-breaking new TV show.

I phoned the number in the ad and found myself talking to someone called Melanie at Sparkle Productions.

I couldn't wait to give her my answers. 'Hi, the first one is two. James Coburn on a bicycle and Charles Bronson in a rowing boat with John Leyton. Who used to be a pop star. And did you know that Charles Bronson was one of fifteen children?'

I rushed on – 'The answer to the second is "clowns". It's taken from the 1973 Stealer's Wheel song "Stuck in The Middle With You".' I can't promise that, at this point, I didn't actually sing the song. 'Gerry Rafferty was on vocals. He used to be in a folk group with Billy Connolly. The song was revived for the film *Reservoir Dogs*.'

I gulped in air.

'Third is all twelve. Every month has twenty-eight days. It's a trick question: you're expecting people to say "February", aren't you?'

Melanie confirmed that they were and that I had successfully answered all three questions. She then asked me the promised other three:

- How many of Snow White's seven dwarfs had a name which *didn't* end in a 'y'?
- In a game of darts, what is the lowest score you *can't* achieve with just one dart?
- If it takes three cats three minutes to catch three mice, how many minutes does it take thirty cats to catch thirty mice?

Once again I answered correctly: Two – Bashful and Doc, twenty-three, and three minutes.

When was I free? When was I *free*? Well, today I was taking a video back to the shop, tomorrow I was having my hair cut, Wednesday I was indeed planning to buy a stamp at the post office ... Fortunately, I ran through all these important plans in my own mind so that after breaking away from the gravitational pull of the Planet Unemployment, I was able to reply, 'Now!'

Forty minutes later, I was sitting in the less-than-plush waiting-room of Sparkle Productions. In those days, before the success of *The Lot*, they were above two shops, a sandwich bar and a rip-off ticket agency, in a narrow road off Cambridge Circus. Still,

I didn't mind. This was *telly* – my one shot at the big time – and I couldn't have been more excited.

A nerdy-looking guy walked out of a door towards what passed for Reception and I heard a voice shout, 'Next!' In my eagerness to get there quickly, I managed to fall over a coffee table, which meant that the first time I met Michael Andrews, I was on my knees. Which wasn't, as I was to discover, at all inappropriate.

Funny thing was, the first time I met Andrews, I actually liked him! Obviously, I didn't know him then but he couldn't have been much nicer: he was Charlie Charm himself. Back then I didn't know that he could turn it on or off at will: I just assumed he was always like that. He does have the ability – some say it's his only ability – to make someone feel special, but that can dissipate faster than candy floss in a hurricane the second he doesn't need you, even if he's going to need you again in ten minutes. It's like being with Mr Hyde and Mr Hyde.

But then, like I say, he was friendlier than an insurance salesman working solely on commission.

'Melanie tells me that you scored one hundred per cent on our little quiz.' I couldn't quite place his accent: was it Geordie? I later learned that he grew up in South Africa but moved to Swansea with his family when he was thirteen.

I tried to look proud, modest and professional all at the same time but succeeded only in giving him that leering face Harry Enfield used to do in the titles of his TV show.

'She also tells me that you were able to give her plenty of information besides.'

'Well, I like to think that—'

He cut across me, but at the time I inferred it as an act of charity, that he was rescuing me from saying something stupid. 'Yes, I like that.'

Suddenly he jumped up, which in my nervous state alarmed me, but also surprised me because I could see just how tiny he was. Sitting down, he looked, I don't know, *normal*. I later learned about his £200 special height-raising cushion handmade in Italy. Standing up, he was at best five foot two. Wound up as I was, Michael J. Fox's Emmy-acceptance speech, 'You made me feel five foot tall' sprang into my mind and it was all I could do to push the words from my throat to my stomach.

Now there was another problem. With his head below my eyeline, I could see the burgundy-coloured birthmark on his bald patch. I tried to look somewhere else, anywhere else – but my eyes were inexorably drawn to his cranium and what looked like a poorly drawn sketch of an old VW Beetle. Then I noticed that he had stopped speaking. He was checking out my reactions to his height and to his birthmark. This was obviously a test – and I was failing it!

Just as I was going through an agony of indecision over whether to acknowledge his very obvious distinguishing feature or not, he clapped his hands and smiled. 'Let me tell you about the game-show.'

He then sat down again while I breathed several surreptitious sighs of relief. Later I realised that, far from doing my prospects any harm, it was my very squirming that had got me the job: Andrews likes to wrong-foot people.

And so it was that he took me through what was then called *Money! Money! Money!*. Now, of course, you'll be familiar with the basic format but I have to say that, back then, listening to him talking about the millions of calls and hundreds of thousands of pounds, I thought he was loopy. Not that I told him so, discretion being the better part of saying goodbye to the dole.

Eventually, Andrews came to my role in the show. I was to be one of what he called the 'Big Three'. Along with two guys he named as Frank and Simon, I was to be responsible for all of the show's questions. In addition, we'd all have to – and I remember him putting his chubby fingers which were clad in lots of rings to his thick-lipped mouth as he said it – 'taste' each other's work for accuracy and for suitability.

'Fine,' I said, as I would have done even if he'd told me that the job entailed munching each other's bogeys. 'That sounds great.'

'Before I give you the job,' he said smoothly, 'I want you to tell me a little more about yourself.'

'Well, you've got my CV.' I indicated the piece of paper that I had put on his desk when I'd walked in. He hadn't so much as glanced at it.

He smiled at me in what I took to be a gesture of kindness rather than the sneer it undoubtedly was. 'I'd rather hear it from the horse's mouth, so to speak.'

'Well, I'm thirty-three. I went to public school in Harrow.'

'Ah, so you're an Old Harrovian?'

'No, no. I went to John Lyon. It's like the day school for Harrow.'

He put his fingertips together and once again I was dazzled by his collection of rings. 'Continue.'

'I went to Bristol University where I studied Philosophy.'

Once again, he smiled. 'How very useful.'

'Then I freelanced for a couple of years, trying to break into the media, did a lot of freelance work before I got the job of writing THE TOTALLY TRIVIAL TRIVIA CHALLENGE for the *Daily News*.'

'Yes, yes, I'm familiar with it. And now?'

'Well, now, I'm looking for er, new challenges.'

'You mean you're unemployed.'

'Um . . . that's about the strength of it.'

'I see. Very well.' He indicated the door.

I stood up, trying to make myself look at least seven inches shorter than my five foot nine. 'Have I got the job?'

'We'll let you know.'

I left feeling puzzled. Up until he asked me about myself, I seemed to have the job sewn up. I fretted and stewed for forty-eight hours (as I later realised he intended me to) before I got the call.

It was the best day of my life.

How was I to know it would all go pear-shaped?

# CHAPTER TWO

I can remember the very first question I ever wrote for *Money! Money! Money!*. It was:

Which of the five senses is – generally – the first to go with age?

a) sight
b) smell
c) taste
d) touch
e) hearing

ANSWER: b) Smell

I thought it was a pretty good question until Simon Peskitt and Frank Stephenson, my fellow question writers and 'tasters', ambushed me.

'Doesn't sound right to me. What do you think, Simon?'

'No, I'd have thought it was hearing. Old people

are always hard of hearing.'

'Or taste. My grandma says everything tastes the same to her.'

'Or sight. Old people all wear glasses – everyone knows that.'

I was sitting at a desk in the office that we were sharing. They were walking around me, talking across me. Frank stopped and asked me directly, 'Where did you get that from?'

'I don't know. I just *know* it. Maybe I read it in a book or something.'

'Not good enough,' said Simon with utter smugness.

'What's your source?' Frank repeated.

'I don't have one.'

'You have to have two sources.'

'Or more if one or both of us challenges it.'

'That's ridiculous,' I said. 'Are you telling me that if I wrote a question like "What is the capital of France?" that I'd have to look it up and confirm it and then do the same thing again?'

They both nodded. 'Yes.'

'Are you mad?'

'No,' said Frank, 'just very, very careful.' He stopped walking around and dragged over a chair to sit opposite me. I heard his knee bash the front of my desk but his face registered no pain. 'Look, David,' for a second his tone was less abrasive, less superior – almost kind. 'Simon and I have been doing this for a couple of years now. We know the

14

drill. See, although you *think* you know the answer – and you may be right ninety-nine times out of a hundred – there's always the chance you've made a boo-boo.'

'And that wouldn't doo-doo,' chimed Simon in what was either a manifestation or an impersonation of campness.

'Don't listen to *her*,' said Frank. 'There is a serious issue at stake. In the other shows we've done for Sparkle, there's only been a car or a holiday up for grabs – nothing sensational. But this time, there's anything up to a million pounds to be won. Might even be more. Michael . . .' I noticed him exchanging a significant look with Simon '. . . can't afford to foul up. Which means that *we* can't afford to foul up. Got me?'

'Yeah, I guess. But did you have any problems on any of your other shows?'

'One or two,' said Frank. 'In fact, it might be instructive for you to learn by our mistakes.'

If patronising colleagues were ever turned into an Olympic event, I think Frank and Simon would be up for a gold medal in the freestyle doubles.

'Go on – but don't forget I've had my own series in a national newspaper.'

'Ooh,' screamed Simon, 'not THE TOTALLY TASTE-LESS TRIVIA CHALLENGE!'

'Close enough.' To tell the truth, I was partly flattered that they'd heard of it at all.

'And what happened when you made mistakes?'

I tried to look laconic. If laconic means what I think it does. 'I didn't.'

'I told you he was a perfect ten.'

Now it was Simon's turn to be serious. 'Listen, *muchacho*, there's a world of difference between a rag that people read on the bog and a TV show where the stakes are higher than your newspaper's circulation.'

Frank stood up and leaned forward over the chair he had just been sitting in, all the better to lecture me. 'This time last year, we were doing a show called *Your Number's Up*. There were twenty questions in the show. The answer to each question was a number. Fifteen of the questions were for the contestants, the other five were for the viewers at home.' Once again, I caught the sneer. 'In one show, one of the questions we asked was "Which number Commandment is *Thou shalt not commit adultery*? Any ideas?'

I felt annoyed by how anxious I was to impress these pricks. 'The seventh?'

'Very good.'

'So what's wrong with that?'

Frank stood up and sniffed. Simon took over the narrative. 'Nothing. We checked it in an encyclopaedia and also in the King James Bible and both agreed that adultery is number seven.'

'Down four places from last week's number three,' added Frank.

'And?'

'And, my dear fellow, it is number seven.'

'Well?' I couldn't for the life of me see any problem.

Simon changed tack. 'Have you ever heard of something called "tyrannical ignorance"?' I shook my head. 'It's where you don't know what it is you don't know.'

'Come again?'

'You not only don't know the answer, you don't even know the question to ask. We weren't sure which number Commandment proscribed adultery. That's ignorance. We looked it up and that satisfied our ignorance. But there was also some tyrannical ignorance in that we didn't know that there was also something else we didn't know.'

He saw the baffled expression on my face and said, 'It turned out that – for God knows what reason – adultery is number eight or number six in the Northern Irish catechism or something. Least-wise, it was the Northern Irish Catholics who gave us all the grief. We didn't know we'd made a mistake because it hadn't even occurred to us to ask. I mean, why shouldn't the Commandments be the same everywhere?'

'Next thing we know,' Frank butted in, 'Michael . . .' there was that exchanged look again, 'is screaming at us.'

'And d'you know what?' Simon said prissily. 'He was right. We should have checked more. We should have checked *enough*.'

17

'But that's my point,' I said. 'If you *know* that something's the answer . . .'

'And that's our point, too. We *did* know the answer. Or at least we thought we did.' If laconic means what I think it does, Frank was far more successful at doing it than I was.

'That's why we've set minimum standards,' said Simon.

I put my hands up in mock surrender. 'OK, guys, whatever you say.'

It was my first day and I'd been really keen, but after my mauling at the hands of the Brothers Grim, I felt flat and deflated.

Truth is, all first days anywhere – school, college, jobs – are an anti-climax, if only because they carry so much apprehension and anticipation. In my experience, it's the *second* day that stings: your adrenaline carries you through the first day, inuring you to everything. On the second day, you're still nervous but instead of allowing for it – compensating for it – you're impatient with yourself and that's when the panic attacks start. At least, that's what happens to me: perhaps I'm guilty of universalising my own reactions and experiences.

The other thing with First Day Syndrome is just what a huge impression you make on the learning curve. Let's say that what I was to find out about Sparkle while I worked there equalled 100 per cent. On the first day, I learned a good 60 per cent of it. Admittedly, it was the other 40 per cent which contained the serious shit but still, there was no other day which saw such an exponential rise in knowledge.

Most important, Frank and Simon filled me in on *The Lot* or, as it was still called then, *Money! Money! Money!*.

Just in case you've been out of this solar system for the past couple of years, I'll run through the basic format. The audience are the contestants and vice versa. Three hundred people – selected via premium-rate phone lines – sit in a TV studio answering multiple choice questions on audience response equipment. As long as they answer correctly, they stay in: a wrong answer means they're knocked out. If they're the last person left playing *and* they can answer a minimum of five questions in the second half without getting any wrong, then they win the jackpot or *The Lot*. If they win but don't answer sufficient questions correctly, then they win just 10 per cent of £250,000 i.e. the lowest jackpot. If the jackpot isn't won, then it's carried over until it is won.

That's the show we now all know. Back then, however, they didn't have the 'knock back in' question which allows contestants – or, as we called them, punters – who have been knocked out to come back in if they're among the ten quickest to answer a question correctly. They were also still using four options per question throughout – like

*Millionaire* does – rather than the five they eventually used in the second half of the show.

The big change – the rollover jackpot that is the hallmark of the show – came about two weeks after I had joined the team. One day, in a production meeting, Frank pointed out to Andrews that if we guaranteed a jackpot in every show, we'd be limited to giving away a maximum of £250,000 a show.

I knew that: I just didn't want to be so pushy.

'Convince me,' said Andrews, for all the world like a fucking Roman emperor.

'OK,' said Frank. 'The object of the exercise is not to have to give away the jackpot in every show, right? So what if we made the second-half questions not just slightly harder but *significantly* more difficult?' He grinned craftily. 'Then we could stipulate that to win the jackpot, someone not only has to be the last one standing, but also has to answer at least five questions in the second half – *without getting any wrong*. See, at the moment, if all or both the people left in get a question wrong, you still allow them to go for the jackpot. What I'm saying is that, in those circumstances, they could still carry on to find the winner but they'd just be playing for the consolation prize.'

Andrews was clearly interested. The burgundy birthmark on his pate seemed to flare brighter. Or did I just want it to? 'Why do you say *at least* five questions?'

'OK. If we make the second-half questions seriously harder, you could have a situation where, after just one question, there's only one punter left in. Where's the excitement in that? This way, he's got to answer another four questions correctly to win the jackpot. Alternatively, you could have two or three punters still in after more than five questions. I'm just trying to cover your back. There's three factors to winning the jackpot: harder questions, they've got to get them all correct – though that doesn't apply to the knock-back in question in the first half – and they must answer at least five of them.'

At that moment, Karen, the office junior, walked into the room with a tray of coffee. As she bent down to serve him, Andrews peered up at her cleavage and then swallowed the resulting saliva noisily. When she over-filled Frank's mug, Andrews told him to 'ignore it'. No one was left in any doubt who 'it' was. 'Tell me,' said Andrews. 'What happens to the jackpot?'

'We increase it by £50,000 for every show it's not won. So if it's not won in the first show, there's £300,000 at stake in the second, £350,000 in the third, £400,000 in the fourth et cetera.' Even if he'd prepared his earlier contribution, I swear he made all that up on the hoof. Still, you had to be impressed by his presence of mind.

Andrews was. 'Until, conceivably, they're playing for a million pounds?'

'Or more.'

'I love it. I *fucking* love it!'

And for that tiny contribution – or so it seemed at the time – Frank was given 7.5 per cent of the action, which has got to be worth – what? – two million quid in overseas royalty rates. Not bad when you consider that, at the time, he was pulling in less than forty k. a year.

My only consolation is that if what I subsequently did ever comes to light, it would poison the well so much that the bastard wouldn't get a penny more.

# CHAPTER THREE

When I got home after that first day at Sparkle, it was a real relief to find Peter still there.

'Why aren't you out jigging?' For reasons that even I can't remember, we used to call 'gigging' jigging. It's just one word in a private vocabulary we shared. But then flatmatery is an intimate relationship: it is, after all, the bridge between living with your parents and marriage.

'Nigel's bust a porkie.' Nigel is Ringo in his band the Best Beatles, and Peter meant 'pinky' as in finger – as opposed to 'porkie' as in lie – but then the poor lad was still learning how to speak working-class lingo.

'Bummer. Don't you have a replacement?'

'We did, but he's now playing full-time with the Blackleg Beatles.'

'You ought to start an employment agency just for Beatles' tributes bands.'

'Dig it.'

'Anyway, I'm glad you're here. It's been a horrible

23

day. The show we're working on is fucking ridiculous, I'm stuck in an office with a pair of bum bandits and the boss is a complete git.'

'Is that it?'

'How much more do you want?'

'Both sides of the paper.'

'All right. The show's called *Money! Money! Money! . . .*'

He started singing the Abba song of the same name.

'Look, fucking don't, all right? I've had just about e-fucking-nough of everything today and I don't need your fucking flippancy, all right?'

'I'll get us some cheers.' It was as useful an act of contrition as anything I could think of.

Cheers is what we call beers. He went over to the battered fridge we'd inherited with the grotty kitchen in this musty two-bedroomed flat in the worst part of Kilburn and took out two cans of lager, one of which he threw at me.

I caught it cleanly, which reassured me that my central nervous system wasn't entirely shot. 'Beers!' I said – that being our word for 'cheers'.

'Beers! So *Money! Money! Money!* Eh?'

'. . . must be funny in a rich man's world.' Now it was my turn to be silly. I took a swig of beer and smiled at Peter. Crisis over.

'What's the format?'

'No audience – just three hundred contestants. They answer multiple choice questions on keypads.

When they get a question wrong, they're eliminated. The last one left in wins the jackpot.'

'Sounds simple.'

'Yeah, except that there are many modifications and qualifications. For example, ten people who have been knocked out get knocked back in again and then there's the rolling jackpot which you can only win if you answer a specified minimum number of questions correctly.'

'Sounds complicated.'

'I'm assured that these things start out simple, become complicated and end up simple. Well, that's how it was described to me.'

'Why's it any different from any other quizzical wankfest?'

''Cos they're giving away hundreds of thousands of pounds.'

'Oh, like *Who Wants To Be A Millionaire?*?'

'No, *not* like *Who Wants To Be A Millionaire?*. That's clever, witty and successful. Besides, we haven't got Chris Tarrant.'

'Who have you got?'

'Are you squatting comfortably?'

'Go on.'

'That's a clue.'

'Kit Connolly?' I indicated that he was right. 'Kit Connolly, Kit Connolly, Kit Connolly . . .' He recited the name as if he were conjugating a particularly regular Latin verb.

'None other. The man who persuaded a whole

generation of sub-teenies to watch ITV on Saturday mornings – simply by appearing on BBC.'

'So why have you got him?'

'Search me. Michael Andrews – he's my boss . . .'

'What's *he* like?'

'What, Michael? He's a dwarf. Well, he's not actually a dwarf – not technically – but he helps 'em out when they're busy. He'd be in their basketball team.'

'I get it. Doesn't need to fly business class.'

'That's right. Put it this way, he thinks the *Radio Times* is a top-shelf magazine.'

We laughed at our cruel witticisms, drained our lagers and scrunched up the cans.

'But he's OK?'

'I don't know. The jury's out. I mean, it was my first day and the only time I saw him, he glared at me and told me to – and I quote – "get out of the fucking way". And there's one other thing.'

'What? A toup?'

'No.'

'A club foot?'

'No.'

'I give up,' Peter told me. 'I'm not going to sit here playing "guess the handicap" when I could be discovering new porn sites. My Adultzone gold membership's only got four more days to run and there's a whole bunch of videos I haven't even begun to look at.'

'You're a sick puppy, my friend. I know it's your computer and that, but it'll be just my luck that you'll be out when the Vice Squad comes knocking.'

'Fuck off! It's all legal. The great thing about Adultzone is that, no matter how hard the porn, you know that all the girls, and the men for that matter, are over eighteen.'

'You should get some shares in Kleenex. What's your habit running at – a box a day?'

'Better out than in, I always say.'

Once again, we giggled. This time it was my turn to push my chair away from the kitchen table and fetch a couple of cans from the fridge. 'Beers!'

'Beers! So what's the matter with Michael?'

'He's got a dirty great birthmark on his bald head. Looks like someone's spilt a glass of indelible wine on his bonce.'

'Maybe they did.'

'Don't be silly. Anyway, as I was saying before I was so crudely interrupted, according to Frank, Michael thinks that Kit is "retro".'

'Dig. Like Nicholas Parsons and Rolf Harris.'

'Yeah, and Bob Monkhouse. But let's face it, he's *not* like them. *They're* popular, *they're* talented, *they're* cool. Kit is unpopular, untalented and so uncool he could heat up a hot tub.'

'So why's he got the jig?'

'That's what I asked. Frank then said that Michael reckons that Kit's *going* to be retro.'

'So who are Frank and Simon? And are they

indeed of a homsexualist predisposition?'

'Don't know yet but they've got this whole camp routine going. You know, "ooh, get her!" '

'We do that.'

'Yeah, but we're not queer.'

'Speak for yourself, daughter.'

'Even if they're not gay, they're oppos. And I'm the new boy.'

'I see.' He swallowed the rest of his drink but, when he finished, he kept his head tilted back as though he was thinking. Eventually, he returned to his usual position sprawled over the table and said, 'Divide and conquer, man. Divide and conquer. It's the only answer.'

'Thank you, Alexander the Great,' I said facetiously.

'Why does it always have to be so complicated for you, David? I mean, if the solution's simple, accept it. You're a clever cat, but that doesn't mean you've worked out all the angles.' He stood up and gave me a playful clip round the ear. 'Come on, you're the one with the job, you can take us both out for a chinky.'

# CHAPTER FOUR

I met Kit Connolly the very next day after my Chinese meal with Peter.

My first impression was that he was darker than he appears on telly. I don't mean in terms of his pigmentation but his character. Strip away the wackiness, the zaniness, and what's left is actually rather sombre, almost sinister. As though he were his own somewhat bitter identical twin brother. Having said that, he looked a lot older than when I'd last seen him but, given that that had been at least ten years earlier on *Suddenly It's Saturday!*, that was unsurprising. Nevertheless, there's something particularly ageing about thinning fair hair coupled with a pot belly. You can get away with one or the other but not both.

It was all I could do to stop myself from telling him the two bits of trivia I had on him: the fact that, like Perry Como and Glen Campbell, he's the seventh son of a seventh son, and also that he was born on precisely the same day as Marc Bolan (I'd love to have known what Kit's horoscope was on the day that Marc died). I was going to mention my trivia to him but something in his demeanour told me that he'd only have sneered at me and, what with Simon and Frank, I wasn't exactly feeling under-sneered-at.

'So you're the latest *Wunderkind*?' were his first words to me.

I didn't know what to say so I just shrugged my shoulders. He looked me up and down as though he were a cat and I were a budgerigar that had just made the career decision to escape from its cage. Then he licked his lips.

As soon as Kit dismissed me by turning round to talk to our mutual employer, Frank whispered, 'Watch your back, mate, I think he likes you.'

I immediately discovered two things: Kit was gay and Frank wasn't. At this point, I should say that I'm not a homophobe. The only thing I can't stand is when gay men insist on telling me all the gory details blow by blow, shall we say? I don't tell them what I get up to, so why should they tell me?

My brother Clive, who's a residential estate agent but otherwise not a bad bloke, has a theory. He says that coming out carries a far greater stigma than promiscuity so that once a man declares himself to be gay, there's nothing to stop him going on (and on) about his sex life.

I once put that to Tim, a friend of mine who is a seriously promiscuous gay but who at least spares me the intricate minutiae. He reckons that with gays – unlike straights – there's no one fulfilling the traditional female role of saying, 'Don't'. Anyway, I myself am a member of a persecuted minority for, like Craig David, David Beckham, Dale Winton, Fred Trueman and Pete Sampras, I've got a Jewish grandparent. So who am I to discriminate against anyone?

I think the thing that shocked me about discovering Kit's sexuality was that he'd always made such a fuss about how *heterosexual* he was. Getting photographed with bleached-blonde lovelies in Stringfellow's, judging beauty contests and *forever* going on about Page 3 girls.

Later that day, when the great star had departed, I plucked up the courage to ask Michael how come he'd picked him.

'What?' He sounded irritable. I wasn't sure whether to repeat my question or just to drop it. I looked around his large office for inspiration but the ornate hat stand couldn't help me, nor could all the BAFTA statuettes, which I later learned were copies and had been awarded to other people on programmes with which Andrews had been only tentatively associated.

'Just thinking, you know. Kit Connolly – interesting choice.'

'Interesting choice, my arse. You think I'm a cunt.'

Actually, I hadn't even considered the possibility until that precise second.

'Well, let me tell *you* something, Mr Old Harrovian. Kit Connolly was making mould-breaking television programmes while you were hanging off your bloody mother's teats.'

I wondered at the time why he should talk about my mother so vituperatively. It was only later – much later, just before my employment with his company ended – that I discovered he had grown up believing his mother to be his sister.

Actually, I might have got that the wrong way round. What I'm trying to say is that his mother had him when she was just fourteen. His grandmother brought them both up as brother and sister. Apparently, it was only when he needed his birth certificate – for a passport application – that he discovered the truth: that his 'sister' was indeed his mother.

Same is true of Eric Clapton, Jack Nicholson and, as I found out just the other day, the late Bobby Darin, who was thirty-two when he discovered the truth.

I was intrigued to know what 'mould-breaking television programmes' Kit Connolly had been in, unless the 'mould' in question applied to 'quality', 'watchability' or, indeed, 'success' but there was absolutely no doubt that Andrews was singularly close-minded on the subject of KC's suitability for *Money! Money! Money!* And, given how shitty the show was looking, who could gainsay him?

'Now look here, David,' said Andrews in what I

took to be a conciliatory tone. 'I'm told that you're having difficulty coming to terms with the way we do things here.'

Frank or Simon: which one of those wankers grassed me up?

'I recognise that you've got good general knowledge – which is why *I* took the risk of hiring you.' It was only later when I was replaying the conversation in my mind that I realised he was congratulating himself for my intelligence. 'However, that's only the half of it. You've got to have *judgement* too.' He patted his head which only succeeded in drawing my attention to his birthmark. Suddenly, it looked like a map of France.

'Of course, when I was at the BBC, I knew many blokes like you: public schoolboys, Oxbridge types and the rest. And where are they now? I'll tell you. They're still fucking there. Scrabbling around Kensington House in their corduroy jackets making documentaries – *docos* – for each other because, sure as hell, ain't no one else is going to watch them.'

He shifted forward in his padded chair. His body language shrieked, 'I'm going to give you a life lesson!' Unfortunately, in so doing, he was giving me an even clearer view of his birthmark or – as it was now established in my peculiar mind – *marque de naissance*. There was what looked like a white-head between Bordeaux and Biarritz. I felt myself starting to giggle.

'All that matters in television is giving the

punters what they want. And what they want in game-shows is accuracy and certainty. What's the matter? Why are you laughing?'

'I'm not,' I snorted, trying to convert my giggles into coughs. 'I suffer from an allergy to . . .' I looked round the room again to find anything to which I could conceivably be allergic '. . . to carpet dust!'

Andrews peered down at the carpet. The shift of blood to the front of his head turned Marseilles an angry red. I was now coughing so hard that I was in danger of rupturing my oesophagus. He looked up at me, his eyes narrowed with suspicion. 'What do you take for it?'

'Oh, nothing. I . . . er . . . just try to avoid the . . . er . . . triggers.' I thanked my lucky stars for *le mot juste* but that phrase in itself took me back to where I'd been. So with eyes streaming and throat rasping, I ran out of the room and lurched towards the loo.

From that day onwards, I was obliged to rub my eyes surreptitiously and/or cough in Andrew's presence whenever I could remember my 'tendency to allergies'.

# CHAPTER FIVE

Following Peter's advice to 'divide and conquer', and taking great care to wait until Simon wasn't around, I invited Frank out for a drink at the end of my first week at Sparkle. He led me to a pub just off Shaftesbury Avenue that, because of fruit machines, giant TV screens and heavy traffic, was horribly noisy even without people talking.

'What are your three best bits of trivia?' he asked when we'd sat down with our drinks – a gin and tonic for him; a pint of bitter for me.

'What, celebrity trivia or trivia trivia?'

'Either. Both.'

I opened a bag of honey-roasted cashew nuts, poured some into my hand and shoved the lot into my mouth. The sugar gave me an instant hit.

'OK. Celebrity trivia first. Nicholas Parsons's GP father delivered Margaret Thatcher.' I looked at his face to register how impressed he was and was gratified to see his eyebrows raise – almost in spite of himself. That's my number one piece of celebrity trivia – the one I always use when asked, which isn't as often as I'd like. The second was harder to find. Not that I didn't have plenty but I wanted it to live up to the first.

'Groucho Marx ate his first bagel at the age of eighty-one.'

'I *like* that.'

'I hoped you'd be – in the words of my flatmate – "hip to it". All right. Now for the jackpot. Melissa Joan Hart – you know, the girl who plays *Sabrina, The Teenage Witch* – she can recite the mathematical expression pi to four hundred decimal places.'

He rolled this revelation around his mouth like a wine-taster. 'Yeah, it's a good fact. A great fact, but I've heard it before, more than once. Got any non-celebrity trivia?'

I took a sip of my drink and ripped up a beer mat into as many even pieces as I could. 'All right. Did you know that all the continents are wider in the north than in the south?'

'Now you mention it I didn't, but it makes sense. Did you know, by the way, that the names of all the continents begin and end with a vowel?'

'What about South America?'

'Hmm. That's a bugger.' He grinned. Suddenly, I found myself liking him.

'The longest word that can be typed entirely by one hand is "stewardesses".'

Typing an imaginary keyboard with one hand, he nodded. 'Sounds about right.'

'Humans are the only animals to sleep on their backs.'

'Yeah, great. I like that. I like all of them.'

Then, on the basis that whenever someone asks you a question, they really want you to ask them the question back, I said, 'What about you? What are your favourite bits of trivia?'

The look in his eye told me that I was right to ask. He took the lemon out of his drink and bit it savagely. Then, like a trivia gunslinger, he rattled off his best shots. Actually, that's a bad analogy: it was more like two lead guitarists trading licks than a gunfight.

'When Paul Gambaccini was at Oxford at the same time as Bill Clinton, it was he who was voted *The American Most Likely To Succeed*. Before marrying his wife, Jay Leno lived at different times with five woman who were all born on 5 September. Jeremy Beadle was the first person in Britain to own a video phone.'

'Wow!' I said, trying to take all this in. More for the fun of it than anything else, I shot back: 'Bet you don't know who the *second* person was to own a video phone?'

There was no catching him out. He answered as if he were a contestant on *The $64,000 Challenge*. 'The second person was Alan Minter, the ex-boxing champion whose name means "splinter" in Cockney rhyming slang.'

Now it was my turn to do the eyebrows-raising

act. 'That's great. You really know your onions.'

He didn't pause to bask in my praise. 'Now for my miscellaneous trivia. The architect who built the Kremlin had his eyes gouged out by Ivan the Terrible so that he'd never be able to design another building like it. Tarantulas can go for up to two years without eating.'

I interrupted him to say that I found it hard to go for two hours without eating. He didn't seem to enjoy my witticism and I realised that this was a man for whom trivia was definitely not trivial.

'Disneyworld is bigger than the world's five smallest countries.'

Now, he was ready for my plaudits and I didn't stint him. However, later I found myself wondering whether he'd played this game before and had therefore improved his own best facts with other people's. More to the point, how long would it be before he added the Nicholas Parsons or Groucho Marx facts to his own repertoire? But I mustn't be churlish. The world of trivia is much like the world of scientific research: we believe in sharing our knowledge. Also, the object of the exercise was not to best him but to befriend him. To this end, I tried to draw him out a little. 'So what did you do before?'

'Before what?'

'Before this malarkey.'

'Oh, I see. This and that.' He was being obtuse and he looked edgy. He couldn't have been more different from the man who did the camp double act with Simon.

'That covers a multitude of sins.'

'Yes.' He paused long enough to indicate that that phase of the conversation was over. 'What are you having?'

'Same again, please.'

He walked over to the bar, his long Army great-coat nearly upending a chair. The coat struck me as incongruous – not because the early February weather wasn't cold enough to warrant it but because I couldn't imagine him going into an Army surplus store, let alone buying anything there. It was so out of kilter with the rest of his neat, department-store appearance.

When he returned, I complimented him on the coat and asked him where he'd bought it.

'I didn't buy it.' I looked puzzled enough for him to add, 'It was my brother's: he was in the Army.'

I don't know what possessed me to ask the supplementary question, 'What does he do now?' unless it was just the desire to make conversation.

'He got murdered in Northern Ireland.'

I didn't know what to say. Real drama – real life – had infiltrated our world of trivia. I mumbled a sorry into my beer and waited for Frank to speak next.

A couple of minutes later, he said, 'You haven't met Tony Bowes yet, have you?'

I shrugged my shoulders. 'No, I don't think so.'

He answered my silent question. 'Tony invented *Money! Money! Money!*.'

'Oh yeah?' It didn't mean anything to me. I hadn't really given any thought to who had invented the game. I don't know why, but for some reason I had assumed that Andrews himself was the creator.

'You'd remember him if you had met him. He's the fattest bastard you ever saw.' Frank grinned, which was a relief to me. 'And the luckiest.'

'The luckiest?'

'You bet. He's going to make a sodding fortune out of this.'

'Really?'

'You sound sceptical.'

I felt a wave of panic as I thought I'd been too indiscreet. 'It's just that . . .' I cast my mind around for an explanation. 'Kit Connolly . . .'

'. . . is a complete tosser but don't let him put you off. The format is brilliant. A sureproof winner.'

'But surely the presenter is an important factor in the programme's success? I mean, look at Tarrant.'

'Sure, he's vital.'

'But . . .'

'Kit Connolly won't be let anywhere *near* the show, you can rest assured on that. By the time we get to series, he'll be long gone.'

'So why is he involved with it now?'

'He's . . .' Frank drummed his bitten fingernails on the table as an aid to thought. 'He's a stalking horse.'

'Explain.'

'That's probably not the best way of expressing it. OK, he's a stand-in. See, the presenter we *really* want is Richie Clark.'

'What? Richie Clarke as in *Richie's Night In*? I approve! Why don't we approach him now?'

'Because Clarke is under exclusive contract to the BBC and will be for another three months or so. Remember, ITV have commissioned *Money! Money! Money!*. Apart from anything, the Beeb would never have bought it: the show could only work on commercial television.'

'Then why take on Kit or, indeed, anyone until then?'

'We have to have someone or else Clarke would have us over a barrel. Kit is by way of being a bargaining counter.' He noted my smile. 'All right, he's not the best bargaining counter, but there's also the problem that we have to have a presenter for the pilot. By the time we get through that, Richie Clarke's contract will be up and we'll be able to get him. In the meantime, we've got Kit.' He flicked a stray cashew off the table. It landed in a fake pot plant. 'You've also got to consider the importance of press coverage in building up anticipation, and Kit's still a name even if he is useless. And when the time comes to bid him goodbye, he'll take it on the chin – at least he will if he knows what's good for his career. They're not exactly queuing up for him, you know.'

Frank leaned forward and told me: 'Basically, Kit Connolly's disposable.'

'But Andrews . . .' I was already beginning to think of him by his surname and quickly corrected myself, '. . . *Michael* was saying how brilliant Kit is. He was really quite strident on the subject.'

'Oh, he was just being perverse. If *you* had been enthusing about him, Michael would have said what an arsehole he was. Mind you, I think there's some history there. They cut their TV teeth together in Wales, way back when.' He took a swig of his drink and moved closer. 'Michael likes to keep his cards close to his chest. He doesn't know that Simon and I know about Richie.'

'So how *do* you know?'

He tapped the side of his nose which I found irritating and said, 'Never you mind,' which I found even more irritating.

'Does Kit know?'

'I shouldn't think so for a minute. Listen, for all that he struts around like the biggest *fromage* on the cheese board, he's a two-bob nobody, a pathetic poof. He's the sexual intercourse consultant on the show.'

'The what?'

'When we want his fucking opinion, we ask him for it.'

# CHAPTER SIX

It's never ceased to amaze me how quickly I settle into a new job. No matter how apprehensive I am before I start, nor how strange it all seems once I actually do start, within a couple of weeks I've developed a routine.

At Sparkle, this consisted of leaving home at 9.20 on my moped, as I'd quickly tired of an Underground journey necessitating two changes, arriving at the office at 9.50, popping next door to buy a caffe latte and being at my desk in the office I shared with Frank and Simon at ten o'clock.

The first thing we did was – no, not say hello to each other – but test each other. They always said that it was to set us up for the day, but there was no doubt in my mind that the sole object of the exercise was to set the tone for the day i.e. to score points off each other.

On a typical day, Simon said, 'OK, what are you two like on phobias?'

Frank replied, 'Try me,' and we were off.

'Right, I'm not bothering with Arachnophobia, Claustrophobia, Agoraphobia or Sociophobia or indeed any of the easy ones. Who can tell me what Pogonophobia is?'

Neither of us could but I now know that it's a fear of beards – just like I now know that Chrometophobia is a fear of money, Linonophobia is – bizarrely – a fear of string, Sciophobia a fear of shadows, Dikephobia a fear of justice and not, as Frank guessed, a fear of beer-guzzling women in tweed skirts, Aulophobia a fear of flutes and Blennophobia a fear of slime.

As I recall, I didn't do very well in that quiz. Worse still, when Frank expanded the quiz to include celebrities, I didn't fare any better.

I knew that Howard Hughes was mysophobic (fear of germs and infection) and that Natalie Wood, who drowned, was hydrophobic but I had no idea that Johnny Depp was frightened of clowns or that Judy Garland was terrified of horses.

Eventually, I was so piqued by my ignorance that I decided to make one up. Out of nowhere (well, actually I'd seen the scene-by-scene remake of *Psycho* the night before and I guess that scary movies and phobias go together), the name Sir Alfred Hitchcock came to me. 'Did you know,' I said, 'that Alfred Hitchcock suffered from Glazzophobia, a morbid fear of glass?'

It was Simon who corrected me. 'A phobia about glass is Nelophobia.'

'Yeah, all right,' I replied. 'Some of us didn't get *The Boys' Own Book of Phobias* in last year's Christmas stocking.'

Simon smiled condescendingly and then, in a drawl, added, 'And, as I recall, Sir Alfred Hitchcock had a phobia not about glass but about policemen. The story goes that when he was a boy, he misbehaved and so his father took him down to the police station where he prevailed upon the Duty Sergeant to put the boy in a cell for an hour or so. Afterwards, he was so traumatised that he not only kept to the straight and narrow but also retained a lifelong fear of the boys in blue.'

'It's true,' said Frank. 'In fact, he refused to learn to drive for fear of ever being stopped by a policeman.'

My eyebrows lifted involuntarily at the scope of their knowledge. 'Did you know,' I said when my brows had returned to the horizontal, 'that Sir Alfred Hitchcock was celibate from the age of forty-two which, considering that he only lost his virginity at the age of twenty-seven, didn't give him much of a sex life?'

Either they did know or, worse, they didn't but had come to mistrust me on all things Hitchcockian – or, indeed, on all things – for they merely nodded noncommittally. Before I could take even more earth out of the hole I'd dug for myself, Karen popped into the office and put a sheaf of papers on Frank's desk. I noticed that he didn't thank her: in fact, he didn't even acknowledge her existence.

'What's the S.P. on Karen?' I asked when she'd left the room.

'Why – are you sweet on her?'

'No, I'm not,' I said indignantly, although there was no reason – beyond Simon's camp taunting – why I should have been indignant. Karen was, in the way that my friend Ziggy puts it, 'no pig'. She was early twenties, slim but busty, had lovely chestnut hair and, if she'd had some corrective surgery on her nose to remove the prominent kink, would have been a candidate for a stunnership.

'She's got lovely hair,' I said, and immediately mentally reproached myself for thinking out loud.

For some reason, this provoked sniggers.

I was annoyed and puzzled in equal measure but decided against showing it. Instead, in an approximate imitation of Joe Pesci in *GoodFellas*, I said, 'I make you laugh? I amuse you?'

'No,' said Frank, who was the less giggly of the two. 'It's not you, it's her – or at least her hair.'

'And very nice it is too,' I said evenly.

'So would yours be if you used the same shampoo,' shrieked Simon, who was almost wetting himself.

'Yeah,' said Frank. 'Not so much a case of Wash and Go . . .'

Simon finished his sentence: '. . . as Wash and Come!'

'OK, guys,' I said as patronisingly as possible. 'Explain.'

'Wash and Come,' repeated Frank. 'Geddit? The reason her hair is so lustrous, manageable and tangle-free is not due to the beneficial properties of aloe vera, coconut or even our old friend, jojoba. It's due to our even older friend, jism. Or, if you prefer it, spunk, love juice, cum.'

Like any other man would have done, I wanted more details. 'How do you know?'

'We have it on the word of our esteemed Führer, Herr – or should that be *Hair* – Michael Andrews.'

'And how does *he* know?' But I knew the answer before I'd even finished the question.

'Because, my dear sweet innocent, he was the one who did the vile deed. Which makes him, I suppose, the cummer.'

'And her,' chimed Simon, 'the cummee.'

'But isn't he married?' I asked.

Simon made the sound of a buzzer on a TV game-show. 'Correct. To Emma. But they have what is known as an open marriage.'

'At least *Michael* does,' added Frank. 'I don't think the sainted Emma knows a thing about it.'

'Poor Emma,' said Simon with cruel insincerity. 'She has no *sparkle* in her life.'

'Unlike her hubby . . .'

'. . . who has too much!'

'And he told you about Karen, I suppose, just like that.'

Simon nodded while Frank essayed a cod-Tommy Cooper impersonation, 'Just like that.'

'Did you know,' asked Simon of both of us, 'that Tommy Cooper died on stage – literally?'

'I knew that,' said Frank. 'I also know that Sid James, Leonard Rossiter and the music hall artiste, Marie Lloyd, all died on stage too.'

It was like schoolboys swapping stamps but I couldn't resist showing off my knowledge. 'Everyone knows about *them*. What about Les Harvey, the Stone the Crows musician who was electrocuted by touching a live microphone with wet feet in 1972? Or the opera singer, Richard Versalle who, in 1996, fell off the stage and died immediately after singing the line "Too bad you can only live so long".'

I was too fluent – and the information was too arcane – for them to doubt my veracity. For once, *I* was able to trump *them*. What I didn't add, then or later, was that I had happened to learn those facts myself that very morning, whilst on the loo reading some out-of-print book of lists.

They weren't impressed enough to say so but it did shut them up for half an hour. Which was a lot more valuable to me than their praise.

# CHAPTER SEVEN

Knowing what I did about Karen and, as I thought of it, her special conditioner, I found myself staring at her at every opportunity. Worse still, I couldn't take my eyes off her hair.

I mean, I've always been pretty well up to speed on sexual trivia. I know the wonderful story about Milton Berle, the comedian, only pulling out enough of his cock to win a bet when he was challenged by a well-hung man. I have collected eight men who died during sex, eleven people who were virgins when they died (thirteen if you include the Irish leader, Michael Collins, over whom there's some doubt and Hans Christian Andersen who, despite being bisexual, didn't actually 'do it' with either sex), nineteen people who married their cousins (including Edgar Allan Poe and Jerry Lee Lewis whose cousins were just thirteen at the time), and fourteen British Prime Ministers who committed adultery.

When it comes to, ahem, 'sexual preferences', I

know that Napoleon Bonaparte and Adolf Hitler were coprophiliacs; that Havelock Ellis enjoyed watching women urinate while standing up, that T.E. Lawrence liked to be spanked; that Algernon Swinburne had sex with a pet monkey which he later killed and ate when it bit one of his guests; that Errol Flynn, Lord Byron, Charlie Chaplin and Elvis Presley were all voyeurs; that Jean Jacques Rousseau would show off his bum in the hope that some disgusted woman would spank it; that James Boswell, in his teenage years, used to enjoy shagging trees; that Howard Hughes liked his women hairy and forbade them to shave themselves and that James Joyce used to carry around a pair of doll's knickers in his pocket.

However, I've never heard of the practice of coming over a woman's hair. And I have to say that I found it disturbing that Andrews should treat his staff in such a way.

Don't get me wrong, I'm no prude. I know that all prudes precede every prudish statement with the words 'I'm no prude but . . .' but *I really am not a prude*. I also believe in freedom of choice – provided of course that both parties are consenting adults.

However, two things disturbed me about Karen and Andrews: one was that I wondered how much Karen was consenting to sex in order to keep her job and the other was that, having presumably been offered a whole raft of choices by the obviously accommodating Karen, Andrews should have chosen to humiliate her by messing up her hair. What kind of a man does that to a woman? What kind of a boss does that to an employee? What kind of person does that to anyone and then tells everyone else all about it?

It didn't put me off him as such but merely aroused in me a growing sense of mistrust. This was further confirmed a couple of days later when he called us into his office (which, in those days, also doubled as the boardroom) to introduce us to his latest recruit.

I looked around the room and tried to place everyone. Andrews sitting behind his desk, Karen scuttling around with glasses of white wine and mineral water, Frank and Simon chatting and, presumably deliberately, excluding me. There, by the *Spotlight* casting directories, was Hugh, the Financial Controller and his secretary, Linda, whom I'd met on my first day. Sitting in what, considering his bulk, looked like an extremely uncomfortable director's chair was Christopher Watney-Howe, the legal affairs honcho and, standing in the corner, reading a poster for a film I only vaguely remembered but which featured Andrews's name in some associated capacity, was someone named Joe something-or-other who didn't actually work at Sparkle but – or so I was told by Frank – was the company's biggest individual shareholder.

That was the full muster as far as I knew, and now we were to be presented to our newest colleague: a tall, slender woman with perfect auburn hair – which I tried not to think of in connection with our mutual boss – wearing a beige suit and silk scarf. Her face, although not unattractive, was so angular, and her lips and eyebrows made up to be so tapered, that it looked as though she'd been given a makeover by Salvador Dalí.

'This is Belinda,' said Andrews, looking and sounding for all the world like a football manager introducing his new record signing to the press. 'She's come to join us to replace Melanie in my office and I'm sure she'll be a very valuable member of the team.'

I later learned that Melanie, who had interviewed me on the phone before I got the job, had left a couple of days before I'd joined because she was tired of having to rebuff Andrews's advances. Fortunately for him, she was too classy to take him to an industrial tribunal where his predatory activities would have come to light but, even so, she'd stung him for a big *ex gratia* payment.

Following Frank and Simon's lead, I mingled with my colleagues. Not having anything to say to any of them – beyond a smile-and-eyebrows combo to indicate that it-was-good-to-see-them-even-if-the-wine-was-rank – I went up to Joe, the shareholder.

'Hello,' I said, extending my hand. 'I'm David Marriott.'

He gave me a firm handshake and said, 'Joe Mackintosh.'

Andrews appeared at Joe's shoulder – well, more like his waist. 'I see you've met David,' he said to his partner, who nodded. 'Don't waste your time on him: I've got more interesting people for you to meet.'

'Thanks,' I mouthed to their backs.

I felt lost so, since she was also alone, I approached Belinda. 'Did you know,' I said to her by way of welcome, 'that Anneka Rice, Mystic Meg, Ulrika Jonsson and Anne Robinson all started out as secretaries and that Caroline Aherne used to be Janet Street-Porter's secretary up at BBC Manchester?'

She didn't so much speak as bark. 'I'm a PA – *not* a secretary!' The words 'hoity' and 'toity' both sprang to mind.

'Sorry,' I said, grinning in what I hoped was an ingratiating way before adding, 'Rachel Stevens – you know, Rachel from S Club 7 – she was a PA in fashion.'

She looked at me as if it were just possible that I was something more senior than the lowest form of office life. 'What do you do here?'

'I write the questions for *Money! Money! Money!*.'

'Oh, I see.' She looked away from me – over my shoulder to a point on the far wall where, from memory, I knew there to be a poster for the 1978 Reading Festival. I never did discover what Andrews's connection was to the event but it was inscribed *To Michael, with love peace and sunshine* and signed illegibly.

Having clearly succeeded in pissing off Belinda – and also being in the mood to discharge vast chunks of trivia – I saw no reason not to annoy her further. 'Do you know,' I said, almost forcing her to look at me, 'what Peter De Savary, T.S. Eliot, Robin Cook and Thomas Hardy all have in common?'

'No,' she said, with a look that assured me that any surprise she was registering was not due to her interest in me or my words, but rather due to my insolence in addressing her in the first place.

'They all married their *secretaries*.' I made sure that I stressed the last word. 'Good luck in your new job.'

Suddenly, I had no problem at all with the prospect of Andrews getting in his employees' hair.

# CHAPTER EIGHT

'Bummer.'

'We're not Corried, are we?' In our lingo, to be Corried is to be restricted, for technical reasons, to just one television channel. Named after the scary time when, because our telly went berserk, every TV station became unobtainable except for ITV which was showing *Coronation Street* at the time.

'No, worse.'

'I can't think of anything worse. All right, give me ten questions to which the answers are—'

'David! You can't turn *everything* into a fucking quiz. Some things are, like, too important,' There was a pause, and then Peter said: 'We're going to be evicted.'

'You what?'

'Chucked out. Made homeless. What part of "evicted" don't you understand?'

'The bit that sees us on the street.' He giggled, as I knew he would, but that did nothing to ameliorate the situation. 'Why are we being evicted?' I asked.

'It's Chris.'

'Chris who?'

'You know, Chris who shared my room here when we first moved in.'

'I remember him. A ginge. What about him?'

'He's only gone and told Wilton.' Trevor Wilton was our landlord, always referred to as 'Wilton' or, when we wanted to be particularly obtuse, as 'the carpet man', as in Axminster and Wilton.

'But Chris was here unofficially. We weren't supposed to have a third person. He knew that. Why did he land us in it?'

'It's not his fault. It's all a ghastly coincidence. Since he wasn't meant to be living here, he never actually met Wilton in the flesh.'

'OK.'

'So when he goes to a new prospective landlord and gives him his last three addresses and that new landlord happens to be . . .'

'. . . the carpet man. I get it. But why do we have to leave?'

'Wilton says it's because we betrayed his trust.'

'Trust, eh? We're not the ones who drew up that ludicrous inventory. We're not the ones who insisted on huge deposits. We're not the ones who . . .' Unfortunately, my rhetoric couldn't match my anger. Peter tried to calm me down.

'Just the way it goes, man. Bummer.'

I was pacified. 'Bummer.'

It was the end of my third week at Sparkle and

I'd got myself into a really good routine, writing sixty questions a day – which doesn't sound many but you have to factor in the sometimes ludicrous 'sourcing' – cross-checking Frank and Simon's work, avoiding Andrews and his birthmark, which recently had come to resemble not so much a map of France as an open-mouthed wolf howling, avoiding Belinda and generally easing myself into the world of TV quiz shows. Our first pilot was still five weeks off and the show itself wasn't due to be recorded for another seven weeks after that.

Actually, I say 'pilot' but it wasn't a pilot in the usual sense of the word. We weren't trying to get a commission: that was already guaranteed on the strength of a presentation which had been made before my arrival. So the 'pilot' we were doing was actually a 'run-through with cameras' and was for our benefit rather than for the commissioning ITV company, though Frank had told me that they would view it with interest.

So I was really pissed off by Peter's bombshell. Domestic disruption was the last thing I needed at this point in my life and I found myself cursing Chris, Wilton, Andrews, life and anything else I could think of as Peter and I sat on the sofa eating a takeaway pizza, watching TV and discussing our options.

'I hate you!' I screamed, as another contestant took 'the walk of shame' on *The Weakest Link*.

'Cool it, man, she's just doing her job.'

'That's what they said at Nuremberg.'

'No one forces them to go on the programme.'

'It's a show, Pete, not a programme.' I was so angry that I called him Pete, in the full and certain knowledge that it would piss him off.

'Ooh – Percy Pedantic.'

'Don't go all fucking camp on me, I get enough of that at work.'

'Listen, man, calm down. Why don't you try some deep breathing?'

'Oh fuck off, hippy.'

Peter changed tack. 'I thought you didn't like this flat. You're always going on about how poky it is, how dirty it is, how inconvenient it is – well, now you're out of it, man. It looks like a result to me.'

'You don't understand, mate. I don't want – I can't *take* – any disruption to my life at the moment. Do you know what I mean?'

'Sure I do.' He took the plates into the kitchen, which was surprisingly domesticated for him, and then returned. 'Look, David, I'm not too busy at the moment: my next gig isn't till next Wednesday. I'll make it my responsibility to find a new flat and move all our stuff over. OK?'

I could have hugged him but you don't do that sort of thing when it's just two blokes sharing a flat. So I simply said, 'You're a mate, mate.'

'Tell you what,' he said, clearly looking to capitalise on my suddenly improved mood. 'Bet I can name more celebrity flatmates – past or present – than you can.'

'Bet you can't.'

'How much?'

'Pint. At the Swan. When you've conceded defeat.'

'Done. Right, I start with David Baddiel and Frank Skinner.'

'Peasy. OK, Marilyn Monroe and Shelly Winters.'

'They have to be alive.'

'Says who?'

'Says me. I called the game, I name the rules. That's how it always works. Or have Frank and Simon turned you?'

'Steady, Peter. All right. Gary Webster and Phil Middlemiss.'

'I was going to say them.' He took a sip of what he called herbal – but which I called 'pooffy' – tea and said, 'Dustin Hoffman and Gene Hackman.'

'Don't forget Robert Duvall. He was also in that flat.'

'Show-off. No one likes a know-all.'

'My turn,' I said. 'Lesley Joseph and Maureen Lipman.'

'OK, Charles Bronson and Jack Klugman.'

'Really?' I asked. Peter nodded, which was good enough for me. 'Mel Gibson and Geoffrey Rush.'

Now it was his turn to look sceptical. I pre-empted his question by nodding vigorously. I could see that he was starting to struggle. Eventually, he said, 'Paul Whitehouse and Harry Enfield'.

'I don't think so. Way I understood it, Harry Enfield dossed down on Paul Whitehouse's floor. They weren't flatmates as such.' Then, noticing his indignation, I said, 'OK, OK, have it,' before muttering under my breath, 'Much good may it do you'.

It was now my turn again. 'Lord Charles Falconer and Tony Blair.'

'No,' said Peter, 'I can't allow that. Falconer's only famous for being a flatmate – Tony Blair's flatmate. He's not a celebrity in his own right.'

'Yes, he is.'

'All right, he is now – but he wasn't then and he only is now because he was. If you get my drift, man.'

'OK,' I said, all St Francis of Assisi, 'that's cool. What have you got against Matt Damon and Ben Affleck?'

'Nothing.'

There then followed a pause. Which elided effortlessly into a longer pause. Until, eventually, I put him out of his misery. 'Can't think of any more, Pete? Well, what about Zoe Ball and John Thomson? You know, him off *The Fast Show*?'

'Nice one.'

'Or you could have said Tommy Lee Jones and Al Gore. Or Ioan Gruffudd and Matthew Rhys.'

'Who's he?'

'What, Matthew Rhys? He was Kathleen Turner's

co-star in the stage play of *The Graduate*. Apparently,' I added for the sheer joy of it, 'they speak Welsh to one another at home.'

Finally, it was time for my *coup de grâce*. 'You also missed out on a very obvious one. Sir Michael Caine and Terence Stamp.'

'I concede,' he said, chucking a piece of ham from off his pizza that had fallen down the side of the sofa at me. 'You're a pro now and you're out of my league.'

# CHAPTER NINE

While Peter was out searching for a flat, I found myself searching for sanctuary at work.

For some reason, Andrews had got it into his head that I was 'useless', 'stupid' and 'a complete wanker'. The first was manifestly untrue, the second a matter of opinion and the third, I'm sorry to say, true only in the literal sense (I wasn't getting any at the time).

Sticks and stones and all that, but it had started to get me down. Apart from anything, I really couldn't see what I was doing wrong. I was writing good questions (even Frank and Simon conceded that), I was beavering away checking their questions and I had even given up my weekend to help with another Sparkle pilot: a game-show entitled *Break the Bank!*, which was supposed to be based on casino games but had a set that made it look less classy than a travelling fairground's amusement arcade.

It started on the Monday morning after Peter

and I were given notice to quit our flat, with a visit from Belinda. 'Michael,' she said in a supercilious tone that made me notice how she always put the emphasis on the first syllable of our boss's name, 'wants to see you in his office. Now.'

Woof woof.

Andrews, who seemed to be absorbed in his laptop computer – though how his pudgy, ring-laden fingers could negotiate the keyboard was beyond me – looked up long enough to say, 'David, yes. No, don't sit down. What the fuck is this supposed to be?'

'What?'

'Don't fucking "what" me! This question: "Which is the only one of these animals that can't jump? a) pig b) elephant c) horse d) lion".' He looked at me and there was rage in his eyes. 'What sort of fucking question is that?'

I cleared my throat. 'It's a question. It's for towards the end of the first half. It's intended to make them think.'

'It'll make them think all right. It'll make them think we're a bunch of prats.'

'I've cited my sources underneath and I think Frank and Simon will have corroborated it.'

'That's not the point.' He bashed the keyboard of his computer. 'What about this one? "Which British TV presenter co-wrote the screenplays for *Isadora* and *Jesus Christ Superstar*? a) Michael Parkinson b) Terry Wogan c) Melvyn Bragg d)

Clive James." Who the fuck cares?'

I should have kept quiet and waited until his tantrum subsided but I couldn't help but defend myself. 'You could say that about *any* quiz question. It's a good question. Some people will know that it's Melvyn Bragg and others will get there by the process of elimination.'

'Oh, so you think it's a good question, do you?'

I nodded.

'Well, I don't – and I was writing quiz questions while you were still getting buggered at your public school! Do you understand?'

I understood that he was throwing all his toys out of the cot.

'I could do your job standing on my head! But I don't because I've got more important things to do!'

I swallowed hard and counted to six – six being the number of thousands I was then overdrawn. I had noticed that, the more choleric he had become, the more his birthmark was metamorphosing into a Wagon Wheel chocolate biscuit with a bite taken out of it. Possibly not a good idea to mention it.

'You'd better pull your socks together fast if you want to stay at Sparkle, I can tell you.'

I could have told him that he was mixing his metaphors, but something in his current mood indicated to me that he was not in the market for my didacticism.

He bade me farewell ('Go on, fuck off out of here!') and I left his office for the relative tranquillity of the writers' room.

'What the fuck's eating Andrews?' I asked of no one in particular. I was so stunned that I forgot to be discreet.

'Ooh,' queened Frank, 'she's in a tizz.'

'You'll be in something much worse if you don't cut it out.'

'Oh, he's *sooooo* butch!'

'I'm warning you . . .'

'What's up?' asked Simon.

'It's Michael.' I pronounced his name in an imitation of Belinda. 'I can't believe it. He's gone mad. He's just completely dumped on me. He says that I can't write questions, that he could write them better than me, that I'm useless, that—'

'Don't worry,' said Simon, offering me an extra-strong mint either out of sympathy or because my breath wasn't making it. 'He does it to all of us at some time or other.'

'What, even to you?'

'Yeah, and to the fairy queen over there.'

'But why?'

'Dunno. Just the way he is, I guess. Figures that he pays us so we're there for his edification. Usually starts off that he really likes you – treats you like a pet dog that can walk on its hind feet.'

'I seem to have missed that phase,' I muttered.

'Then he'll ignore you and then, when he's forgotten what it was like before you arrived – that's to say how much he needed you – he starts to resent you. See, you're costing him money at the moment and he's not getting any payback.'

'No, but he will.'

'That's not how it feels to him on a wet Monday morning.'

'What's the next phase?' I asked with no little trepidation.

'Depends,' said Simon. 'Either you'll survive this and still be here as an important and integral member of the team . . .'

'Or,' added Frank, 'you won't.'

'But he needs me. It's less than five weeks before the pilot and . . .'

Simon completed my sentence: '. . . we've easily got enough questions. Fact is, we've got enough questions for the whole fucking series if and when Michael realises that he doesn't need thousands in a database and allows us to put them together show by show.'

I must have looked glum, for Simon qualified his last statement to say, 'But it's not going to happen like that.'

Frank chirped in, 'More's the pity: I'd have really liked that kind of power.'

'Michael's already promised the commissioning

editor that for security reasons if for nothing else he'll have a database of several thousand questions.'

'That's OK then.' I said it but I didn't feel it. I suddenly felt really low. The anxiety had receded and left me totally flat. The fact that I should have been at my happiest working in a job requiring my trivia talents only served to make me feel more glum. I was considering going home for the day when Frank derailed my self-pitying train of thought by calling over to Simon. 'Did you hear? We've got Walter Willis as our producer.'

My immediate reaction wasn't to ask who he was but to say, 'That was Bruce Willis's name at birth – Walter Willis – but he dropped his first name in favour of his middle name, Bruce.'

'Small world,' said Frank.

'Phew!' said Simon, and pretended to mop his brow.

'Who is he?' I asked.

'Only the best light entertainment producer out-side of the Beeb.'

'I'd say inside too,' said Simon. 'Mind you, we'll have to watch our backs. He's got a reputa-tion for chasing pretty boys like us around the office.'

I found myself wondering how it was that Frank and Simon always had all the news and knew who everyone was. It only took a few seconds for me to realise that the two were, of course, interconnected.

Hearing about this Walter man tempted me to tell them my story of how Frankie Howerd once chased me around a room at his agent's with the words, 'I could stick my cock up your arse any time I liked' – to which I had replied, 'I'm sorry, Mr Howerd, the newspaper doesn't pay me enough.' Then I decided that they'd only take the piss out of me and, in my present mood, I didn't feel up to handling that.

'OK,' said Simon, 'in Walter's honour, how many gays can you name?'

'Boring,' pronounced Frank. 'How many gays can you name who married?'

'Gays or bisexuals?' I asked, my appetite whetted in spite of my vestigial despondency.

'Gays. Out and out gays.'

I was about to 'ooh er' but stopped because once those guys got going – and I confess to having been as bad as them – innuendo takes a back seat (ooh er, in this context) to trivia.

'Oscar Wilde.'

'Lord Alfred Douglas.'

'Peter Tchaikovsky.'

'Rock Hudson.'

'W.H. Auden,' said Frank.

'Are you sure?' asked Simon.

'Yes. He married a woman to save her from the Nazis and he also urged – unsuccessfully –

Christopher Isherwood to do the same.'

Frank then trotted out – rat-a-tat machine-gun style – a whole list: King Edward II, Kenny Everett, Raymond Burr, Vaslaw Nijinsky, Jimmy Edwards, Cole Porter and Yukio Mishima, the Japanese writer. By the time he'd finished, Simon and I were a little pole-axed but he managed to offer Charles Laughton and, of course, Michael Barrymore, while I came up with Ronnie Kray, Tom Driberg and Antony Sher.

'Stakes are raised,' said Frank. 'Can you think of any famous women who married gay men?'

I immediately tried to remember the gays we'd all just said to see if any of them had married famous women. 'Elsa Lanchester, she married Charles Laughton. And . . .'

But before I could add anyone else, Frank leapt in: 'Vanessa Redgrave married Tony Richardson.'

'I think he was bi, not gay,' said Simon.

'All right, then instead I offer you Judy Garland and do I get any credit for adding that both Judy and her daughter, Liza Minnelli, had gay fathers?' I asked.

'No,' said Simon sternly, 'any more than I do for naming August Strindberg and Harold Nicholson as men who married lesbians.'

'I can beat that,' said Frank.

'I've no doubt you can, big boy. You seem to be particularly well informed on this subject.' There was an edge in Simon's voice.

'I'm particularly well informed on *every* subject. You missed out Rudolph Valentino.'

'How?'

'He married a lesbian. In fact, he married *two* lesbians.'

'Now that's what I call a threesome.'

It was time for me to give my self-esteem a much-needed boost. Once again, a recent session on the bog had provided me with some superb ammunition. 'Can either of you two name a celebrity with a gay mother or father?'

Cue much head scratching. Eventually, and reluctantly, they conceded defeat.

'Well,' I said, 'where should I start? Patrick MacNee's mother was a lesbian. Jacqueline Kennedy Onassis's father was gay. As was Anne Heche's father.'

'I'm with Mencken: "I never met a dyke I didn't like".'

Quiz over, I went on to my computer, on to the program Andrews had had specially written for us with its prompts for where a question fitted into the show (first question, early first half, middle first half, late first half, last first half; first second half, early second half, late second half et cetera), the spaces for the four (or more) possible answers and for the sources – as well as name boxes for the two checkers to tick when they/we were completely satisfied.

I'd enjoyed my moment of triumph but mentally dismissed it as luck that I happened to have read a useful article. It was only after I'd finished work that it even began to occur to me that Frank had done precisely the same.

# CHAPTER TEN

I had never even begun to think about where we would find the contestants for the show, which was, by now, officially called *The Lot*, having had its name changed when it was discovered that not only could we not use the Abba song in the titles, we couldn't even use the song of the same name from *Cabaret*.

Fortunately, this had already occurred to Andrews. I'll give him that: although he was an autocratic shit and an appalling man manager given to childish tantrums, he was good at putting game-shows together. Or, at least, this game-show.

I had always assumed that, if you held a game-show, people would come – rather like in *Field of Dreams*, I guess. The truth is that someone has to find them, ticket them, get them to the show, feed them, water them, nursemaid them and, finally, put them on the show. After that, they can fuck off back to oblivion.

You see, that's what you get like when you come

into contact with Members of the Public (MOPs). You don't see them as a collection of individuals. The same is undoubtedly true in other jobs: a friend of mine who works for an airline tells me that he and his mates regularly refer to passengers as 'self-loading cargo'.

I first became aware of the existence of such a personage as 'contestant researcher' one lunchtime. Frank and Simon had gone out together *again* – Peter's divide and rule strategy couldn't get round the simple truth that they clearly preferred each other to me. I was in the writers' room eating a delicious poached salmon and watercress sandwich from Pret À Manger and reading a short item about Andrews in *Private Eye*: *Michael Andrews, midget founder and owner of pisspoor production company Sparkle, earned himself a slap round the face from a lissom hackette he tried to interest in negotiations of a Ugandan nature at the Groucho Club*. I was just trying to figure out whether Andrews would be more pleased by the mention in *Private Eye* than he would be mortified by the story when I heard someone cough.

Surprised, I looked around and saw that Karen had entered the room. I gathered that her cough was a stage cough, a timid way of announcing her arrival. She smiled shyly and said, 'Do you have any friends you want to invite to the pilot?'

'What do you mean?'

'The pilot's coming up in four weeks' time and

I've been told to put together an audience – well, contestants really as they're one and the same thing, aren't they?'

'Yes, they are. So what happens then? We all just ask people to come along?'

'That's the idea. Friends and family.'

I had to think fast. I also had to remove my eyes from her perfect breasts. I was somehow aware that my value system obliged me to follow up a leer with a pass and I wasn't sure I wanted to go where Andrews had been before.

The trouble with the pilot was that, obviously, I didn't want any friends of mine – still less family – witnessing what could very well be a complete débâcle. More to the point, I couldn't risk any of them saying something untoward to Andrews who would undoubtedly be in screaming mode. On the other hand, I didn't want Karen – or anyone else at Sparkle – to be under the impression that I was David No-Mates or that my family didn't give a toss about me.

'Leave it with me,' I said eventually. 'I'll ask around and get back to you but,' I motioned her nearer to me as though I were confiding in her, 'since it's my first show . . .'

I had hoped that she would infer enough from those words without me having to explain further but her confused face indicated otherwise.

'Look, Karen, this is the first TV show I've ever been involved with: it's important to me to get it right. I want to be able to concentrate on my job and not worry about my Auntie Betty.'

'I've got an Auntie Betty too.'

'Small world.' But the sarcasm was wasted on her. Truth is, I don't have an Auntie Betty but Karen was not someone to whom you'd want to explain a figure of speech. 'Perhaps you'll give me some tickets for a future show – you know, once the run has started.'

'Oh no, I won't be able to do that. That will be the job of the contestant researcher.'

'What's that? I know that a can-catcher is the person who has to make sure that cans at the end of the conveyor belt don't crash into each other and get dented. I am familiar also with a foot-straightener as the person who screws the feet on clock dials into place and I've heard of a boner – no, Karen, it's not what you think: it's the person who puts stays into women's corsets. But I've never come across a contestant researcher.'

'She's the person who researches contestants.'

'Serves me right.' I laughed; she giggled. 'So if you're not the contestant researcher, who is?'

'A girl called Gaby Taylor. She starts on Monday.'

'Sounds a bit of a doss job. All she's got to do is . . .' And that was when it occurred to me that I had absolutely no idea how a contestant researcher operated. Was there, I found myself wondering, an agency which matched TV shows with wannabes? Or was there something on the web? Or was it simply a question of getting in touch with large companies and seeing if they wanted to organise a works' outing? Did such things as 'works' outings' even exist outside of an old-fashioned comedian's patter?

Once again, I was beset – or would have been if it had mattered to me – by ignorance.

'One thing's for certain though,' I told Peter that evening as we drove to Richmond to check out a new Beatles' tribute band, imaginatively named The Ballad of John & Paul. 'She will be shallower than the shallow end of a kiddie pool designed for the children of midgets.'

'Gotta figure, man.'

'Contestant researcher is like a failed personnel officer.'

'Dig it.'

'OK, she's under five foot three, with a fat arse and badly dyed and permed blonde hair.'

'I thought you hadn't met her?'

'I have the gift of second sight.'

'Bollocks!'

'Yes, I do. Didn't I give you the first two home in the Grand National?'

'Yeah. When there were two horses left in the lead.'

'Well I put them in the right order.'

'That's not second sight, dummy. Sod!' This latter word wasn't addressed to me but to the back of the Volvo driver who had just cut us up. I say 'us' but it was, of course, Peter who was doing the driving as I, like Michael Jackson, Claudia Schiffer, Ken Livingstone and Gordon Brown, am a non-driver. It isn't that I had a licence and lost it, nor am I physically incapable of driving (witness the fact that I've never – touch wood – had a crash on my moped) and I'm hardly so important and wealthy that I don't *need* to drive. It's just that, if I have a talent for anything, apart from trivia, it is for failing driving tests.

I've taken eleven tests so far and failed the lot. I fail for different reasons: poor reversing, going too fast, going to slow, use of gears etc. but, if you took my eclectic best over all the tests, I could have passed several times over.

Still, so long as mates like Peter and Ziggy were prepared to ferry me round, I had no problem using a mixture of public transport, taxis and my moped, for which I had passed a test a hundred years ago. It's true that girlfriends were chosen as much for their geographical proximity and/or their ability to drive as for their other attributes, but my not being able to drive always seemed to bother other people more than it ever bothered me.

'I think I might have found a flat,' said Peter *à propos* of nothing.

'Bo!' Bo – a contraction of 'Bonzo' – was the highest form of approbation. 'Where?'

'Marylebone.'

'Triffic.'

He turned to look at me which is something he does far too often when he's driving. Not that I can complain, of course, being Douglas Bader (i.e. without a leg to stand on) when it comes to driving. 'Well, Lisson Grove, more like, but it's cool. Big, airy, really good acoustics.'

I gave an 'as if' look. I wanted a flat, not a rehearsal studio.

'Yeah. Only trouble is, it's three hundred a week and it's got three bedrooms. Can you think of anyone we could get to share?'

'Ziggy.'

'And don't say Ziggy.'

'Ah, come on, man. I love him: he's great.'

'He's a prat.'

'Steady.'

'OK, I'm being unkind. He's not a prat but he's a prattler. He doesn't stop prattling. And when he's not talking about some fucking fad diet, he's going on about bleeding *EastEnders*.'

'Yes. Well. Granted he's got a tendency to be a little – how can I put it? – *monomaniacal* about his interests but, shit, we all do that. Look at you with your porn.'

'That's different. That's more of a personal hobby.'

'All right. What if I banned him from talking about television?'

'And the diets?'

78

'I can't stop him doing them, but I'll have a word with him and ask him to stop proselytising about them.' I couldn't blame Peter for his wariness. The trouble with Ziggy – or Gary, to give him his real name – is that he can't help sharing his passions with anyone who has the misfortune to be in the same room as him. So one day he'll be telling you how the only way to eat is to separate carbohydrates and proteins, and he'll be deaf to your perfectly reasonable response that you like eating your spag and your bol in the same meal and not five hours apart. Or he'll have an opinion – no, not an opinion, a conviction – that, say, a certain cricketer is the best all-rounder in history and nothing can safeguard you against his passionate advocacy.

This passionate advocacy should, in theory, help him with his work as a barrister but the funny thing is that, once he gets into a courtroom, he freezes. It's true, I've seen him in inaction and to describe him as 'tongue-tied' is to overstate his fluency. Whether it's fear, which he furiously denies, or just a matter, as he claims, of 'over-checking my exuberance', he's spectacularly unsuccessful.

I decided to articulate my thoughts. 'Look, mate, you know what Ziggy's like in court . . .'

'King William the Silent?'

'*Précisément, mon brave*, so why don't we put him in a wig? That'll shut him up.'

Peter laughed in that high-pitched way he does when he can't help himself. 'OK, you've got it, man. But . . .'

'I know, I know.' And I knew. Above all, I knew that what really bothered Peter was not Ziggy's crazes – which were at worst enervating – but the fear of losing me to him. By joining him in a (legitimate) slagging off of Ziggy, I was reassuring him that our relationship was still more important. In time, I hoped that the two of them would become just as good friends with each other as I was with them. Well, nearly.

'We're here,' said Peter unnecessarily as he parked opposite a magistrate's court.

I got out of the car and shut it carefully as I know that Peter's got a thing about people slamming his car's doors.

'Oi, man, don't slam the fucking door!'

'I never!'

"kin did!'

"kin didn't!'

We sorted out our difference of opinion in a typically mature fashion by pushing each other on to the bonnet of a parked Jaguar. It earned us a disapproving 'tut' from a passing old bag.

'What do you reckon to the jig?' I asked as we walked down the road.

'It'll be crap.'

'You hope!'

'I know.'

'So why go?'

'Just to make sure.'

An impromptu see-who-can-gob-furthest-while-we-walk contest ensued before I said, 'Tell you what . . .'

'Des Lynam.'

'What do you mean?'

'Des Lynam says, "Tell you what!" Wasn't that your Des Lynam impression?'

'Don't be a prat. I wasn't doing an impression, I was just about to offer you a triv. challenge.'

'How so?'

'Beatles.'

'Cool.' He rubbed his hands. Peter's never lost a Beatles trivia quiz to anyone – not even to me.

'Real people namechecked in Beatles songs.'

'OK, you called it; you go first.'

'Edward Heath: "Taxman". Oh yeah, that's another thing: you can only use one person per song so, like, you can't have Harold Wilson who's also in "Taxman".'

'I understand. The Queen: "Penny Lane".'

He was looking confident but I could think of at least two more which might just beat – or, at least, tie – him. 'Edgar Allen Poe: "I Am The Walrus". "Man you should have seen them kicking . . ." '

'I got a rule too: no bloody singing.'

'Ooh, get her!'

'You've been spending too much time with your bum chums.' He kicked someone's discarded lager

81

can off the pavement and into the gutter. ' "Dig It."
It's a song on *Let It Be* just before the title track. It
mentions lots of people. Heroes, that kind of thing.
I'll say Sir Matt Busby.'

'And I'll say Charles Hawtrey in the intro to
"Two of Us" on the same album.'

'Very good, David, I'm impressed. My turn and
it's Mao Tse-tung on "Revolution".'

I was now struggling. 'Are there any more?'

He nodded and was about to speak when I
stopped him. There was someone's name mentioned in 'The Ballad of John and Yoko' but I was
damned if I could remember who it was. I started
singing it to myself – as quickly as possible – until I
got to 'Peter Brown called to say' . . . 'Peter Brown!'

'I'll let you have that. My turn, Bob Dylan: "Yer
Blues".'

I did a gesture of something going straight over
my head. 'Are you bunnying me? "Yer Blues"? I've
never heard of that.'

'Don't blame me for your own ignorance. It's on
the *White Album*.'

'I'll take your word for it,' I said without hesita-
tion. Peter is the most honest guy I know.

I couldn't think of any more real people in
Beatles songs. Not besides the people I'd already
said plus the Queen and, if I'd thought about it
long enough, Chairman Mao. Fortunately, we'd
reached the venue. 'Sorry, Peter, it looks like the
contest's over.'

'It will be as soon as you concede that you're stumped.'

I held up my hands in mock surrender. 'I concede!'

'Then you'll curse Sir Walter Raleigh for being such a stupid git . . .'

'. . . "I'm So Tired". You bastard, I knew that!'

'Tough tit, babe. But you did well, man. You came second.'

# CHAPTER ELEVEN

Because of pressure of work, I ended up agreeing to Peter's choice of flat without even seeing it. But then, given his generosity in offering to handle the move – not to mention his capitulation over Ziggy – it would have been churlish of me to have insisted on an inspection.

As for Ziggy, he was thrilled. 'Groovy. I was just about to embark on a quest for a new billet and now you've saved me the hassle.' He really does speak like that sometimes: a curious mixture of old buffer and 1970s swinger – a sort of cross between C. Aubrey Smith and Peter Wyngarde.

The plan was for Peter to supervise the 'man with a van' on the Friday and make the place habitable. Then Ziggy and I would move in on the Saturday to help tart it up – i.e. put up posters of scantily clad females, arrange the boxes of cereal and jars of pasta sauce and, most important, sort out a comprehensive (by genre and thence by alphabet) display of all of our CDs. We would store them all together but with a colour coding. Mine, we had decided, would be marked with a blue spot, Peter's with a white spot and Ziggy's with a yellow.

Later, when we had achieved this Sisyphean task – which took twice as long as all the other jobs put together – I was staggered by how old-fashioned my flatmates' musical tastes were. Of course I understood that Peter was obliged to own the entire Beatles output together with most of their solo work but that didn't explain Donovan, the Incredible String Band and Cat Stevens.

At least my vintage CDs include the great R&B classics from the Yardbirds, Them, the Who and the Kinks. I also have a respectable collection of great Stones albums – from four decades – but Peter holds this strange belief that you can't like the Beatles *and* the Rolling Stones. In his own warped words, 'It's like supporting Spurs and Arsenal, man.' No it's not, dummy.

Meanwhile, as well as those albums, my collection also includes a healthy number of CDs by Coldplay, Craig David, Moby, Muse, Gomez and Radiohead. I've even got an Eminem CD which, if truth be told, I only bought (and play) to wind up Peter and Ziggy.

In his own way, Ziggy's collection is even more tragic than Peter's. The only 'contemporary' CD he possesses is Steely Dan's *Two Against Nature*. I say 'contemporary' but it's still a throwback to 1970s jazz-rock-fusion. For what it's worth, I've got nothing against Steely Dan – in the right place at the right time i.e. a university bedsit in the 1970s. They're certainly better than the Nick Drake and early Joni Mitchell that he puts on when he's not listening to 'The Dan'. And what, while we're about it, is Pretzel Logic anyway?

Apart from sorting out all our CDs, whilst attempting to give the lads a musical education – which only succeeded in uniting them against me – my other contribution was to point out the real significance of our new home. 'Marylebone,' I announced, for we had decided that if we couldn't think of our flat as being in Marylebone as opposed to Lisson Grove then how could we persuade visiting women to do so, 'holds an important claim to fame. Its station is the third most often landed-upon square on the Monopoly board.'

Eyebrows were raised which meant that my authority was being challenged. 'Listen, children, and learn. If there were no Jail and no Community Chest and Chance cards, you'd have an equal chance of landing on any square. However, there are and you don't. Look, there's three ways of going to jail in Monopoly: via the cards, by landing on a square or by throwing three doubles in a row. Where is Marylebone Station? Precisely five spaces after you emerge blinking in the sunlight from jail. What is more, there is even a card that invites you to take a trip to Marylebone Station. QED.'

Ziggy pondered my fascinating fact. 'You say that Marylebone is the third most often landed-upon square – my God, they didn't teach you syntax at your minor public school, did they? So what are the first and second most landed-upon squares?'

I looked at them both in the eyes. For the first time, I noticed that Ziggy has perfectly brown eyes: something I don't think I've ever seen before as, if you look closely enough, most brown eyes are flecked with green. The lads were torn between needing to know the answer and wanting me to fail. I happened to know the answer but wished to tantalise them a bit longer. On the other hand, I didn't like the idea of them thinking that I was taking my time in order to make up answers, so I broke my silence. 'Trafalgar Square and Go.'

'How do you know?' asked Ziggy. He isn't a barrister for nothing.

'Read it once in an American lists book. A scientist factored in all the statistics into a computer and those were the results. All I did was transpose them from the American game.'

They were visibly impressed. Why, Ziggy even stopped scratching his balls – one of his least lovely hobbies – to give me a Paul McCartney-style thumbs up.

For good measure, I also told them that Free Parking and Marlborough Street came, respectively, fourth and fifth on the same list – though, by that point, I could have said the Conservatory and Irkutsk and they would have taken my word for it.

If only it had been as simple at work. There, not only did Frank and Simon have the drop on me most of the time, but also, there wasn't the same reservoir of goodwill and affection. The truth is, just like I loved outwitting them in trivia challenges, they adored discovering my mistakes – which, somehow I think, made them nastier to me. For example, I had written the following question: What was the first song ever played on *Top of the Pops*?

a)  'She Loves You' the Beatles
b)  'I Only Want To Be With You' Dusty Springfield
c)  'Hippy Hippy Shake' The Swinging Blue Jeans
d)  'You Were Made For Me' Freddie and the Dreamers

ANSWER: b) 'I Only Want To Be With You' Dusty Springfield

Simon read it aloud to Frank and said of me as though I wasn't in the room, 'I think he's made an 'ickle error.'

'Oh yeah?' I said, surprised at the force of my desire to push his prominent Adam's apple to the back of his throat.

'Can't you see it, David?'

I stopped to think about it for a second – just in case I had indeed made a mistake. 'No, I stand by it. I've checked – as you'd know if you'd bothered to actually read my sources list – with reference books, the internet and even with the BBC TV press office, and they all confirm that Dusty was the first person on *Top of the Pops.*'

'Tell him, Frank.'

Frank looked up from his copy of *Empire* magazine and, in a bored voice, said, 'No one's doubting that she was the first person to *sing* on the programme, but that's not what you've asked. In your question, you've asked: What was the first song ever played? That suggests something entirely different. That suggests a record played on a gramophone rather than one sung.'

I immediately saw his point but wasn't giving up without a fight, especially as I also realised that I had been ambushed, that they had obviously colluded in advance in order to sap my morale. Just because I was paranoid didn't mean the bastards weren't out to get me. 'Fair dos. But even if – and I stress the *if* – the question's open to misinterpretation, the answer isn't: the only answer to the question is Dusty.'

I could tell by the triumphant look in Simon's eye that he was ready for me. 'Perhaps. For all we know, the first record played on the show – as opposed to performed by an artiste – was one of those three "wrong" answers you gave. I've seen recordings of early editions of *Top of the Pops* and they actually used to put a record on a turntable and spin it. Now suppose the first time they did that, the song was "She Loves You". Where would you be then?'

'But it's perfectly clear what I was getting at. I mean, "the first song on *Top of the Pops*" means something, "the first song not performed live" is meaningless.'

'Aha,' said Frank, 'the value of precision. However, that isn't our problem at the moment.'

'So what is?' I said sulkily, knowing that I had been bested on the last point.

'Michael is not happy.'

'Ooh,' said Simon, 'we can't allow that, can we?'

'He says we're being too clever.'

'What do you mean?'

'OK. What are the last three questions you've written?'

I looked on my computer and read out the questions I had just finished composing. They were: In which African country would you find the Etosha National Park? In which Shakespeare play would you find the line 'The wheel is come full circle'? Who won the 1976 Miss Orange County Beauty Contest? The answers being, respectively, Namibia, *King Lear* and Michelle Pfeiffer.

Frank nodded with what looked like something

approaching approval but his words belied it. 'And what do you notice about those three questions?'

I didn't know. 'I don't know. Not contemporary enough? I can't believe they're not varied enough, and if it's a problem about where I place the correct answer . . .'

'No, the solution is staring you in the face. They're all too difficult.'

'What? Do you think so?'

'It's not what I think that counts: it's what Michael thinks, and he thinks that we've made the questions too hard.'

'Yeah, but there are only four choices . . .'

Simon interrupted. 'Actually, I think you'll find that four options gives you *three* choices.'

'Ignore Patsy Pedantic,' said Frank. 'That's not the point. Michael says we're overestimating people's intelligence. Michael says – and I quote, "Only patronising wankers upset the punters who pay their fucking wages". Michael says . . .'

I couldn't resist it. 'I thought the game was "Simon says".'

Frank shrugged. He didn't seem bothered by my jibe. 'He who pays the researcher . . . Maybe he's right.'

'The truth is,' said Simon, 'we write harder questions because they're more interesting to write – more of a challenge and less of an insult to our intelligence to research. There's nothing wrong with dumbing down even if it's more boring for us. We're not here for our own edification.'

'All right,' I said. 'I'll be dumber than Danny Dumb's backward younger brother.'

'Speaking of which,' said Simon to Frank, 'did you know that the starfish doesn't have a brain?'

Frank went into an old-style patter routine. 'I didn't know that the starfish doesn't have a brain. How does it think?'

'Hang on, Morecambe and Wise,' I said. 'Did you know that the flea can jump 350 times its body length? That's like a human jumping the length of a football field.'

'Ooh, hark at her, so she's an entomologist,' said Simon, before reverting to his proper voice to deliver a devastating catalogue of insect trivia. 'A cockroach will live nine days without its head, before it starves to death. A male spider's reproductive organ is located at the end of one of its legs. The average caterpillar has 2,000 muscles in its body, as opposed to humans who have 656. Anteaters can stick their tongues out up to 160 times a minute. Mother tarantulas kill 99 per cent of the babies they hatch. Queen bees only ever use their stingers to kill other queen bees. Queen termites can live for up to 100 years. Gram for gram, a bumblebee is 150 times stronger than an elephant. An ant can survive for two weeks underwater.' He paused for breath and then asked me, 'Did you know all of that?'

I was speechless. It was like a trivia machine-gun attack – and just as deadly. I might have overtaken Peter but I still had a long way to go to catch up with those bastards.

# CHAPTER TWELVE

Just when I was beginning to think that, like the sergeant who complains that everyone's marching out of step except him, I was the only human being at Sparkle, two people joined who made me revise my view. Dramatically, in the case of the second person.

With two weeks to go before the pilot, the producer, Walter Willis, arrived to head up the team. I have to admit that I had been slightly apprehensive about working with him. I'm not a homophobe – nor, for that matter, am I pretty – but, if his reputation was anything to go by, I was going to have to fend him off. And what with Andrews sneering at me, Belinda snubbing me and Frank and Simon scoring off me, I already had my work cut out.

Fortunately, within minutes of meeting him, I knew that not only was my bottom safe but, more importantly, my arse was too. I was going to be working for what Ziggy calls a 'mensch'. True, he was an absolute screamer but he was also the sort of guy you could josh with. So when he asked me – straight out – 'What are you doing tonight, handsome?' I was able to respond, 'My Mummy warned me about strange men like you.'

'What did she warn you about?'

'She said that they'd promise me jelly babies.'

'And so I will.'

'That's all right then. I was only worried that you wouldn't deliver.'

'Oh, I deliver all right. The question is, do you?'

''Fraid not, Walter. My body's strictly off-limits.'

He blew me a kiss. 'Pity. What a waste.'

I realised, with a slight shock, that I had been flirting with him but it was totally harmless. I think the truth was that, with his short pudgy body, thinning greying hair and a round face distinguished only by the most crooked teeth I've ever seen (he himself described them as looking like 'piano keys which bear the imprint of one too many symphonies'), he looked so unprepossessing that his sexual predatoriness – although clearly earnest – came across as cartoon rather than dramatic.

It's funny I should use the word 'earnest' when writing about Walter because 'earnest' was a codename for 'homosexual' used by Victorian gays. Hence the title Oscar Wilde gave to his play, *The Importance of Being Earnest*.

Interestingly though, Simon and, to a lesser

extent, Frank both seemed cowed by him – as if they were somehow scared of him and I don't know how significant it was but they never went into camp mode whenever he was around. Which was a blessed bloody relief.

Walter's arrival meant that, for the first time since I started work at Sparkle, I had a structured, supervised working environment. Until then, Frank, Simon and I had been careering around like prisoners yoked together inside a gigantic wheel: working, yes, but also bitching and snarling which is, ultimately, counter-productive.

Of course, the three of us already had a boss in Andrews but, for whatever reasons, he liked to see us squabble. The more divided we were, to adapt Peter's theory, the more he ruled. The fact that, as the Managing Director of Sparkle, he was acting against his own interests, only marked him out as a total tosser.

The following Tuesday, Belinda summoned me to Michael's office. 'Sit down, David,' he said. I coughed and looked away as the sight of his birthmark, looking now like the stern of a World War Two battleship, threatened to make me giggle.

That was when I saw Gaby.

Later, when I rationalised it, I discovered that there was nothing particularly special about her. Shoulder-length brown hair, snub nose, light freckles, brown eyes and a little bit tubby. Her only distinguishing feature was a pair of matching dimples in her cheek which went in as she smiled. However, at the precise moment I met her, she was Cleopatra, Helen of Troy and Marilyn Monroe rolled into one perfect person.

*Perfect*. That was my instant reaction. *I've met the perfect woman.* I couldn't catch my breath, not because of excitement but fear – the fear that I might muck up my one shot at true happiness.

Don't be an idiot, I told myself as Andrews introduced us and asked me to take Gaby under my wing. You're exaggerating this. You don't believe in love at first sight – do you? Anyway, even if you do, which you don't, this is hardly likely to be it. Not here, not at bloody Sparkle.

Andrews left the room which meant that there was a silence. It would have been embarrassing for me to stand there staring at her, even though that was what I wanted to do more than anything else in the world. 'Where have you come from?' I couldn't believe how inappropriately mundane my question was.

'The BBC.' It was Gaby, talking to me. Talking. To. Me!

'Oh yes?' I gibbered. 'Which department?' As if *I'd* know.

'Light ent.'

It meant nothing to me but I'd heard Walter Willis and Simon having a conversation along those lines earlier and I desperately wanted to appear au fait with the media in front of this lovely girl so I nodded intelligently.

That was the word: lovely. Even at that moment, as I stood there drinking in her gorgeousness, I think I might have just about – on some level – worked out that this was a personal loveliness, for these eyes only. But that just made her even lovelier. Anyone can fall in love with Julia Roberts, albeit from a distance: Gaby Taylor was beautiful just for me.

'So you'll already know Walter Willis then?'

She smiled. 'Everyone knows Walter. He's wonderful. I used to be his PA before I became a contestant researcher.'

'Er, I'm not actually inviting any friends to the pilot.' I don't know why I volunteered this – unless it was nervousness at being in her presence.

'No skin off my nose. I'm not responsible for that. I'm here for the series. Besides, television pilots are like Monopoly money: no use in the real world.'

I liked her. 'Ah, but we've got Kit Connolly.' I searched her face, mostly because I found it so utterly appealing but also for a reaction. It came.

'That prat?' she said scathingly. 'Is he just here for the pilot or the series as well?'

'So you've heard?'

'No. About what?'

'Richie Clarke.' If I was thinking of spending the rest of my life with this woman then I might as well get into the habit of telling her everything.

'Richie Clarke as in *Richie's Not In*?'

'Isn't it *Richie's Night In*?'

'Not at the BBC, it isn't. Richie's never in. At least, he's never where he should be as he's always off shagging.'

'No!'

'Oh yes. They don't call him Clarke the Cab for nothing.'

'I don't get it.'

She lowered her eyes in a pretence of being demure. 'He comes and he goes.' She noticed I was puzzled, so she elaborated. 'He picks 'em up – usually at the Club in TV Centre – takes 'em back to his place and then, when the deed is done, he calls a cab and he's off.'

'And you know this for sure, do you?' I shouldn't have but I couldn't resist it.

She pouted and I felt stirrings in my groin. 'Ladies don't tell. On the other hand, I can disclose that Richie Clarke is not my type. It's not that he's narcissistic, it's just that he spends all his spare time looking in mirrors in the hope that he'll find one that kisses back. So you see, young man . . .'

'. . . not so much of the young man. I'm thirty-three. What are you? Twenty-eight, twenty-nine?'

'How dare you! I'm twenty-seven.'

'When are you twenty-eight?'

'Three weeks' time.'

'Well then.'

'Well then.' To an outsider, it would have looked as though we were almost squaring up to each other but I knew that both of us were involved in top quality badinage.

'What date?'

'The twenty-seventh.'

'Care to come with me to a gig? My flatmate Peter is taking part in a Battle of the Beatles Tribute Bands at the Hammersmith Apollo.'

'Sounds gear.'

'So you'll come then?'

'Wild horses . . .'

'That's the Stones . . .'

'. . . written by Mick for Marianne Faithfull.'

'Top triv,' I said, genuinely impressed. I had been holding myself back in that area, fearful that I might lose her if she suspected me of nerdiness. Caroline, the girl I lived with for forty-eight hours (when I put my back out) had dumped me for that. 'Come back to me when you've got some experiences of your own to tell me about rather than those of celebrities,' she had said after giving me my marching orders. And I, as I recall, had replied, 'Funny you should say that: Noel Gallagher used to be a roadie for the Inspiral Carpets, Courteney Cox was the first person on US TV ever to use the word 'period' – in an ad for Tampax, Alan Davies bought the *Big Brother* diary room chair for £30,000, Sir Anthony Hopkins used to be able to hypnotise people by pulling their earlobes.' I had carried on chuntering out celebrity trivia until she'd been obliged to run away.

It hadn't bothered me then. I didn't feel anything for Caroline beyond the physical, and the fact that she'd echoed my mother's words to me, 'The trouble with you is, you know everything there is to know about rubbish and nothing about what really matters' hadn't worried me in the slightest. Truth is, *I* know I'm not a nerd – and so do all my friends in the trainspotting crowd (just kidding).

But now, I couldn't afford to alienate Gaby by spouting trivia at her. On the other hand, if she was to want me at all, then she had to know the real me.

Fortunately – and amazingly – she settled my dilemma. 'There's more where that came from.'

'Oh yeah?' I said with my heart fluttering.

'Oh yeah. You mentioned the Beatles, right? Well, I can tell you that "Something" was written by George Harrison for his wife Patti.'

'Everyone knows that. Just like everyone knows that Eric Clapton wrote "Layla" and "Wonderful Tonight" for her too.'

'OK, did you know that Paul McCartney wrote "Things We Said Today" and "We Can Work It Out" for Jane Asher?'

'Yes, I did, and I also know that he wrote "You Won't See Me" for her too.'

'OK, clever clogs,' she said with a smile that

involved her eyes, her mouth and, of course, her dimples, 'who inspired the line "I know what it's like to be dead" in "She Said She Said"?'

I was torn between loving her for her evident love of trivia and annoyance at my ignorance. 'Don't know,' I was forced to admit.

'It was written by John Lennon who overheard the actor Peter Fonda talking about a near-death childhood experience to George.'

'Wow! And do *you* know who inspired the song "Dear Prudence"?'

She looked at me in much the same way that Dr Stephen Hawking would have looked at a GCSE Physics student who asked him if he was familiar with Boyle's Law. 'Yawn. It was written to encourage Prudence Farrow, that's Mia Farrow's younger sister, to stop meditating so much – "won't you come out to play" – during the Beatles' time in India.'

I heard Andrews (or someone) walking towards the office. Like a wartime spy, I had just seconds to pass on my vital message. 'I love you,' I whispered.

# CHAPTER THIRTEEN

Hard as I tried, I saw very little of Gaby over the next ten days. When she wasn't out and about rustling up audiences, I was buried in endless meetings discussing the minutiae of questions, arguing interminably over, for example, whether Miss Marple could reasonably be described as 'a detective' or if the word 'Oscars' could include British Academy Awards as well as American.

The biggest argument was over a question I wrote. It was for the second half of the show and it went like this: How many British Prime Ministers were there in the twentieth century?

a)   17
b)   18
c)   19
d)   20

I reckoned the answer was twenty and, with my usual diligence, had appended the full list. What could possibly be wrong with that, I wondered – but I had reckoned without Simon's genius for hair-splitting.

'It's misleading,' he pronounced.

I gritted my teeth. 'Oh? How?'

'You claim there were twenty different Prime Ministers but Harold Wilson was Prime Minister twice. That makes it twenty-one by my estimation.'

'But that's ridiculous,' I said. 'I asked how many Prime Ministers there were – not how many different times. Besides, twenty-one isn't even one of the possible answers.'

'But someone could argue that we misled them.'

'Come off it, Simon, you're mad. You're worse than pedantic: you're paranoid.'

It needed the wisdom of Solomon to sort it out but we had to make do with Frank. 'How about we change the wording to "How many different people served as Prime Minister in the twentieth century"?'

'All right, I suppose,' I said sulkily.

'No,' said Simon, 'I don't like that. Clement Attlee deputised as Prime Minister during the war when Churchill was away.'

'So fucking what!' I shouted. 'Attlee's on our fucking list!'

Simon looked defeated but now it was Frank's turn to be nitpicker-in-chief. 'What about Butler?'

'Butler? What, as in "I hate you, Butler"?' Their blank looks betrayed their ignorance of the seminal 1970s sitcom *On The Buses*.

'No. R.A. Butler – Rab Butler. He stood in for Eden when he was ill and later for Macmillan.'

'And your point is?'

'He never became Prime Minister and yet he *served* as Prime Minister.'

I exploded. 'Which is how you fucking worded the question! Now you're arguing against yourself. This is crazy.'

'This,' said Simon with enviable coolness, 'is professionalism.'

And that's how another brilliant question got binned.

The night before the pilot was horrible. I've never thought of myself as the nervous type but I found myself pacing round the large kitchen-breakfast room of the (new) flat like an expectant father.

'Cool it, David,' said Ziggy, who was spooning unfeasible amounts of yoghurt and honey into his mouth. 'You're putting me off my tuck.'

Peter arched an eyebrow. 'Didn't think anyone was capable of doing that.'

'I'm sorry,' said Ziggy coldly, 'isn't there any porn on the net at the moment?'

'Having watched you eat, man, I think we're going to have to redefine the word "porn".'

In my agitated state, I couldn't bear to see my closest friends bickering. 'Girls, girls, girls. Hand-bags down. Peter, please. I tell you, what with

Frank and Simon and now you too, I feel like one of Harry Enfield's Scousers: either in a row or stopping one. Ziggy, you just keep shovelling that muck down your gob. By the way, I thought you were meant to be on a diet.'

His chins wobbled as he tried simultaneously to swallow a particularly large mouthful and defend his reputation. 'This is a diet.'

'Yeah, man,' said Peter, indicating the acoustic guitar on his lap, 'and this is a trombone.'

'Please, guys,' I whined. 'Don't do this to me. I'm feeling so strung out about tomorrow, I can't handle it.'

Each of them tried to help me the only way they knew how. 'Here,' said Peter, offering me a joint he'd just lit, 'have a toke on this.'

'No thanks, Peter, you know I don't. It's not because I've got anything against dope, it's that I don't want to get hooked on tobacco again.'

'I've got some chocolate if you want,' said Ziggy. 'It's seventy per cent cocoa. Finest kind.'

'Thanks, Zig, but no – it would just make me sick. I feel really nauseous as it is.'

Ziggy stopped eating – a real sacrifice that I appreciated. 'What, specifically, is bothering you?'

I put on a Brando accent. 'What have you got?'

'Seriously.'

'Seriously? I'm worried that I'm going to fuck up tomorrow.'

'How?'

'That I'll get a question wrong.'

'But they've all been checked, haven't they?'

'Yes, but there's always the chance that a rogue one's slipped through.'

Peter put down his guitar and his joint. Another magnificent gesture. 'From what you've been telling me about the procedures there, that would be impossible.'

'Not impossible but, I have to concede, unlikely.' I bent down to pick up a piece of bacon fat that Peter would have dropped at lunchtime. He's a vegetarian but his definition of vegetarianism includes bacon sarnies.

'There you go,' said Peter. 'Why should you fuck up then? Are you thinking of Paxton's?'

'What's that?' asked Ziggy.

'Tell him, Peter.'

'Do you remember when David worked in that features agency?'

'Sort of.'

'Do you remember when David left?'

'Sort of.'

'Did you ever wonder why he left?'

'No. I presumed that he had found a superior position elsewhere.'

'Well, he didn't. He went from there to the DSS. Do you know why he left? He was caught with his hand in the till.'

'Peter! That's not fucking fair! I wasn't caught – and nor had I been stealing.'

'Yes, you were and yes, you had been.'

'OK, but Ziggy, you've got to believe me that it wasn't exactly as Peter tells it. True, I helped myself to five hundred quid out of petty cash and yes, I was asked to leave – although they were never able to actually prove it.'

'That didn't stop you from pacing up and down outside the magistrate's court for days on end . . .'

'Yes, because I felt guilty – but the fact is, *they* ripped *me* off. I came up with this celebrity puzzle idea called *Seven Down* – it's a pun on the soft drink, get it? – which basically gave readers seven clues to identify a celebrity. Bog standard stuff, right?' They both nodded obediently. 'Now the agreement I had with Ron – Ron Paxton, the boss of the agency – was that because he was paying me so little, I got to keep ten per cent of the proceeds of any idea I initiated. But the funny thing was, my ideas never seemed to get used: he was always changing them – not by much but by just enough to claim that they weren't mine and he could therefore deny me my dosh.'

I paused.

'Well, with *Seven Down*, he made the mistake of not only selling the puzzle as I'd created it, but also of keeping the name. When I saw the puzzle in a supermarket magazine, I showed it to him and demanded credit, but he tried to bullshit me by saying that as the magazine wasn't on sale to the public, our agreement didn't hold. Bollocks! I knew it; he knew it. So I bided my time and when the opportunity arose to claim restitution, so to speak, I claimed it – with both hands.'

I raised my shoulders in a 'what else could I do?' gesture.

'Ron never knew for sure it was me but his guilty conscience told him that I was prime suspect so he called me into his office and gave me the Roberta Flack.'

'The *what*?' asked Ziggy, licking the last of the yoghurt off his finger.

'The Roberta Flack, the tin tack – *the sack*, for God's sake.'

'You just made that up.'

'No, I didn't!'

'Yes, you did. Peter, what do you think?'

'Much as it pains me to agree with you, Gary,' it's very rare for Peter to call him Ziggy: I think he thinks it's too intimate, 'I reckon you've got him bang to rights. As he himself revealed, "tin tack" is the Cockney rhyming slang for "sack". Not Roberta Flack – or indeed Cilla Black.'

'Aha!' I said. 'I never mentioned Cockney rhyming slang. And I think you'll find that Cilla Black means "back" in that. No, I was talking about *New* Rhyming Slang. And in *New* Rhyming Slang, Roberta Flack means "sack". Just like Giorgio Armani means "sarnie", Calvin Klein is "fine", Kate Moss – "toss", Fat Boy Slim – "gym", Ronan Keating – "meeting", Britney Spears – "beers".'

'Got you,' Peter interrupted. 'Come on, David, get in the Britneys. Ziggy? Does your so-called diet allow you to drink beer?'

'I'm off to watch *The Sweeney* on Granada Plus,' said Ziggy, departing with as much hauteur as a man with yoghurt and honey smeared all around his mouth could muster.

I called after his retreating round-shouldered corpulent frame, 'But you've watched every episode a thousand times. How often do you need to watch Jack Regan saying, "You're nicked"?'

Peter put his arm around my shoulder. 'Don't, Guv, he's not worth it.'

We both laughed and I realised with pleasure and relief that I was no longer feeling so wretched.

# CHAPTER FOURTEEN

The nerves had returned – with interest – by showtime.

At seven o'clock, Simon and I were sitting in the green room at the studios just south of the river. I'd never seen a green room before and was – albeit foolishly – surprised to find that there wasn't a trace of green in it.

I mentioned it to Simon. 'If you think that's funny,' he said, 'you should know that this whole studio is a mistake.'

'What do you mean?'

'This is next door to a major teaching hospital, right? Well, this place was endowed by an eminent surgeon who intended to leave his money to an operating theatre but, thanks to a misunderstanding, a theatre theatre was built instead.'

'No!'

'Yes, apparently so. It's a good story at any rate.'

I was pleased to find Simon in rare human-being mode. Maybe he was as nervous as I was but

111

couldn't show it. Mind you, he wouldn't have known that I was bricking it – not unless he was counting the number of times I went to the loo. Thirteen in the past hour.

'Nicholas Lyndhurst, John Travolta, Kurt Russell, John Grisham.'

'Your point is?' he asked.

'They're all pilots. They've all got pilots' licences.'

I was sorry I had spoken but it had at least whiled away a few seconds. I hadn't realised just how much empty time there is in a television studio interrupted every few hours by an unbelievably hectic and intense three minutes in which you're required to know the answer to every problem thrown at you.

Now, with the audience in their seats and Andrews and Walter temporarily satisfied, Simon and I were alone: the original two spare parts. In fact, we weren't entirely on our own. In the corner, doing some needlepoint, sat a middle-aged woman with a beatific smile on her face. Someone's mum, no doubt, or else one of the hundreds of people who were evidently vital to the whole process. And to think it wasn't even a proper programme: in fact, not even a real pilot – just a 'run-through with cameras'.

'Poor old Frank,' I said, delving into an impressive fruit bowl for a bunch of grapes.

'What do you mean "poor old Frank"?'

'Getting stuck up there with Andrews while we put our feet up here.'

'I think you mean "lucky old Frank". He's the one on a percentage.'

'Yeah, but Tony Bowes is the main man.'

'Just so, but there'll be plenty enough gravy for all the Bisto Boys.'

'Really?'

'Not us, young David. We're the deserving poor.'

Part of me was rather enjoying my new found alliance with Simon. I spat a grape pip on to the floor: the woman in the corner looked at me over the top of her needlepoint and, for a second, her face registered disapproval. It didn't bother me. I scooped up a handful of peanuts and ate them greedily – despite the fact that I had had a massive supper just an hour earlier. I was eating out of boredom. Judging by the huge arses of most of the women crew I'd seen in the studio, it was an occupational hazard. Still, no worries, it was going into my mouth and going straight through me without hanging around in my digestive system. That's the funny thing with me: nerves don't seem to affect my appetite – even if they play havoc with my guts.

'Did you know that Russell Grant presented the pilot of *Every Second Counts*?' Simon asked. 'You know, the show that Paul Daniels went on to host?'

No, I didn't. 'No, I didn't. Did you know that Kit

Connolly presented the pilot of *The Lot*? You know, the show that Richie Clarke went on to host?'

Simon smiled.

'Poor Connolly,' I said without a trace of sympathy. 'He's such a . . .' I was about to say 'cunt' but, out of deference to the lady in the corner, I changed it to 'such an arsehole'.

'He's getting more than thee and me for tonight's work.'

'How much *is* he getting?'

'Not shy of ten thou.'

I whistled.

'Yes,' he continued, 'but you've got to bear in mind that he's had to put in the odd appearance at the office and then there was the rehearsal yesterday.'

'Even so. That's mucho moolah.'

'Richie'll get more.'

'Is he on board yet?'

He nodded. 'Nothing's signed, at least not as far as I know, but it's all over bar the sacking.'

'Poor Connolly,' I said again. 'Just his luck to be working for a bastard like Andrews.' I stood up and stretched. 'Need to go to the little girls' room again. That goulash I had for supper must have been off.'

'Oh, by the way, David. On your way out, say hello to Emma who's sitting over there. She's Michael Andrews's wife.'

£  £  £

Looking back on it now, immune from the nerves that were almost paralysing me, I have to say that the pilot – sorry, 'run-through with cameras' – went far better than we had feared. I later learned from Frank and Gaby respectively that there was pandemonium in the gallery and on the studio floor, but watching it on the monitor in the green room, it looked remarkably polished – in fact, like any 'real' game-show.

Of course, I was feeling simultaneously stomachy and pukey: the former due to my nerves and my gluttony, and the latter to the strong probability that, after dissing the boss in front of his wife, I was about to be made redundant. What an absolute bastard Simon was. He knew that Emma Andrews was in the room. He could have bloody warned me but, instead, he let me witter on, just knowing that I would eventually make some derogatory reference to our boss.

As it happened, I didn't lose my job. Either Emma was as saintly as she looked or else she told her old man and he accepted it as fair comment.

I have to say that Kit looked the part. Wearing a blue blazer, grey flannel trousers and a shirt and tie that looked like they'd come out of a supermarket's shirt 'n' tie Christmas set, he introduced the show as though it were a programme watched by millions every week.

'Hi, folks,' he said with a Hughie Green-style wag of the finger, 'and welcome to *The Lot*, the show that delivers the lot! This is the only game-show in the world with no audience and no contestants. That's right. The audience are the contestants and the contestants are the audience! Confused? You shouldn't be! It's simple – as simple as Benny out of *Crossroads*.' He then went into a patter about *Crossroads* and how he had once had a bit part in it, before he turned back to the show.

'Here's how it works,' he told us. 'There are three hundred of you out there – or at least there will be when we come to do the show proper. For the purposes of tonight, there are one hundred friends, family and freeloaders! Each of you should have an audience response pad with four buttons on it marked a, b, c and d. I'm going to ask you a series of questions I've put together . . .'

'Cunt!' I shouted at the TV screen, temporarily oblivious of the presence of Mrs Andrews and a skinny old man in a suit who was cupping his hand around a cigarette and whom I later discovered was Kit Connolly's driver. 'How dare he say that? "Questions *he's* put together"? My arse!'

'Cool it,' said Simon. 'He knows it's bollocks and he knows that any pro watching it will know that too but he just can't resist promoting himself.'

'Even at our expense?'

Simon smiled. 'Especially at our expense.'

'So basically,' I heard Kit say, 'if you answer a question wrong, you're out. If you keep answering questions correctly, you're in. If you're the last person left in, you're the winner and you get a fantastic prize – a night out with me. The runner-up gets . . . two nights out with me!'

'Boom, and indeed, boom,' yawned Simon.

'There's just one other thing,' said Kit busily. 'Just before the second half we play "Knockback". This is a question for all you poor people who have been knocked out. The first ten to answer correctly will be knocked right back in again. Understood?' He paused, then: 'Right, are you squatting comfortably?' Two people recognised his catchphrase and gave a weak cheer. 'Aha,' said Kit triumphantly, 'I've got my fan club in. OK then, here's the first question. Who are Posh and Becks?'

a)   Queen Elizabeth II and Prince Philip
b)   The Speaker and Deputy Speaker of the House of Commons
c)   A pair of TV puppets from the 1960s
d)   Victoria and David Beckham

The audience/contestants were given ten seconds to consider their answers: ten seconds which were accompanied by a musical sting so horrid that I swear I knew even then that it would become a big talking-point.

I couldn't believe that anyone would get the question wrong but, incredibly, two did and Kit picked on them mercilessly. This was, of course, the whole point of the first question: to put everyone at their ease but to make fun of one or two unfortunates. The fact that, as they explained, they knew the answer but their keypad wasn't working didn't cut any ice with Kit, who told them that 'poor workmen always blame their tools'.

'Doesn't look good for the programme, does it?' I asked Simon.

'Nonsense, it's fine. We'll just cut their complaints out of the final edit.'

The second question was: Which one of these London streets can be found on the Monopoly board?

a)   Cannon Street
b)   Regent Street
c)   Victoria Street
d)   Wimpole Street

ANSWER: b) Regent Street

Ninety-two of the remaining ninety-eight got it right. The other six selected Victoria Street or Wimpole Street. Kit located them and invited the others to 'point at them', which they did.

The next question surprisingly managed to knock out twelve people. I say surprisingly because, having known the running order of the questions beforehand – as it was only a pilot we weren't using the question database – we had all marked down the number of people we thought would be knocked out in each round. So far, I hadn't been too far off the pace (having predicted none for question one and five for question two) but for this question, I had guessed that only four would get it wrong. Maybe the guys were right when they said that contestants are thick – or maybe the invited audience reflected the stupidity of the friends who had asked them along.

The question in question was: Which actor's name is an anagram of BLOB RECREATION?

a)   Pierce Brosnan
b)   Sean Connery
c)   Bob Hoskins
d)   Robbie Coltrane

ANSWER: d) Robbie Coltrane

Surely ten seconds is all you need to answer that correctly? I mean, the length of the anagram and name alone should be enough of an indication, you would have thought.

The next question was, I admit, trickier but still gettable. In fact, I thought it was a really good question – even if it was one of Simon's: What was first sighted in AD565 by St Columba but only became famous after a 1933 newspaper article?

a)   Halley's Comet
b)   The planet Venus

c)    The Loch Ness Monster
d)    The Blue Whale

ANSWER: c) The Loch Ness Monster

I had expected that we'd lose 15 per cent. In the event, we lost precisely 20 per cent: twenty people – taking us down to sixty.

Now I started to panic that we'd get through all the contestants too quickly – perhaps in just another two or three questions – and that we wouldn't have a show any more.

'Relax,' said old hand Simon, when I told him of my fears. 'For a start, 'taint your problem if the format's wonky and, anyway, it isn't.'

'But we just lost twenty per cent!'

'The thickest twenty per cent. Also, you're clearly ignorant of mathematical progressions. We could carry on for – gosh, several more questions – losing twenty per cent at a time.'

I silently damned him for his superiority and blessed him for his reassurance.

He was right, of course. We lost just twelve people on the next question: What took place for the first time in 1872 at the Kennington Oval in London before a crowd of 2,000?

a)    The Calcutta Cup
b)    The FA Cup Final
c)    The Grand National

d)    England v. Australia Cricket Test

ANSWER: b) The FA Cup Final

Then we lost thirteen on this one. In which country were Joanna Lumley, Spike Milligan and Sir Cliff Richard all born?

a)    Ireland
b)    South Africa
c)    Canada
d)    India

ANSWER: d) India

And just nine on this: Who created the literary character Hannibal Lecter?

a)    Sir Anthony Hopkins
b)    Thomas Harris
c)    Leslie Thomas
d)    Robert Harris

ANSWER: b) Thomas Harris

On the next question: What was Michael Caine's surname at birth?

a)    Morrison
b)    Mountjoy

c) Micklewhite
d) Marks

ANSWER: c) Micklewhite

we lost ten people and thus fell below twenty which was the trigger point for the knockback question. This was a deliberately easy question intended to reward the quickwitted i.e. the first ten of the eighty-four who had been knocked out earlier to answer correctly. The question was: In which city were the Summer Olympic Games held in the year 2000?

a) Beijing
b) Melbourne
c) Sydney
d) Cape Town

ANSWER: c) Sydney

Seventy-six answered it correctly but 3.12 seconds turned out to be the cut-off point for being knocked back in. So now there were twenty-six people left in. The first half of the show would come to an end when that number dipped below ten. I thought the next question would achieve just that and said so to Simon but he looked down at the running order of the questions and just shook his head. The question was: Which sport derives its name from the Japanese for 'gentle art'?

a) Karate
b) Kung Fu
c) Judo
d) Aikido

ANSWER: c) Judo

Simon, of course, was right. We eliminated just eight people – leaving us with eighteen. However, during yet another one of the interminable recording breaks (so much for 'run-through with cameras') I was rewarded with a lingering shot of Gaby's beautiful bottom – by courtesy of a bored cameraman and an indulgent director.

'Will you look at dat?' said Simon in a cod-Oirish accent. 'Two scouts fighting under a blanket.'

'I think she looks absolutely wonderful,' I said without thinking. Immediately, I added, 'For a girl!' but it was too late.

'So David's smitten, uh-huh?'

I could have lied – I *should* have lied – but he'd caught me in a vulnerable moment so I just shrugged and, to my horror, blushed which was, of course, far more revealing than any words might have been.

'Needless to say, your secret is not safe with me.'

I was about to warn him of the consequences

of . . . of . . . when the show started up again with a question that *did* manage to take us below ten: What does a deltiologist collect?

a)   Greek urns
b)   Ties
c)   Postcards
d)   Shells

ANSWER: c) Postcards

That took out precisely half of them which meant that we had nine people – the maximum – for the second half. Inevitably, this precipitated in the crew the sort of panic I'd previously associated with news footage of refugees fleeing an advancing army. Equally inevitably, it triggered in me an urgent need to run to the loo.

When I returned, the chaos had, if anything, become even worse so I made my way over to a splendid finger-buffet that had materialised during my absence and proceeded to get outside it until the show's ghastly sting summoned me back to my perch next to Simon on the orange sofa.

'Welcome back!' said Kit with a cheesy grin and point of his fucking finger. 'We're down to our fabulous finalists who have joined me here on stage! I'm going to find out a little bit about them. Let's see what answers they've got to my *personal* questions!' Looking back, maybe he thought he was being ironic in *pretending* to be a complete tosser but I've always subscribed to the idea that if it looks like a duck and it walks like a duck and it sounds like a duck then it is a duck.

Anyway, after nine turgid vox pops that only revealed just how boring all the invitees were (like me, Simon and Frank had resisted the offer to recruit their friends and families), we had the first question. Like all second-half questions, it had five options: What is the third book of the Old Testament?

a)   Genesis
b)   Ezekiel
c)   Exodus
d)   Leviticus
e)   Deuteronomy

ANSWER: d) Leviticus

Three people got it wrong and were summarily ridiculed by Kit who would never have known the answer himself. The six people left were then asked: What do Eminem, Jude Law and Sarah Michelle Gellar all have?

a)   Tattoos
b)   History degrees
c)   An extra toe
d)   Twins

e)    Dual nationality

ANSWER: a) Tattoos

Someone in the audience shouted out, 'Easy-peasy.' Given that it was only a run-through and that the audience were friends and family, I suppose it wasn't surprising but, frankly, I agreed with them. That was never a second-half question: even if you didn't know the answer it was easy to work it out by process of elimination.

In the event, two people guessed wrongly and the surviving four were asked: What are White Winter, Black Winter and Black Summer?

a)    Breeds of horses
b)    Types of truffle
c)    Styles of ballet
d)    Weather fronts
e)    Breeds of pigs

ANSWER: b) Truffles

Only one person got that wrong. Now we were down to three and, even judging by the tension in the green room, it was getting seriously exciting.

Typically, Kit dampened it down by telling some totally irrelevant anecdote about meeting Leslie Crowther at a party – as if we cared – before asking: The Roman God of War was Mars. Who

126

was his Greek equivalent?

a)   Aeolus
b)   Ares
c)   Artemis
d)   Athena
e)   Athaeneum

Two contestants guessed Aeolus but a guy named John in shirtsleeves and sweat patches under his arms correctly chose Ares and we had our winner.

Kit congratulated him – managing to be simultaneously unctuous and patronising, a rare feat – and said, 'You're right to be proud of yourself, John, 'cos you're a lot cleverer than your Uncle Kit and I'm pleased to say that, whatever happens, you're guaranteed to walk away with a prize. But if you want to win *The Lot*, you have to answer five second-half questions right. You've managed to get four – d'you want to try for *The Lot*?'

'Of course he does, fool!' I shouted at the monitor. 'That's the whole bleeding point of the show!'

'Calm down,' said Simon. 'He's just trying to wind up the tension.'

'OK then, John,' said Kit, putting his arm around the man, 'to win *The Lot*, answer this: How many US States start with the letter M? The options were:

a)   5
b)   6
c)   7
d)   8
e)   9

The camera went tight on John's face and then we saw his middle finger alternating between buttons c and d. With less than a second to go, he pressed button e. The answer, as Kit told him with the sort of sympathy you'd ordinarily expect to get at a funeral parlour, was 8 (Maine, Maryland, Massachusetts, Michigan, Minnesota, Mississippi, Missouri, Montana).

John, of course, looked as if he couldn't have cared less as he was merely getting a magnum of Champagne instead of a jeroboam. Simon, on the other hand, couldn't have been more thrilled. He jumped to his feet and, addressing the green room as a whole, announced, 'Ladies and gentleman, a hit is born.'

And who was I to argue?

# CHAPTER FIFTEEN

'I tell you, man, she's unique,' said Simon.

'No, she's not,' said Frank. 'I'm sure I saw Paula Yates do it once on *The Big Breakfast.*'

'Maybe, but not standing up – or at least not without a standing start.'

'That I grant you, but even so, I don't see what's so special about a girl being able to waggle her vagina.'

Simon expressed mock outrage. 'You don't see what's so special about a woman being able to waggle her vagina? Good Lord, do you have no soul, are you completely bereft of a sense of aesthetics?'

'Hang on,' I said, keen to join in the fun, 'I have a few questions. Like when, where, why – and, indeed, who?'

'Serves you right for getting in late, *muchacho,*' said Simon testily.

'Ah, come on, guys, share it with the rest of the class.'

'Nah,' they chorused.

'I'll give you a nugget of ace trivia if you do.'

'OK.'

I cogitated for a few seconds. 'All right. Florence Nightingale used to travel everywhere with a pet owl in her pocket.'

Frank was just about to say, 'Nah' again when he caught Simon giggling at my wonderfully trivial fact. 'A'right, lad, you've earned your goss. We're talking about Belinda – Michael's secretary.'

'PA,' I interrupted in a not-bad imitation of Belinda's improbably cut-glass accent.

'Sorry, I stand corrected. *PA*. Simon here says that he's seen La Belinda waggling her vagina.'

This was wonderful but I was determined not to appear too impressed by anything they told me. 'Belinda, eh, and her performing poon? Well, Simon, where did you see that?'

'I was in Michael's office and he called her in for some reason. She ignored me as usual . . .'

'. . . Oh, I'm glad I'm not the only one . . .'

'. . . but she turned to Michael and bestowed a smile upon him that spoke wonders for the whitening achievements of the toothpaste industry and then she did it.'

'What, she waggled her fanny?'

'Yup.'

'No warning? No foreplay?'

'No.'

'Key question. Did she move her hips while she did it?'

'Aha, David, you are clearly a man of hidden depths. No, she didn't.'

'*Magnifique!*'

'*Voilà!*'

I noticed that Frank was keen to get in on the conversation now that Simon and I were being so chummy. Well, I thought, just let him see how much *he* enjoys being the third side of this fucking triangle. 'So, Simon,' I nearly called him 'Si' in my enthusiasm – 'in your informed and erudite opinion, do you reckon he's giving her one?'

Simon considered my question with all the intensity of thought that intelligent men devote to such trivial matters. If, on the other hand, I'd asked him what he thought was the meaning of life, he'd have felt honour bound to give a silly instant answer. 'Tough one. I'd say that he's been sniffing around there, certainly . . .'

'At his height, he'd have no choice.'

I laughed at Frank's gag but even as I did so, I was storing it for the future: just in case I should ever need to demonstrate my loyalty to Andrews. God, I hated myself sometimes – but less so than my colleagues whose disloyalty had corrupted any sense of solidarity I might have felt.

'I don't know how you can say such things about our beloved *Führer*,' said Simon, and I could see that his mind was working along the same sort of lines as mine. For a second, I was reminded of Oceania, Eastasia and Eurasia in *1984* – constantly falling in and out of warfare and alliance with each other. 'But I don't think he's consummated any lust he might have for Belinda.'

'Why?'

'Three reasons. Firstly, I think if he had, then she wouldn't be waggling her vagina at him, would she? Secondly, I don't think he likes 'em too keen. He gets off on making them squirm and she's too up for it for him to be able to do that.'

'You said three reasons. What's the third?'

Simon grinned, and momentarily his mask of condescending superiority slipped. I caught a glimpse of someone who could have been a mate. 'Her hair doesn't look like it's had the Wash and Come treatment.'

We all laughed. 'So Belinda isn't getting a work-out,' I said, just thinking aloud more than anything but Frank pounced on it. 'Why, David, were you thinking of volunteering?'

Before I could make some sort of reply along the lines of, 'Not with yours', Simon had leapt in with, 'Don't be silly, Frank, he's sweet on Gaby.'

I couldn't believe that – what? seconds ago – I had been entertaining amicable thoughts about the bastard. I had to nail this one – and do it fast. 'She is, I will concede, on my shopping list but I have yet to go to the checkout, so to speak.'

'If she were on my shopping list,' said Simon deliberately, 'she would be under pet food. The woman looks like a hamster, for Christ's sake.' He then sucked in his cheeks and puffed them out again in a pathetic attempt to imitate her dimples.

'Oh, I don't know,' said Frank. 'I think we're talking "dog" rather than "hamster". Leastwise, if I could fancy it at all it would be doggo-style. And even then I'd risk giving myself a hernia circumnavigating her huge posterior.'

I felt the fury rising but, even as I did so, part of me was saying to myself, This anger is good; this proves that you love her.

'Alas,' continued the loathsome Frank, 'from what I can gather from an *extremely* good source . . .'

'Are we talking Karen by any chance?' asked Simon in camp gossip mode. 'I mean, given that you and she are so intimate.'

'Can one call sex doggy-style intimate? If so, then yes, you are right. The other night, we were making the beast with the wheelbarrow and Karen said she reckoned that the boss had designs on Gabriella's dumpy little body.'

'On her hair, more like.'

They both laughed – at him, at her, *at me* – while I seethed, totally unable to dissemble my feelings. Their comments, however vile, were nothing compared to the appalling news that Andrews was apparently interested in inflicting his disgusting self on my gorgeous Gaby. Not that I had any fears that she might reciprocate his interest – well, not too many fears – but I didn't want her to be harassed out of her job and therefore out of my life. And anyway, I really couldn't bear the thought of him leering and pawing and . . . and . . .

'Oh look,' said Frank, pointing at me. 'She's upset. She's going to cry.'

'Look, fuck off, all right?'

'Ah, the spirit of Oscar Wilde lives!'

'That's rich coming from you. Both of you.'

'Meaning?'

I no longer cared about dividing, ruling or anything. 'You know what I mean. If you don't mock me for being straight, I won't mock you . . .' I let the words fall away. It wasn't even true and I knew it. What's more, I knew that they knew that I knew it but I was really wound up.

Simon put his hand up to acknowledge my obvious anger. 'Fear not, ardent lover, we will forbear to embarrass you or in any way prejudice the course of true romance. Provided, of course . . .'

Frank took over. 'Provided, of course, you let us know when you've shagged her.'

Oddly enough, this cheered me up. They'd gone from somewhere really rather nasty into the familiar, comfortable world of laddishness. More to the point, they were clearly keen to mollify me which meant . . . I didn't know what it meant but, for the sake of my own professional survival, I was determined to construe it as optimistically as possible.

Besides, I could hardly lay claim to any great

intimacy with Gaby. At least not yet. Since our wonderful meeting, I don't suppose we'd shared more than a few inconsequential chats. True, there was the occasion when she'd taken me into a corner after a meeting to whisper that Kirstie Alley bans anyone wearing perfume in her house because of its destructive effect on the ozone layer but if passing on triv. were the criterion for a budding relationship then I'd have long since married Peter.

No, I was totally fixated on the twenty-seventh, her birthday, when I'd arranged to take her to the Hammersmith Odeon. That was when I would plight my troth – ridiculous expression for any man not wearing doublets to use but I couldn't think of anything better. If I asked her out before then, I risked going off half-cocked and our future happiness was far too important to do that.

I was just marvelling at my new-found maturity when Walter Willis walked in carrying a massive box of papers. His chubby face was wet with perspiration.

'Ooh, this is heavier than a priest's testicles! Will one of you lovely boys take it off me?'

Simon was closest to him but I was there first. I've always had the knack of sucking up to Teacher.

'Sweetheart,' said Walter, mopping his brow. He smiled and yet again I was irresistibly drawn to his teeth. He looked like one of the old cons in the film *Papillon*: hadn't he heard of orthodontists? 'You're in for a raise, young David, but then I get a raise every time I look at you.'

Frank and Simon wolf-whistled.

'OK, guys,' said Walter in a surprisingly (for him) strict voice. 'Don't you have any work to do?'

Frank looked peeved. 'Please sir,' he said, 'it's only three days since the pilot and—

'—and you're still being paid to work, so get on with it.' Walter dipped into his box of papers, picked up what, from my vast experience of television shows, looked like two programme scripts and chucked one to Simon and the other to Frank. 'These are P and Cs' (that's what it sounded like to me) 'from past game-shows I've worked on. I don't want you stealing questions as such but there might be some good ideas amongst them.'

Frank's face registered annoyance. 'We've no shortage of ideas.'

Walter narrowed his eyes even further than nature had originally done. He looked like Christopher Biggins doing a Clint Eastwood imitation. 'The evidence would suggest otherwise.'

'If you've got a problem,' said Frank, 'then just say so.' I noticed that Simon was silent but was biting his lower lip.

'I thought I just did.'

I put my hand up and then put it down again in case he thought that, like Frank, I was being a sarky schoolboy. 'Excuse me, Walter, what about me? Do you want me to go through those scripts too?'

He reverted to his normal, ebullient self. 'Dear boy, I have other plans for you. Come with me.'

Following Walter out of the room, I shrugged my shoulders to the others. Simon mouthed 'teacher's pet' so I mimed a wanker sign at him and immediately worried that he would think I meant Walter and not him.

'This way,' said Walter, motioning me out of the front door of Sparkle and taking me into the café next door.

We ordered our coffees – he chose a caffe latte which I was going to choose so I asked for a cappuccino just so he didn't think I was incapable of making an independent decision – and sat down on the smart but uncomfortable wooden chairs.

I hate silence so I broke it. 'You were being a little hard on the Brothers Grim.'

'You think so?'

'No.'

'Exactly. They're prats. TV's full of them: superior shits with nothing to be superior about.'

'But did you mean what you said about the questions?'

He waved a pudgy finger at me and I saw that he was wearing what looked to be a genuine signet ring. It was entirely possible that he was, as my mother would have said, out of the top drawer. The magnificently rotten teeth were, of course, entirely consistent with that. 'No, they're fine. Best thing about the show – at least until we get Richie.'

'That's cut and dried, is it?'

'Home and hosed.'

The waitress, who would have been pretty had it not been for her Mr Spock-like ears, brought us our coffees. I sipped mine whilst maintaining eye-contact with Walter in the hope that he would appreciate the sort of colleague who maintained eye-contact.

'Date for your diary, David. Thursday fortnight. The Institute of Independent TV Production Companies is having an annual quiz night. Michael wants all of us to make up a table. Three-line whip. He says it's essential we win and I, for one, wouldn't want to disappoint our head honcho.'

'Is that what you wanted to see me about?'

'No,' he drawled. 'No, the reason I dragged you here is far less prosaic: I want to pick your brains. As you might know, I'm not on staff, I'm on contract.' I didn't know but the distinction meant nothing to me. 'Consequently, I am, in theory, allowed to pursue my own outside interests. One of these is a little quiz-show format.' He corrected himself. 'Actually, it's more of a game-show than a quiz show.'

'What's the difference?'

'Hard to say, really. It's more to do with tone than anything else. The received wisdom is that contestants sit down in quiz shows and stand up in game-shows, but *The Weakest Link* and *Fifteen To One* are both quiz shows and the contestants stand throughout. What probably differentiates a quiz show from a game-show is the prizes. Quiz shows don't have prizes – or at least not big ones. So *University Challenge*, *Mastermind*, *Countdown* – these are all quiz shows, but *The Price Is Right*, *Strike It Lucky*, *Family Fortunes* are all very much game-shows. Lots of hand-waving and all that.'

'So what does that make *Millionaire*?'

'Good question. It is, I think, a sort of hybrid – hence its success.'

'And *The Lot*?'

'Oh, that's clearly a game-show.'

'Hence . . .'

'Hence nothing. You can't infer anything from a label and *Take it Away* – my game-show – will succeed or not for how good it is and not for what category it falls into.'

'What's it about?'

'What, *Take It Away*? It's a show in which contestants *start* with prizes and then lose them throughout the show. At the end they get the chance to win them all back.'

'Sounds fun.'

'It sounds *feasible*. The point is – and this is crucial – I have someone who's waiting for it. Roger Wyatt at Jump.'

The name meant nothing to me but I nodded

knowledgeably anyway. 'Where do I fit in?'

He drained his caffe latte and tilted his chin upwards. For a second, he was *joli-laid* instead of just *laid*. 'I've heard you swapping titbits' – he pronounced it 'tidbits' – 'with the creeps in the office. I've also heard you with Gaby.' He gave me a sly smile. I put a finger to my lips as if to shush him. 'You're an expert on celebrity trivia. Well, my show is driven by celebrity trivia.'

'You've certainly come to the right place.'

'Ah, but it's not just any celebrity trivia: I want trivia that links pairs of celebrities.'

'Give me an example.'

'OK, here's one I put in the proposal: Clive James and Sylvester Stallone both used to clean out lions' cages for a living.'

'Wow, that's fantastic! Top triv., Walt!'

'I just took it out of a book.'

'Doesn't matter where you found it, it's still ace.'

'Yes, well, I'm going to need lots more where that came from, and you're the man to do it for me.'

I was at once excited and apprehensive: this was a heaven-sent task and yet, given that Walter was also my boss for my day job, the stakes were higher than they would otherwise have been.

I think Walter sensed something of my ambivalence for he patted me on the wrist and said, 'Don't worry, sweetie, this has nothing whatsoever to do with Michael or Sparkle. Of course I'll be paying you, but there's no way they'll know. I'll even give you cash if you prefer. Now, come on,' he said cheerfully, 'whet my appetite; is there anything you can give me off the top of your pretty head?'

I'm normally quick off the mark when it comes to trivia but this was applied trivia, so to speak. As usual, my mind raced to the most recent thing I'd read: specifically a newspaper profile of Rod Stewart in which it had been revealed that the great man was colour-blind. I could vaguely remember that there was someone else who was also colour-blind. Paul Newman – that was it! 'Yes,' I said, more nonchalantly than I felt. 'Paul Newman and Rod Stewart are both colour-blind.'

He clapped his hands. 'Perfect!' Then he thought for a moment and said, 'I don't know about colour-blind but I once very nearly went blind myself.'

'You're joking,' I said.

'No, it was 1970, the year I started masturbating and I swear that I was within an inch of losing my eyesight.'

# CHAPTER SIXTEEN

Walter had impressed upon me the need for speed. 'When do you want them by?' I had asked as we'd left the café. 'Yesterday,' was his reply – and so I'd had no choice but to rope in my flatmates. It has to be said that I have done my bit for them. I have listened to countless renditions of 'Here Comes the Sun' and the fact that Ziggy hasn't yet been disbarred is testimony to my having talked him out of an appalling line of defence (unlike Horace Rumpole, he doesn't defend out of conviction but out of necessity: the CPS won't have him) on more than one occasion.

And yet, I was still seriously grateful that the moment I explained my predicament, the guys immediately switched into work mode. True, I was obliged to point out – far more forcefully than I should have had to – that, no, the audience and contestants did not consist exclusively of Beatles and *EastEnders* fans, but once they'd grasped that, they were keen as mustard.

''Kay, man,' said Peter, looking up from a pile of magazines. 'I think I've found a bo connection. What do Telly Savalas and Tommy Lee have in common?'

For fear of dampening his enthusiasm, I forbore to tell him that they were unsuitable because one was dead and the other needed qualifying as Pamela Anderson's ex-husband. 'I don't know.'

'Both had mothers who won the Miss Greece beauty contest.'

'That's fantastic! I was wondering about the celebrities but the link is so superb I'll include it.'

'Won't you have to give a clue?'

'No, it's not necessary. As I understand it, Walter will put up pictures of the two celebrities, then ask the contestants to choose which one of five connections applies to them.'

'I see.'

'Well, I don't,' said Ziggy. 'Why can't they just tell these people the answer without putting them to any bother.'

'Because,' I said through teeth that had lost nearly all their sharpness from having been gritted so often in recent weeks, 'that is the whole point of a quiz.' I'm never quite sure when Ziggy is genuinely confused or simply being obtuse. If it's the latter, then I've no doubt that he'd be perfect as one of those judges who asks, 'What are these Rolling Stones?' or, 'Who is Gazza?' The only trouble is that you can't become a judge without enjoying *some* success at the Bar.

Ziggy nodded and went back to scouring the internet. 'So they can only be pairs then?' he asked just as I had managed to find my place again in the book of celebrity lists I had been reading. Really, it is sometimes hard to measure the difference between Ziggy and no bloody help at all.

'No, child, just give me any two people – preferably the best two people – out of a list of celebrities. Unless, of course, like Peter, you come up with a connection that I'm sure could only apply to two celebrities.' I sensed Peter swelling with pride (which was sort of intentional) and Ziggy wince (which wasn't): I hadn't intended Peter's carrot to be Ziggy's stick but then needs must when you've only got a few hours to put together a hundred – *one bloody hundred*! – examples of celebrity connections.

At any rate it must have worked because within a couple of minutes, Ziggy was jumping up and down in his chair yelling, 'Yowser! Eureka! I've got a list of celebrity Manchester United supporters!'

'How many of them actually live in Manchester?' asked Peter.

I headed them off at the pass. 'Don't go there, guys. OK, Ziggy, who have you got?'

'Shane Richie, Eamonn Holmes, Zoe Ball, Steve Coogan, Angus Deayton, Ulrika Jonsson, Ian McShane, Morrissey, Gary Rhodes . . .'

I interrupted him. 'Great, mate. I'll take Zoe and Angus.'

'But what about the others?'

'I won't take them.'

'Oh.' He sounded flat but I didn't have the time to pacify the little lamb as I was scanning a list of karate black belts and trying to decide between Sharon Stone, Dane Bowers and Nigel Mansell as a partner for Guy Ritchie for the connection 'have black belts in karate'.

'Hey, man,' said Peter, 'I've got a good one. Tim Roth and Davina McCall both had their nipples pierced.'

Ziggy snorted. The sound reminded me of a recent wildlife documentary on wild pigs in Germany. 'Trust you to find the sex angle,' he said crossly. 'Does your mind ever emerge from the sewer?'

'Why?' Does yours ever emerge from the larder?'

'Children!' I shouted. 'Stop it or Mister Hand is going to meet Master Bottom and Master Bottom is going to come off second best. Peter, nice try but I don't think that pierced nipples are suitable on mainstream telly.'

'Pervert!' said Ziggy but without malice.

'Slob!' said Peter in a similar vein.

'Loser!' they shouted together and, fortunately, giggled.

After seven hours of desperate research – leavened

only by beers, pizzas, Maltesers, some truly bad gags (from them) and some stern reprimands (from me) – I had my hundred connections.

Actually, to be fair, what took so long wasn't writing the connections but ranking them. Peter and Ziggy insisted that we wouldn't have finished until we had voted for the top ten. The way we did this was to print out the hundred facts and then each rate them from one to a hundred. A fact rated number one received a hundred points, number two got ninety-nine points . . . all the way down to the fact rated one hundred which won just one point.

At the end of all this, we had our Top Ten facts which, from worst to best, were:

10. David Bellamy and Graham Greene each entered a competition to imitate himself – and lost

9. Richard Madeley and Michael Parkinson have both had vasectomies

8. Charles Manson and Stephen Stills both auditioned unsuccessfully for the Monkees

7. Mel Gibson and Brian Lara are both one of eleven children

6. Hugh Grant and George Michael have both been models for teen photo-romance stories

5. Gavin Rossdale (Chelsea) and Des O'Connor (Northampton Town) both had trials for Football League clubs

4. Brad Pitt and Chris Tarrant both used to live in their cars

3. Britney Spears and Anna Kournikova have both had computer viruses named after them

2. Olivia Newton-John and Mariel Hemingway both have grandfathers who won Nobel Prizes in the year 1954 (Olivia Newton-John's grandfather, Max Born, won for Physics; Mariel Hemingway's grandfather, Ernest Hemingway, won for Literature)

1. Jane Seymour and David Bowie each have eyes of different colours (Jane Seymour has one green and one brown while David Bowie has one green and one blue)

I actually voted for the Olivia Newton-John/Mariel Hemingway connection as my number one – and not just because I found it. In truth, I was responsible for at least three-quarters of them, including the Jane Seymour/David Bowie fact. No, what I loved about my number one connection was the fact that I was able to specify the year – 1954.

What happened was that I was looking through a mini-biography of Olivia Newton-John in some rock encyclopaedia when I discovered that she was the granddaughter of a Nobel Laureate. Fine, but how to connect her up? So I went through a list of every other Laureate this century but there didn't seem to be anyone else . . . until I remembered that Ernest Hemingway's granddaughters were

Margaux and Mariel Hemingway. Margaux (or Margot as she became) is no longer with us but Mariel is certainly plenty famous enough. Then I noticed – oh bliss! – that Olivia and Mariel's grandpapas both won their Nobel Prizes in the same year: 1954. What a fantastic coincidence!

For about the fourth time that night, I said as much to Ziggy and Peter but the former was fast asleep on the kitchen table and the latter was too stoned/drunk to understand anything beyond the fact that, by helping on this project, he had earned himself a free chinky meal (Menu D – which was usually off-limits).

'Beers!' was all my mate could say as I explained to him, in intricate detail, just how clever I was.

'How can Ziggy sleep when we've got so much to discuss?' I raved as I paced around the kitchen. 'I could have used David Emanuel, Benny Goodman or Lewis Carroll for that one about being "one of eleven children". And Lenny Kravitz also used to sleep in his car but in fact it was a Ford Pinto van and Hilary Swank and her mother often slept in a car when she was a kid. When Hilary Swank was a kid – not when her mother was a kid. Paul Ross and George Melly have also had vasectomies and—'

I broke off from my stream of trivia consciousness for a second to consult the next connection down – or, rather up – on the list. 'Oh gosh, there's loads of celebrities who've had trials for Football

League clubs: Rod Stewart, David Frost – scored eight goals in his trial for Nottingham Forest – the Duke of Westminster, Audley Harrison, you know, the guy who won a Gold Medal in boxing at the Sydney Olympics, David Essex, Angus Deayton – that's a trick one: it wasn't Manchester United who he supports but Crystal Palace, Rod Stewart . . . have I said him? Oh yes, Gordon Ramsay, the chef, he played twice for Rangers. Did you get that, Peter?'

'Beers!'

I might as well have been talking to myself. Hell, I *was* talking to myself. I went to the sink, poured a glass of water and sipped it slowly in an attempt to come down from my trivia-and-carbohydrate high.

As I started to relax, I felt the tiredness replacing the adrenaline – well, for Christ's sake, it was four in the morning. *Four in the Morning*? That was sung by Faron Young, wasn't it? He had had a vasectomy, too – I knew, I had just read about it. He also fought in the Korean War. So did Jamie Farr who played Corporal Klinger, the one who dressed up as a woman to get out of the army in *M*A*S*H* and yet he was the only member of the cast to have actually served in Korea. Now who else served in Korea besides him and Young and Michael Caine and James Garner?

I was about to cram some more taco chips into my mouth as an *aide-mémoire*, but stopped. I was meant to be unwinding, wasn't I? Just stop thinking, man. Relax. Deep breaths. A warm glow spread through me. With the help of my trusty pit-props I had absolutely mastered Walter's brief. He would be so pleased, he would be so proud and I would get some money.

How much? I had no idea, I really didn't. I would be happy with whatever he gave me, wouldn't I? But what if he asked me how much I wanted? On the one hand, I didn't want to seem like a breadhead, on the other, I didn't want to sell myself short, as Dad had always accused me of doing. Two hundred quid – that sounded about right, though I'd accept less. Of course I would! More would be brilliant: I could really use the dosh. Although I was getting £25,000 gross, this came down to not much more than £1,500 a month after tax (for some reason – not unconnected with Andrews, I suspected – I was still on emergency taxation) which was fine but, with so many loans outstanding, I was always playing catch up.

What I needed, I decided as I nimbly stepped around the now-prone figure of Peter on my way to bed, was an earner: a pay day. A couple of hundred, out of which I'd have to buy a chinky feast for three, was all very well but it wouldn't help me buy a place of my own, would it? And although I had always mocked people (Dad again) who wittered on about 'getting a foot on the housing ladder', I had for some time harboured middle-of-the-night fears that I would never be able to afford to buy somewhere.

I mean, it was all very well flat-sharing in my thirties, but did I want to be doing that in my forties? And what about marriage and children? Much as I had always despised (or affected to despise) the semi-d., the Jag. and the 2.4 kids, what was the alternative? Living in a grotty flat and feeding my children on a catch-as-catch-can basis? or worse, a flat in a council estate – all concrete, graffiti and syringes. No, that was not an option. It might have been in theory once, but not now. Not now that, thanks to Gaby, my mind was beginning to focus on such things. Now, I was moving away from the general, the principle of the thing, and on to the specific and I didn't like it or my prospects one bit.

For example, I had always been consistent in my opposition to public schools. I can remember passionate discussions in which I – an ex-public schoolboy – would explain why such privilege was unfair and outdated. Why, I would argue, should one parent be able to *buy* (I would spit the word out) a better education for their child? Well, maybe that was right and maybe I would stick to my beliefs and send my son (as this putative child had become) to the local comp. but that night, I suddenly found I would at least like to have the choice.

And there could be no choice without money.

I flopped into bed without even bothering to undress – let alone brushing my teeth. I wanted to switch off my brain and get some sleep. However, there was one part of my brain which desired not rest but resolve. What was I going to do about my future? How was I going to earn some proper money?

Didn't they amount to the same thing?

Who did I know who might be able to help me? Dad? Uncle Ronnie? No, they were 'comfortable'. I would settle for 'comfortable', but I had to at least try for more. Besides, any advice they might have given me would have involved getting a 'proper job' and with advice like that, who needed discouragement?

Walter flitted into my mind. Not surprising since I had just been working for him. He seemed savvy enough. I wouldn't mind a job like his one day. Yeah, but not working for a wanker like Andrews. My thoughts turned reluctantly to my boss: somehow I knew that I would have to consider him, at least mentally, if this process were to have any value.

He was wealthy, wasn't he? I'd heard stories about his house-with-a-swimming-pool-in-Berkshire (it was always said in a hyphenated way) and what with Sparkle and his flash Merc . . . well, he must be as near as dammit a millionaire.

But at what cost? Was he a complete bastard

because he was rich or was he rich because he was a complete bastard?

I knew that I was allowing myself to be side-tracked down a well-worn path. Maybe it was because I was so tired. Surely the middle point between extreme fatigue and a mind that won't stop racing is sleep? Don't alkalis and acids neutralise at some point? Suddenly, I was aware of having established a great truth – which goes to show just how much we delude ourselves, when we're knackered or stoned, into thinking that we've found the meaning of life.

*It was money, dummy: that and Gaby.* No rocket science needed – which was just as well for a man who got a grade D at GCSE Chemistry & Physics.

Game-shows. Walter was doing one: this one. Maybe there was money in them? Then I remembered Tony Bowes – the creator of *The Lot* – and drinking in that pub with Frank and him saying that he – no, not Frank, Tony Bowes – was going to make a sodding fortune. That could have been me: that *could* be me. That WOULD be me!

I sat up in bed – as much to mark the moment as out of any need or reflex. I would come up with a game-show idea and I too would make a fortune.

I had some idea that it was all a lot harder than I might have imagined: I had no idea what the game-show would be about. But that night – at five-something in the morning – was the point at which my life changed and led me (almost) directly to where I am today.

# CHAPTER SEVENTEEN

I don't want to give the impression that – rather
like in those successful Brit flicks *Four Weddings*,
*Notting Hill* and *Bridget Jones* – my friends only exist
for me, that they care passionately about every
nuance to do with me and my life and that I care
nothing for them or theirs. The night before my
first proper date with Gaby, did I pace around the
flat fretting? No, I did not. And why not? Because
my friend Peter needed me. He was anxious about
the Battle of the Beatles Tribute Bands and so I
ceded the floor to him.

'Like, it's not fair.'

'What's not fair?'

'Life.'

'Can you be a little more specific?'

'The universe.'

I tried the tough approach. 'Listen, Franklin, you
ludicrous hippy, you're not responsible for anything more profound than your own pathetic self.
So what is the fucking matter?' He stopped pacing

up and down the kitchen like an expectant father. 'It's tomorrow night.'

I successfully suppressed the urge to tell him that it wasn't tomorrow night. 'What about tomorrow night? It's just a jig like any other. No, that's not true: you've only got one song to do. Sounds a bit of a doss to me.'

'That's the whole trouble, man.'

'Explain, my child. Pausing only to pass me a packet of Nik Naks.'

He threw the packet of snacks at my right ear. I picked them off the floor and sat astride a chair. 'I'm all ears.'

It came out in a torrent. 'If we've only got one song then I say that we should do our best song and that is *not* "I Am the Walrus" because a) Roy is *not* our best singer and b) even if he were it's not the best Lennon song and c) it should have been me.'

'Wasn't that Yvonne Fair?'

'What?'

' "It Should Have Been Me"?'

'David, don't.'

'OK. So why isn't it you?'

'Because Roy and John say that we have to do a John or Paul song.'

'Sounds fair to me.' His face turned thundery and so I qualified my reaction. 'I mean, *you're* the best singer in the Best Beatles – no question – but John and Paul were clearly the most important singers in the real Beatles. Surely you can see that?'

'Yeah, I guess, but it doesn't stop me feeling pissed off. One chance, one bloody chance to win this contest and we're doing "I Am the Walrus". I mean, why can't we do "Norwegian Wood" and at least then I could show off my sitar playing.'

I cast my mind back to the sounds I'd heard coming from his bedroom the other night. I had been on tenterhooks waiting for the RSPCA inspectors to burst through the front door to rescue that poor cat. 'Best not, mate,' I said sympathetically. 'On the other hand,' I said through a mouthful of Nik Naks, 'I do take your point about "I Am the Walrus". Why aren't you doing "A Day in the Life"? There's enough distortion to cover up Roy's lack of vocal inspiration.'

'Tell me about it. There's twenty bands competing tomorrow night and the organisers wanted to make sure that the same song wasn't played more than once.'

'OK.'

'So they put the names of all the bands into a hat and drew them out to see who got first choice of song.'

'Ah, I see.'

'By the time they got to us, all the best songs were taken.'

'Oh come on, Peter, there are plenty enough songs to go around.' I paused to recall their best songs. 'What about "A Hard Day's Night"?'

'Taken by . . .' he consulted a sheet of paper . . . 'the Fab Four.'

'All right then, what about "Penny Lane"? I don't want to be the one to pass praise but John sings a mean "Penny Lane" – even if he does sometimes switch the verses around.'

He looked at his crib sheet again. 'It's being done by the Beetles. That's "Beetles" as in insects.'

'If they're the band I'm thinking of' – his nod assured me it was – 'that's Beetles as in shite. All right, all right, what about "Hey Jude"? Again, it's only one number so it doesn't matter if Roy really goes for it and loses his voice – like he did that time at Pontin's.'

'It wasn't Pontin's, it was Butlin's. Southcoast World. And, once again, it's been taken.' A quick shufti. 'By the Gold Beatles.'

'So that leaves you with "I Am the Walrus"?'

'It was that or "Help!" '

'That's the one where Roy sounds like Jimmy Savile imitating Gerry Marsden.'

'Yup.'

'And I take it that you knocked that one on the head pdq?'

'I didn't have to: Nigel did.'

'Oh really? I didn't think Nigel ever raised his head above the drumkit.'

'Doesn't usually but he hates playing "Help!" Reckons it's a trap for drummers.'

'What? A snare?'

He tutted but he did at least smile. 'You should take up crossword writing.'

'It might very well come to that.'

In the event, Peter's band managed to come a respectable fifth – not least because of Peter's inspired guitar work. The winners, as selected by a panel of judges that included an ex-Page 3 model, someone who had been evicted early from *Big Brother 3* and a wrinkled old prune who had once played in a band with Rory Storm (he of the Hurricanes fame), were Get Back! whose 'John' did a wonderfully nasal 'Ballad of John and Yoko'. Just to confuse everyone, the Ballad of John & Paul – who Peter and I had seen in concert recently – came third with 'Get Back'. Meanwhile, the self-styled John Paul George & Ringo finished second with a technically competent but, to my ears, uninspired rendition of 'Ticket To Ride'.

I figured, correctly as it turned out, that Peter would be quietly pleased with the result. The truth was that all he, they or any of the bands were trying to achieve was some exposure to potential bookers. So, by that measure, it was a moderately successful evening.

There was nothing moderate about the success of my evening. It was, as I triumphantly told Peter and Ziggy at the following evening's inquest, the first date of the rest of my life.

Gaby had picked me up from the flat. Ordinarily, on a first date, this might have put me at a disadvantage but a) we already knew each other and b) she wasn't doing me a favour as I could have got a lift with Peter. Also, concepts like being 'at a disadvantage' were so alien to how I saw my relationship with Gaby. Or at least how I *hoped* our relationship would develop.

The start of the drive over to Hammersmith was a little uncomfortable because neither of us was quite sure of our ground. Was this a date? Well, yes, as far as I was concerned it was but I wasn't entirely sure that she knew it. And, anyway, I found myself thinking, What *is* a date? And if it is what I think it is, does it necessarily involve some sort of sexual contact?

Both of us sensed that it would have been a bit of a social solecism to discuss work or colleagues, and yet there lay almost all of our potential conversation.

Ironically for someone who prides himself on his knowledge, it was my ignorance that broke the ice. 'What sort of car is this then?'

'It's a Clio.'

'What? I've never heard of that. Is it a Ford?'

'Idiot,' she said not unaffectionately. 'It's a Renault, a Renault Clio. You must remember Nicole and Papa?'

I brushed the top of my hair back to convey that such things go over my head. She turned to me in (only part) amazement. 'Honestly, David, you are such a girl!'

'I know. I am a girl. A complete girl. I have never denied it. I can't drive – or at least I can, but I can't seem to persuade the bloody driving-test examiners that I can – I can't do DIY, I'm not remotely practical and, promise not to tell anyone, I'm not particularly interested in sport. Apart from cricket, I suppose.'

'David!'

'It's worse than that. I can't programme the video recorder, I can't even map-read – which is something that all men are supposed to be able to do. I enjoy shopping, a chick thing if ever there were one. I've also got great intuition and I like gossiping.'

'QED, you're a girl.'

'Ah, yes, but I don't fancy men . . .'

'I'm relieved to hear it.'

'Which makes me a lesbian woman.'

She clapped her hands together – which is no mean feat when you're manoeuvring your way into an NCP car park. Then she said, 'I love sport – all sport – and I'm very practical. And I can read maps. So what does that make me?'

I waited for her to negotiate the alarmingly tight parking space. 'Assuming that you don't fancy women?' I raised my eyebrows. A shake of her head confirmed that she didn't. 'Then you are a gay man.'

We enjoyed the show more for the awful acts than for the good ones. The Beetles' 'Penny Lane' was execrable but not even a tenth as bad as the Beatles For Hire's attempt on 'Day Tripper'. When I say 'attempt on', I use it in the same way as one might describe a would-be assassin's 'attempt on' someone's life. I don't know much about the technical side of music but even I know that the opening guitar riff should be in the same key as the song. And the vocalist was a real nowhere man.

As we left the theatre, my mind turned to the logistics of how and where I might engineer our first kiss. By which I mean OUR FIRST KISS.

It was no good. I loved her far too much to try to engineer anything. 'Oh, sod it!' I stopped walking and turned her round to face me. 'Look here, Gaby, I know we haven't been to bed together yet and we haven't even kissed but I . . . I . . . love you. I do, you know, I . . . I . . .' then, realising that I had possibly gone too far, I adopted a Scouse accent, 'I bloody adore you, me.' I switched accents again to upper-class Englishman in a 1950s B movies. 'Is there any chance that you might possibly feel the same way about me?'

She pushed me away but her coquettish smile, which stretched all the way to her big brown eyes, indicated that she wasn't completely indifferent to me.

I moved back towards her with my lips puckered as if to signal my intentions. She smiled again, a bigger smile which brought her dimples into play. For a split second I could see the hamster resemblance. I considered mentioning it but decided that there might be a better time to do so. Or maybe not even to do so at all. When I was sixteen, I told Stephanie Jones that she looked a little like Michael Heseltine. The fact that I also told her that she was extremely beautiful – which she was – didn't stop her chucking me.

Gaby put her finger to her lips. 'Sorry, David. If you want me, you're going to have to win me.'

'What?'

'It's pop quiz.'

'WHAT?'

'If you want to kiss me, first you're going to have to beat me.'

'I'm not that kind of guy.'

'You know what I mean.' She beeped her car from her electronic key fob and we clambered in. She put the key in the ignition so that she could open an electric window but didn't start the engine. 'All right, Mr Trivia. Name me – shall we say? – seven Lennon and McCartney songs never actually released by the Beatles – except on the anthologies.'

'What the hell are you talking about?' But even

as I said it, my brain was ticking away. I gave it a few seconds, composed myself and said: ' "Nobody I Know" and "A World Without Love" were written by Paul McCartney for Peter and Gordon – that's Peter Asher, as in Jane's brother – but they were credited to Lennon and McCartney.'

'That's two.'

'Cilla Black also did a couple of their songs. "Step Inside Love" and no, don't tell me . . .'

'I wasn't going to.'

'Hang on, it's coming . . . "It's For You". I knew I knew it!'

'That's four. You're getting close.' I moved towards her. 'But not close enough!'

'There's another one. By Billy J. Kramer and the Dakotas. It's on the tip of my tongue.'

'That's five.'

'What are you talking about?'

' "Tip of My Tongue". But it wasn't by Billy J. Kramer: it was by Tommy Quickly.'

'Never heard of him. But I know there was a Billy J. Kramer song and I also know it wasn't "Trains and Boats and Planes" . . .'

'. . . which was by Bacharach and David.'

'I knew that.' I had a flash of inspiration. 'I also know the song it was. "Bad To me".'

She looked impressed – as she was bloody entitled to be. 'That's six. One more, David, and you can do with me what you will. Up to a point.'

As if I needed the inducement to win a trivia

contest! But, as hard as I tried, I just couldn't think of any more.

Eventually, she put me out of my misery – unfortunately, they'd recorded 'Misery'. 'You could have had "Like Dreamers Do" recorded by the Applejacks, "That Means a Lot" recorded by P.J. Proby, "I'm In Love" released by the Fourmost or "One and One Is Two" which was by the Strangers with Mike Shannon.'

The fluency with which she'd listed them, particularly that last one, made me suspicious and it must have shown because she confessed, 'I've been swotting.'

'You . . .! You . . .!'

She put a finger to my lips and then, suddenly, as though she were using it to mark the spot, replaced it with her own lips. Soon, our tongues were entwined and I was drinking in her saliva, breathing in her fabulous aroma.

When, after a few minutes, we separated in order to recapture our breath, I said, 'Hold on, I thought I had to get seven right?'

'That's right. You didn't, so I won. This is *my* prize.' And she started kissing me again.

# CHAPTER EIGHTEEN

Over the next few days, I had a split personality. At home, with Peter and Ziggy, I did nothing but talk about Gaby; at work, with Frank and Simon, I did anything *but* talk about Gaby.

The former came naturally; it was the latter I found impossible. But it was essential to keep *shtum*. Gaby had once had a relationship with someone at the BBC and while everything was fine, everything was fine but when it finished, the fact that everyone knew them as a couple only added to the pressures of the split. Consequently, she made it extremely clear to me that if anyone discovered that we were an item, we would cease to be one. I intended to heed her words – as soon as I finished wallowing in the blissful fact that she acknowledged that we were an item.

It was just as well that I was the Serotonin Kid because everything and everyone else seemed to be conspiring to bring me down. At work, Frank and Simon were resenting – big time – Walter's supposed patronage of me. Fortunately, they were far too subtle to make anything much out of it.

'I'm surprised he can sit down,' said Simon camply.

'I take it the "h" in sit is silent?' answered Frank as if they had been rehearsing their routine – which, for all I knew, they had.

'But is W.W. silent when he's getting up David?'

'I don't know, but he's certainly getting up to no good with him.'

'Actually that's a good nickname for David. "No good". As in Walter's getting up to no good. What do you think?'

'I think it should be "to no good" – 'cos Walter's getting up "to no good".'

'Like it!'

I butted in. 'Well, *I* don't. Is that it or have you had enough?'

'Is that what Walter asks you?'

'No, he just asks me which one of you two creeps we should get rid of.' I sounded sufficiently pissed off – and plausible – to shut them up but now I had to contend with their brooding silence and, if anything, I preferred their bitchiness to their moroseness.

The interesting thing was, I had just chucked it out as a half-hearted putdown. Why would either of them take it so seriously? Especially Frank. If anyone was fireproof, surely it was him? He was on a percentage of *The Lot* and clearly Andrews's blue-eyed boy. For all Walter's talent and eminence, he was working for Andrews who could, presumably, veto any decision he might make to fire a question writer. There was obviously something else, something more, bugging the didactic duo.

Then I realised what it was. They weren't bothered about *their* position; they were pissed off about *mine*.

There was a hierarchy of Frank and Simon – or Simon and Frank (although I think Simon was quite prepared to play second fiddle) – followed by David. Now, thanks to my 'friendship' with Walter, this was threatened. And the bastards didn't like it one bit.

The truth was that, beyond his friendly advice the day he took me out for a coffee, Walter hadn't mentioned Frank and Simon once to me. Our relationship was almost entirely predicated on my freelance contribution to his game-show. Although I wasn't going to let those bastards know that.

Later on the day of that conversation, they only deigned to speak to me for two reasons. The first was to pick holes in a question I'd written: Which one of these is a grandchild of Queen Elizabeth II?

a)   Ella
b)   Erica
c)   Eugenie
d    Enya

ANSWER: c) Eugenie

'Euston,' said Frank, 'we have a problem.'

'I'm sorry?' I said, not feeling at all apologetic. 'How could there possibly be a problem with that question – unless you want to query where it might be used in a show.'

'How do we know that Her Majesty hasn't got a grandchild named Ella, Erica or Enya?'

'Because we do.'

'Sources?'

'We must have sources,' chimed in Simon.

I understood where they were coming from – and it was Pedants' Corner. 'OK, how precisely am I supposed to prove a negative?'

They clucked unsympathetically in unison.

'That's the way it goes,' said Simon.

'But hang on,' I said, 'we know that the Queen has a grandchild named Eugenie. She's the daughter of Prince Andrew . . .'

'. . . and the Duchess of York. But how do *you* know that Prince Andrew didn't have a lovechild named Ella, Erica or Enya?'

'Exactly,' said Frank. 'Or Prince Charles.'

'That's crazy,' I said. 'No reasonable person could object to the answer "Eugenie". It's correct, for Christ's sake!'

'I know it's correct. No one's disputing it's correct. What we're saying is that another answer might also be correct. As for your reasonable person, the trouble is, dear boy, the world is not composed of reasonable people. There are far too many *un*reasonable people.'

I felt my shoulders slumping. 'Oh, I give up.'

Just before we left the office, Simon managed the extraordinary feat of making me hate him even more when he asked me, in a fake casual voice, whether I'd 'porked the hamster yet'.

I felt an adrenaline rush which would, I knew from the time I fell off my moped, give me the illusion of time slowing down and therefore valuable moments to think. It was essential that I kept my cool as Simon would immediately pick up on any anger or distress.

'Come on, Simon,' I said evenly, 'Gaby and I are boring. What the world *really* wants to know is when are you and Frank going to get it on.'

Keep the bastards guessing. That was how I would conduct myself at the office. At home, however, I could afford to indulge myself and, I am now ashamed to admit, I did.

'Have I told you lately that I love her?' I asked Peter.

'Only like three million times.'

'Do you think we should be David and Gaby or Gaby and David?' I enquired of Ziggy who was in the middle of eating his eighth chicken breast.

He stopped eating for a second which, I suppose, was a compliment. 'I could care less.' By which, I think he meant he couldn't care less. It's obviously an American idiom that he's picked up watching television. It's all he ever seems to do. Apart from eat.

'You know something?' added Peter. 'Whoever coined the phrase "all the world loves a lover" obviously hadn't met you.'

'Guys, guys, guys, anyone would think you were jealous.'

'David, David, David, anyone would think you were the first man to meet a girl he liked.'

'Did you say *liked*, Peter? *Liked?* I don't *like* her, I love her, I adore her, I . . . I . . .' I grasped for the right word. 'I *cherish* her!'

Even I realised I'd gone too far and I started to blush. Ziggy looked over at Peter who was perched on the work-top next to the cooker and traced a weirdo sign with his forefinger.

'Look,' I said to them both. 'I know I've said this before about a girl . . .'

'Yeah, like not many.'

'But this time it's different. This time, it's for keeps. I want to marry her. Honest.'

'That's what you said about Lois. Cheer?'

'Beers!'

Peter chucked a can which only just missed Ziggy's left ear. Fortunately, given that he's got the digestive system of a ruminant, it didn't put him off his tuck.

'That was different, man. That was lust. Once

we'd done the business, I lost interest.'

'Isn't that the story of your life?' There was enough of an edge in Peter's voice for me to wonder where he was coming from.

'I guess,' I said in a non-committal voice and then added with just a little bit of my own needle, 'On the other hand, nothing ventured . . .'

I'd expected Peter – who's such a commitment-phobe that he'd rather have no sex (apart from sex with himself) than risk getting involved with someone – to react but it was Ziggy who slammed down his plate, leaving half a chicken breast and a pile of greens, picked up his 100 per cent fat-free banana smoothie, and stormed out of the room.

'What's up with him?' I asked Peter.

'Fuck him. Anyway, he's *your* friend.'

'I thought you two were getting on like a house – well, if not a house on fire then at least a house where the heating can be turned down without risk of hypothermia.'

'We were, I suppose but now . . . fuck him.'

'So you say. Your vocabulary seems to be some-what restricted.'

He stood up and kicked a loose tile across the floor. 'Look, if you must know, I'm a little pissed off about the other night.'

'What – the Battle of the Beatles jig?'

'Yeah.'

'I thought we'd discussed it. Fifth place isn't too shabby and—'

'It's nothing to do with that. It's Ziggy. He didn't come.'

'I don't get it. He said he was going. In fact, when Gaby and I' – I momentarily savoured the words – 'left, he said he'd be leaving later.'

'Well, he didn't.'

'Why? Did the car break down?'

'No, he had to stay in to watch *EastEnders*.'

'I thought he was taping it.'

'That's what he said he'd do but like, as it turned out, he couldn't bear to wait for even a second,' he did an imitation of Ziggy but succeeded only in sounding like a cross between Michael Winner and the late Frank Muir, 'to find out what happened in his beloved soap opera.'

I trod carefully. 'That would seem to be an unreasonable excuse. Has he apologised?'

'Not in so many words.'

I tutted and left the kitchen to have a word with Ziggy, feeling ever so slightly like Kofi Annan on a shuttle diplomacy mission.

He (Ziggy not Kofi) was sitting in the lounge in what had become *his* chair watching an American satellite TV show which wasn't *Buffy* or *Sabrina*. 'What's happening?' I asked him.

He turned, thereby knocking over a bowl containing a pound of grapes that had been wedged precariously between his stomach and the arm of the chair. As he moved to see how much fruit he could salvage without actually leaving his chair, three remote controls fell down in sympathy.

'I didn't need that dig.'

'What dig?'

'That thing you said about me not "venturing" to have a girlfriend.'

'If it was a dig . . .'

'If it *were* a dig. Subjunctive.'

'If it were a dig, then it was – *were* – aimed at Peter. You've had girlfriends. Well, one or two when you can be bothered to get off your arse and find them. It's Peter who's scared of being tied down. That's why he's so big on porn and all that. It's DIY, isn't it? Shit, he's the only man I know who's joined the mile-high club on his own.'

Ziggy forgot his annoyance for a second. 'Is that true?'

'Well, I don't know if he's the *only* person but he certainly did, you know, have a quick one off the wrist in the loo on a jet. He told me. But don't tell him I told you.'

'Don't worry, we're not really on speakers at this present moment in time. Besides, I wouldn't tell him if he were on fire. Nor would I piss on him.'

'Listen, mate, from what I hear, he's the one with the grievance.'

'Oh really, why?'

'Well, you didn't show up at his gig.'

'You're dead right I didn't. And do you know why not?'

'No.'

'It's because he deliberately scrubbed my *World's Strongest Man* tape which I had been saving for a day when there was nothing to watch on telly. He admitted it. He said he didn't think I'd mind. Well, I bloody do.'

The day hasn't dawned when there hasn't been something on television crappy enough to satisfy Ziggy but I was trying to mend fences, not batter them down. 'Come on, Ziggy. This is no way to live. Surely there's more that unites the two of you than divides you.'

He pondered. 'Yes, there is something that unites us. We're both sick to death of hearing about you and Gaby. Now will you stop hassling me? I'm trying to watch *Tucker*.'

I considered returning to the kitchen for another round of shuttle diplomacy but decided instead to go to the pub at the bottom of Gaby's road. We'd agreed – at her suggestion – to have an evening apart but it wouldn't count, surely, if we bumped into each other by accident?

# CHAPTER NINETEEN

I didn't see Gaby that evening but it was enough for me to escape Peter and Ziggy and to be geographically closer to her. I even found myself humming 'On the Street Where You Live' (if I remember *My Fair Lady* right, the street in question was Wimpole Street).

The truth is, I was absolutely potty about the girl but, back then, it was all getting a bit too much for me. Besides the obvious problem of conducting a surreptitious relationship at work, I was also coping with having my emotions engaged properly for the first time in my life. It was all so foreign to me. I was like a school exchange student in a French family home: I had the vocabulary but I simply couldn't speak the language.

Not my smallest problem was the fact that we had yet to consummate our relationship. There had been opportunities – not so much at my flat where one of my flatmates could always be relied upon to play gooseberry, but at her place where

Phoebe, her flatmate, was a nurse who worked shifts – but I had kind of shied away from them. I told myself – and intimated to her – that it was because I was trying to make our relationship different, more special than all the flings that had preceded it, but I was also aware of another dimension within myself. Fear.

Not, I hasten to add, fear of my ability to perform properly. I don't put 'kind and considerate lover' on my CV but I have had quite a few testimonials to that effect and even the ex-lovers for whom the earth didn't move indicated to me that they'd quite enjoyed the encounter.

Trouble is, none of 'em came back for more.

All right, not none but certainly not very many: maybe three? But if I am honest with myself, it wasn't my partners who were reluctant to repeat the experience, it was me. It's true – even though I know it sounds unlikely. I'd much rather it was the other way round. Being a serial rejectee would be a lot more palatable for my self-esteem than acknowledging the fact that I am emotionally incapable of sustaining an adult relationship.

I know I laughed when Gaby told me about Richie Clarke being known as Clarke the Cab for the way he legged it in a taxi as soon as he'd done the business but, aside from the mode of transport (I was a moped man myself) and the fact that I wasn't as famous as him, there wasn't much difference.

I suspect that Clarke was motivated by precisely the same thing as I was with a woman: curiosity. Curiosity to discover whether she'd have sex; what she was like naked; how she behaved during sex. The only curiosity we lacked is what it would have been like to stay. For Clarke and me, there was absolute certainty there: we weren't going to get tied down, not when there was so much curiosity to be satisfied.

So that's what was holding me back with Gaby: the fear that as soon as we had sex, our relationship would end. I would discover – as I had so many times before – that what I thought was love was merely sexual anticipation; the scales would fall from my eyes before I'd even made my excuses and left. Somehow, I *knew* that what I felt for Gaby was different, but that only made me all the more apprehensive about putting my feelings to the test. In other words, my very love for her stopped me from making love to her.

Hindsight makes philosophers of us all, but back then, I was a horrible mixture of passion, insecurity and fear. I've got this theory – I suspect it's the closest I'll ever get to a philosophy all of my own – that what mars enjoyment of the present is fear of the future. In the past, all that fear is settled, one way or the other, but only now that it is the past and no longer the present.

I found myself wishing that I could talk to someone about it. To someone who didn't have a fucking axe to grind. Which ruled out my mother ('you are *so* immature, David'), my father ('does she play golf?'), my brother ('Hilary and I are *so* happy') and, I guess, any friend ('it'll be just like all the rest: you'll be off as soon as you've had your wicked way').

Funnily enough, I got succour where I least expected it: at work. Walter invited me out for a coffee to discuss *Take It Away*. After handing over a cheque for a wonderful five hundred pounds, he asked me casually, 'So how's it going with you and Miss Nesbitt?'

'Who?'

'Gab C Nesbitt – Gaby Taylor.'

The question was asked with absolutely no side or spin – just kindness – and so it would have been churlish to stonewall him. 'Great. What can I tell you? I love her!'

'Thought so.' I must have looked alarmed. 'Don't worry, I doubt anyone else has noticed: I'm more attuned to these things than most people.'

'I'd be grateful if you'd, er . . .'

'No need to say another word. But if there's ever anything I can do to help the course of true love . . . just think of me as your fairy godmother.'

I squeezed his hand. 'Walter, I don't think I'll have too much problem thinking of you as a fairy.'

The following evening found me in the company of another gay friend, Tim, who's much less camp than Walter but, I would wager, a damn sight more promiscuous. I'd invited him out for a drink to discuss astrology. No, I hadn't been taking pills to lower my IQ, but I had this idea for a game-show based on astrology and I wanted to run it past him. For in the same way that I know it's a load of cack with absolutely *no basis* in scientific fact, he truly believes in it and even lives his life by it – which is no easy thing to do when you're the partner in a lease evaluation company.

'You do know that it's complete bollocks, don't you?' I said by way of introducing the subject.

'Just so long as you're going to be open-minded about it,' said Tim, downing a pint of bitter.

I took a sheet of paper out of the pocket of my new jacket (just like the one I saw on Jonathan Ross the other night and only £37.50 in the sale), 'OK, Gypsy Lee Tim, I'm going to give you the names of various celebrities and I want you to match them up to the celebrities who were born on the same day of the same month of the same year.'

'And your point is?'

'My point is that if two people born on the very same day don't share similar characteristics, then how can two people born in the same month in different years?'

'I understand, but that's newspaper and magazine astrology: it's meaningless.'

'How can it be meaningless if professional

astrologers cast – if that's the right word – horoscopes for people based on such criteria?'

'Look, the most that can be said for a star sign is that people born under it will have a tendency to behave in a certain way. Real astrology requires much more information than a date of birth. You take your celebrities born on the same day. They might have been born at different times of the day and, almost certainly, in different parts of the world. Still, if it makes you happy, little David, I'll take your quiz.'

'No,' I said, pretending to be piqued. 'But I will give you a few pairs of twins and you can tell me what, if anything, they have in common. OK, here we go. George W. Bush and Sylvester Stallone.'

'Born on precisely the same day, were they?' Tim asked thoughtfully.

'Yup.'

'Well, I should say that Bush and Stallone have a lot in common. A strong mother to start with.'

'All right. Little Jimmy Osmond and Nick Berry?'

'Haven't they both had number one hits?' Tim was getting right into the spirit of the thing.

'Yes, they have. Try this one then. Julian Barnes and Dolly Parton.'

'He's a top, heavy writer and she's a top-heavy singer.'

'Very good, Oscar. What about Tina Turner and

John Gummer. Surely they've nothing in common.'

'Oh, I don't know. Didn't she become a Buddhist and didn't he become a Catholic?'

'Good point. All right, one more pair: Robert De Niro and John Humphrys?'

Tim threw a pork scratching in the air and caught it with his teeth. 'Easy. De Niro is today's greatest actor while Humphrys is *Today's* greatest interviewer.'

'OK, smartarse. If I accept that there are differences of time and place between my twins, what about genuine twins: are you saying that they always have the same horoscopes?'

'Broadly speaking, yes.'

'That's interesting. Elvis Presley, David Jason, Liberace, Freddie Starr, Edgar Allen Poe, Leonardo Da Vinci, Lewis Carroll and Oscar Wilde all had twins who died at birth or in childhood. So how come *both* twins didn't die?'

He cocked his head and stared at me. It was disconcerting. 'Are you really stupid or are you just pretending to be?'

I thought I'd been making an intelligent point and, let's face it, debunking astrology shouldn't be that hard, but suddenly, I was feeling dumb. It doesn't help that, notwithstanding his interest in the zodiac, Tim is clearly so much smarter than me – and better looking. When they make a film of my life, he'll be played by Rupert Everett.

'I think I'm pretending,' I said meekly. 'Let me

get you another drink. I didn't in fact invite you here for a debate, I was actually trying to pick your brains.' I returned with a pint of beer for him and half a lager for me. As I set them down, I couldn't help remarking, 'Shouldn't this be the other way round?'

Tim groaned. 'I know you to be a decent fellow, David, and I've no doubt that you're tolerant too, but your understanding of other people's lives is transparently shallow. Anyway, you didn't ask me here to raise your consciousness.'

I wished I'd kept my mouth shut. 'Tim, let me run a game-show format past you.'

'Am I obliged to wave my hands in the air?'

'No. Here's how it goes. I was thinking of calling it *Star Wars*. . .'

'. . . shame George Lucas beat you to it.'

I didn't break stride. 'I *was* thinking of calling it *Star Wars* but since that's already taken, I'm going to call it *Astro Wars*.'

'A commendable nomenclature.'

'Here's how it goes. Twelve groups of six people are divided into their star signs. Each group is mixed up with all the other groups so that there can be no collusion within the group. A question is asked but it isn't a question that has a right or wrong answer; it requires people to specify a preference or to say how they'd respond to a dilemma. So it might be: Which of these holidays appeals more? Or; If a friend asked you to lie to their partner for them, would you? People vote for their preference and—'

'How do they vote?'

'They use audience response equipment.'

'OK. Just testing.'

'After they vote, the more that people within a star sign have agreed with each other, the more points that team i.e. that star sign gets. The team with the most points wins.'

'And then?'

I sipped my lager. 'Then that team plays the endgame. I should explain that all game-shows have an endgame: that is what makes them game-shows instead of quiz shows.'

'I understand. Or at least I think I do.'

'In the endgame, the team answers more questions to find the two people who agree the most. Those two people are then offered a choice of prizes; ranging from an amazing car to a worthless booby prize. If they choose the same prize, they win that prize. If they choose different prizes, they automatically get the booby prize. So . . .'

'Hang on a minute. Why wouldn't they agree to choose the same prize?'

'They wouldn't have a chance. This is the first time they've met – there's no chance to collude.'

'I can see that, but why wouldn't they both choose the best prize?'

'Good point. For a start, they might be offered

the prizes in a different sequence to each other – with one of them going into a soundproof box. Also, who's to say that both of them would choose the car over a holiday worth more or a cash prize worth slightly less?'

He nodded. 'All right, that's plausible enough, but what I don't understand is what you're trying to achieve here?'

I shrugged. 'A game-show format that might make it on to TV and, from there, sell abroad and make me a shed-full of money?'

'I didn't mean that. What I meant was, for someone who doesn't believe in astrology, you're setting an awful lot of store by star signs.'

'No, that's where you're wrong, Tim. The great thing about this format is that it works whether you believe in astrology or you don't. The believer watches this and says, "Look at all those Taureans agreeing with one another," whereas the non-believer says, "See, those Cancerians are hopelessly split. It proves it's all bollocks".'

I let it sink in before continuing. 'My idea is that we'd have a sceptical presenter who'd spark off the resident astrologer. So the presenter would ask the astrologer to explain the voting and then gently take the piss out of her findings. I should say that I think of the presenter as male and the astrologer as female.'

'I suppose she'll be wearing a headscarf and gigantic earrings?'

'Look, you should be in favour of this programme. Who knows: it might even do something to prove that astrology works?'

'Don't patronise me. There's absolutely no intention of taking the science of astrology seriously.'

'I'm sorry, if astrology is a science . . .'

'. . . which it is . . .'

'Then it's a science for people who flunked science at school. In fact, I'd go further. The only genuine scientific fact in astrology is that, at a party, it's always the thickest girl in the room who asks you what star sign you are.'

Tim rewarded me with a grin which he turned into a leer at the young barman who came to our table to clear away our empty glasses. When he'd gone, I asked Tim, 'How do you know he's one of them – one of you?'

He giggled gleefully like a naughty boy who's just discovered a cache of sweets. 'How do you know he isn't?'

'Touché!' I did the universal mime for 'do you want another drink?' He shook his head. 'Look, Tim, I accept that it's only a bit of fun but what I like about it is that, regardless of the viewer's opinion of astrology, while his star sign is still in the game, he's got a point of identification, a team to support. So, forgetting the astrology bit, what do you think of the format as a TV show?'

'I think it's extremely good.'

'Well, you're a Virgoan, you would say that.'

'No, seriously, I think it would work. What telly seems to lack these days – and you must remember that I am a mere viewer and not a pro like yourself – is *events*. Is it not possible to, I don't know, scale it all up?'

'What – you mean have twelve people per team instead of six?'

'No, I mean have a thousand people per team.'

'But that's twelve thousand people!'

'Your maths does you credit.'

'You'd need a football ground to fit them all in!'

'And so?'

That was when I saw it. 'So we'd get a football ground. So we'd do it every week in a different football ground. And we wouldn't restrict it to a thousand people. We'd allow in as many people as the ground could safely seat. Wow! I love it!'

Tim smiled indulgently as though he'd known this all along.

'Hang on,' I said suddenly. 'How would we get people to vote? We couldn't afford audience response keypads for everyone.'

He considered my question. 'OK, why not do it like this? Instead of separating the star signs, you give them each an area of the ground. Each star sign has a celebrity . . .'

'. . . a micro-celebrity who belongs to that star sign . . .'

'Yup. And he or she has a giant keypad. When the question gets asked, he canvasses the opinion of any twelve of his fellow star signers and presses the buttons on the giant key pad twelve times, one for each vote.'

'And the more votes they have for one particular option, the more points they win.' I thought about it for a second. 'Ah, but what would stop the micro-celebrity from cheating, from pressing the same answer twelve times?'

'I don't know. I guess you have to rely on the honesty of the micro-celebrities. Perhaps you could also have invigilators.'

'I like it! Yes, they would ensure that there was no collusion and they could also make sure that all twelve people gave their answers simultaneously. Actually, we're making it too complicated. Let's not have a giant keypad: let's have twelve ordinary keypads that circulate through the star sign throughout the game and let's have the micro-celebrity as the invigilator.'

'Sounds perfect. But what would you do with them when you had your winner? How would you play your endgame?'

'OK. For the endgame, we take six people, three men and three women – at random – from the winning star sign and split them into three pairs. These pairs compete against each other in a series of physical tasks e.g. a three-legged race, constructing a model, operating a fork-lift truck blindfolded while the partner guides them. Whichever pair performs best – is most in tune with each other – is offered a choice of different prizes as before, and if they choose the same prize, they both get it.'

I rubbed my hands together in satisfaction. 'So, Tim, what do you think?'

'I think we're both geniuses.'

# CHAPTER TWENTY

The next day I doorstepped Andrews as he went into his office. 'Excuse me, Michael.'

'I'm busy. Fuck off. What is it?'

'Are you interested in an idea for a TV game-show?'

'Is it yours?'

'Er, yes.'

'Then it's mine already. I employ you. I own you. I own your ideas.'

I'd anticipated his reaction. 'Fair dos. I just wanted to know where I stood.' I turned and started to walk away.

He was nettled. The thought of losing something to a competitor disturbed him. 'Hang on a minute. Yeah, all right. Tell you what, if you come up with an idea that ends up getting used, you'll be on a percentage.'

I decided to press home my advantage. 'How much?'

'Twenty per cent. But not now. I'm busy. Bugger off.'

Typical of Andrews: just when I wanted him to be at Sparkle so I could pitch the idea to him, he chose the next few days to be out at meetings for *The Lot* which was now just a few weeks away from recording and (a day later) transmission.

The first time I knew that I'd be seeing him for sure was at the Institute of Independent TV Production Companies' annual quiz night, so I took along a beautifully bound copy of my treatment for *Astro Wars*.

The venue for this quiz was the massive hall of one of the London livery companies. I remember wondering whether, one day, there would be a Guild of Quiz Question Writers. There were eight people at our table: Frank, Simon, Walter, me, Joe Mackintosh (Andrew's sleeping partner), Tony Bowes (the creator of *The Lot*), Gaby and Andrews, who deigned to arrive two hours late.

Actually, in Andrews's absence, we were able to relax and enjoy a surprisingly good dinner, given that the caterers were providing food for over six hundred people. Seared tuna was followed by rack of lamb and then Fruits of the Forest Pavlova.

An auction came next in which funny money, i.e. in excess of a thousand pounds, was paid for items like an Arsenal footballer's signed shirt or a weekend for two at a London hotel, then a raffle and a couple of speeches by independent TV producers telling us what fine people they were for supporting this important event. Perhaps that's why Andrews was late – because he hadn't been invited to make a speech.

Our boss still hadn't arrived by the time the quiz started and so, interestingly enough, Frank assumed the role of chairman. He appointed Gaby as the team's scribe and gave us a team talk that wouldn't have been out of place at Twickenham. 'Last year, we came second and I, for one, can remember the taste of defeat. I never want to experience that taste again. Michael expects us to win and, given that some of us sitting around this table write quiz questions for a living, he has every right to do so, especially as most of the other tables are only here for the crack. We'll face *some* competition from Tangent and from PXL Communications, who somehow fluked a victory last year but, if we really concentrate and work hard with and for each other, we will triumph.' He was, by now, slightly red in the face – from exertion or, more properly, out of embarrassment for spouting such jingoistic crap, I couldn't tell – but Walter took our attention away from him by saying, 'Cry God for Sparkle and St Michael! And what I wouldn't do for a bloody Mary!'

The format of the quiz itself was necessarily simple, given the number of people present, many of whom were a couple of bottles to the worse. There were eight rounds of ten questions, with each round devoted to a different subject. Each correct answer would be worth one point – except in the round where a team played its joker, when each correct answer would score two points. Teams had to nominate in advance in which round they were going to play their joker and we decided, with no dissent, to play ours on the final round: TV & Movies.

The four rounds in the first half went well. We scored maximum points on Current Affairs, Books, Science and Quotations to lie joint top with PXL Communications and some rather noisy outfit named TV Dinners, which was presumably a pick-up team.

Frank, Simon and I were responsible for almost all of the answers, with Joe Mackintosh and Walter relaxing in the style of directors of a successful football club. Having said that, Joe was the only person on our table to know all four of Prince Charles's Christian names and Walter bailed us out on a Robert Frost quote.

I was the only person to know the name of the author of *Goodbye, Mr Chips* (James Hilton) although, by watching me carefully and then nodding sagely, Simon was able to pretend that he'd known it too. I did the same to him in the Science round – I can't even remember the question, I think it was about plants, let alone the answer – but, apart from that, Simon, Frank and I were answering the questions pretty much simultaneously – as well we might, given that this was, as Frank kept pointing out, 'a quiz for civilians'.

Gaby (bless) clearly knew as many of the answers as we did but her lack of testosterone (double bless) meant that she didn't put in her two bob's worth. Nevertheless, she saved us all by knowing that Barry Unsworth's *Sacred Hunger* shared the 1992 Booker prize with Michael Ondaatje's *The English Patient*.

The big surprise was Tony Bowes. Given that he'd invented *The Lot*, I'd thought of him as a bit of a quiz king but no, he seemed hopelessly out of his depth. Joe and Walter gave the impression that they couldn't be bothered; Tony was evidently keen to contribute but kept offering the wrong answers. It also didn't help that he seemed to be devoid of a whisper button.

'You're not only wrong,' hissed Simon, 'but you're wrong at the top of your voice.'

'Relax,' said Frank. 'If any other team's spying on us they won't get the right answer from him.'

Bowes looked upset and close to tears. He appeared vulnerable in the way that only a man with more than two chins can. I'd have almost felt sorry for him if I hadn't been busting a gut for the past few months to make him a fortune.

Andrews arrived at half-time and was, as he bloody well ought to have been, all smiles. He shook hands with Joe and Bowes before addressing the rest of us. 'First equal, eh? How are my troops?'

'We're right behind you, sir,' said Simon, only half joking.

The next round was Advertising and, once again, we scored a maximum ten points. I was beginning to wish that we'd played our joker – as PXL Communications did – to gain our extra ten points but, as Frank explained when I mentioned it, it was psychologically better to do it at the end. We were now lying second, ten points behind PXL Communications, and one point ahead of TV Dinners.

Round six was Geography – not my strongest subject. With Andrews watching us like the proud owner of a pack of performing seals, my intention where I didn't know the answer was to nod vigorously with whoever did and then say, 'Wait a second, I'm sure you're right but would anyone like to offer an argument?' – thereby looking like a Man of Judgment. I did this to good effect on two questions before – oh bliss! – finding myself in a position where I was the sole person to know that the capital of Gabon is Libreville. Walter, meanwhile, earned his supper by telling us, most insouciantly, that the mountain K2 is in the Karakoram Range.

We scored yet another perfect ten but were now in fourth place with sixty points, behind PXL Communications on seventy, TV Dinners on sixty-six and Spectrum Productions on sixty-two points but then, as Walter was obliged to explain to Andrews, they had all played their jokers.

The penultimate round was Music. This was such a doddle that even Andrews was able to answer a couple of questions correctly. He made up for this by suggesting – no, insisting – that Peter Green replaced Brian Jones in the Rolling Stones: it took Walter to overrule him with the correct answer of Mick Taylor.

The only difficulty for us was the nationality of the composer Jean Sibelius. Most of the table, me included (although I wasn't too vociferous), thought he was French but Joe seemed so quietly sure that he was Finnish that we went with him. Thanks to Joe, we scored full marks while PXL Communications – hurrah! – dropped a point, presumably on the Sibelius question. With TV Dinners falling away and Spectrum Productions unable to make up ground, all we had to do was hold our nerve in the final round – our joker round – and we were home and dry.

The first eight questions were so easy that we were all – or almost all, as Joe was holding back and Andrews and Bowes were pretty clueless – chanting them together.

And then we came to question nine: Who played the female lead in *Paint Your Wagon*? Well, that halted us in our tracks.

'Clint Eastwood and Lee Marvin were the male leads,' said Simon.

'Thanks for telling us what we already know,' snapped Frank.

I was thinking hard with my head buried in my folded arms so that there would be no visual distraction to my thought processes. From I don't know where, a face was forming. It was a blonde face and now I was trying to put a name to it, but every time I got near, it seemed to recoil. I'd have to get close enough and then suddenly snatch it – just like that! – from out of the air.

And then I heard myself saying, 'Mary Ure.' At first, I was diffident, but soon I was growing in confidence. 'Yup, that's right, Mary Ure.' How I knew, I didn't know – but then I had no idea where the answer Libreville had come from. Then, as if it supported my answer, I started adding extra biographical information. 'She was married to John Osborne. She's dead now.'

'She was also in *Where Eagles Dare*,' added Simon. If he was hoping to impress Andrews, he was going to have to stand in line behind me, tonight's blue-eyed boy. I was also enjoying basking in the admiration of Joe and Walter and, from the corner of my eye, I could see Gaby's dimples pumping. Even Frank was looking at me with what might have been respect. Only poor old Bowes dissented. 'I was sure it was Jean Seberg,' he said dolefully. I leant across to pat him on his corpulent frame and to reassure him. 'She was in *St Joan*,' I explained.

Then there was nothing to do but sit back, relax, and wait for the answers and the final scores which would see us crowned as Quiz Kings.

I think the moment I heard the name 'Jean Seberg' as the answer to number nine was, without doubt, the worst of my life.

'But she was in *St Joan*!' I shouted in my own defence.

'Does that mean she couldn't have been in *Paint Your Wagon* as well?' snarled Frank.

Before I could answer the unanswerable, the final scores were read out in reverse order. We finished with eighty-eight points but it wasn't enough to beat PXL Communications who scored eighty-nine.

Andrew's reaction to me and my unintentional error was as brief as it was brutal. 'You cunt!' He then, somewhat unsportingly, stormed out of the hall before the trophy was handed over to the winners.

I judged that it was probably not the best time to hand him the proposal for a game show.

It wasn't, however, an entirely wasted evening. Gaby and I (surreptitiously) went back to her place and, finally, had sex. It was the first time in my life that I've ever genuinely made love.

# CHAPTER TWENTY-ONE

It was also the first time I've ever woken up with a girl without feeling awkward.

Usually in such circumstances, I can't wait to leave. Oh, I do the right thing. I'll have sex – I've usually got a stiffy in the morning and, anyway, my cock is totally separate from my brain and my emotions; I'll give them a cuddle in a look-I-know-this-is-part-of-the-deal-but-could-we-not-make-a-big-thing-of-it, I'll even eat breakfast with them but there's no doubt in my own mind that I'd much rather be at home on my own with a bowl of Sainsbury's Honey Nut Bran Flakes in semi-skimmed milk and a black coffee in the certain knowledge that, because I'm up after Ziggy and before Peter, I can have a good fifteen minutes on the bog without being disturbed. That's just the way I've always been.

Until I spent the night with Gaby.

When I awoke after four hours of really deep sleep, she was lying next to me, looking just like

Gaby. That might seem obvious but, because of my past record, I had expected her to have lost all her allure. Now, I would see her as she really was and not as I had built her up to be. But there she was, with a few strands of hair almost covering her tiny nose, looking simply gorgeous.

The intensity of my gaze must have awoken her. 'Hello, David,' she said, her face immediately settling into a smile that caused her dimples to do their dimpling thing. 'Did you sleep all right?'

I felt overwhelmed: not by lust but by love. It's true that my response was to make love to her, but that was only because, in my attempt to hold her as close as possible, I had to find *somewhere* to park my morning flag-pole which, for once, was completely in harmony with the nation state it represented.

When we'd finished making love, we lay in each other's arms as though we were holding a silence of remembrance. In my case, I was remembering as much as I could of the sweetness of being with her just in case this turned out to be a one-off.

Eventually, she murmured in my ear, 'We have to go to work.'

Feeling like her husband, and enjoying the feeling, I rolled out of bed and went to the loo, pausing only to cover up my naked genitals when her flatmate, Phoebe, looked out of her bedroom to find out who was singing 'Love Will Keep Us Together' at the top of his voice at quarter to nine in the morning.

She didn't seem particularly bothered. She'd met me with my clothes on and, as a nurse, she must have seen many naked men before – in and out of hospital.

Gaby made us a simple breakfast of toast and jam and coffee and then, because the two of us were, of course, going to the same office, decided it wasn't too profligate to take a cab to work.

I hadn't talked about the quiz evening because I hadn't wanted to spoil something far more important but, now, on our way into the office, I couldn't restrain myself. 'Andrews will sack me, I know he will.'

'Don't be stupid. He needs you too much to do that.'

'You don't know him.'

'Don't I?'

'You don't? You didn't? You haven't?'

She blew at me in annoyance. 'What do you think?'

'I don't know.'

'Then you don't know me.'

The rest of the ride passed in an uncomfortable silence. Just before we got to the office, I squeezed her hand and apologised. 'I'm sorry, Gaby. I'm not normally jealous.'

'You're not normally stupid. Andrews sniffs around me because that's what dogs like him do, but it doesn't mean anything.'

'I love you.'

She kissed me. 'And I love you too. Even if you are about to become unemployed.'

But everything turned out fine. As I learned later, Walter had contacted Andrews to tell him that I was a vital member of the team.

'Thanks for that, Walter, but why didn't you also explain to him that it was partly because of me that we were in a position to win the quiz in the first place?'

'Because, dear boy, I was trying to appeal to his needs – which are great – rather than to his sense of fair play which is, I regret to say, non-existent.'

It was especially decent of Walter to stand up for me, although he wasn't overstating my importance to the team and the show. The fact was, we were within two weeks of our first show and, although we had plenty of questions, we still didn't have as many as we'd promised. For the most part, the pressure had a beneficial effect on the question writers: we simply didn't have time to play silly buggers. On the other hand, when we did disagree, it was worse than our normal bickering.

'Look,' said Frank to me, 'I know that tomorrow is only yet another run-through, but that doesn't mean we can afford to be complacent.'

'Who's complacent?' I said irritably.

'Well, you've asked: "Which one of the Marx Brothers had the real name of Leonard?" '

'Yes, I did. The answer's Chico. Do you have a problem with that?'

'No,' he said through gritted teeth, 'but the way you've phrased it, it could mean surname rather than Christian name.'

'But he was Jewish. He didn't have a Christian name.'

'Don't be a jerk.'

'I'm not being a jerk. *You're* being a jerk. You're nitpicking and when I make a perfectly reasonable point – that none of the Marx Brothers had Christian names because they were Jewish – you tell me I'm a jerk.' As usual, the third writer was brought in to judge. 'Well, Simon?'

'I think you're both jerks.'

Given that he and Frank invariably sided with each other, I was prepared to put that one down as a victory on points.

That afternoon, I met Richie Clarke for the first time. Frank, who seemed to have become the *de facto* Chief Question Writer, took a call and said to us, 'The talent's arrived: we have to go to Michael's office to be on parade.'

Not for the first time, I wondered about Frank's past. Were his Army references because of his brother, or did he himself have a services background? Still peeved with Frank because of before, I said to Simon, 'Arsehole thinks he's in the Army.'

'He wasn't; I was. And you're the arsehole for

associating the Army with arseholes.'

If I hadn't had to go into a meeting, I'd have allowed myself to be even more flabbergasted than I was. Camp Simon in the military! As what? An officer in charge of the entertainment troupe? Captain Ashwood in *It Ain't Half Hot, Mum*? It was all too incongruous.

When I got into Andrews's office, the first thing I noticed was Richie Clarke all over Gaby – *my* Gaby – as though he could smell the sex on her and wanted some of it. I was going to go over and separate them, with a crowbar if necessary but, perhaps fortunately for my career, Andrews chose that moment to launch into one of his welcoming speeches.

'Friends,' he said, trying to sound all democratic but coming over instead like a cheesy salesman, 'it is my pleasure to welcome Richie Clarke into our happy family and I hope he's going to put a little "sparkle" into our "lot".'

'Blimey,' I muttered to Simon. 'How long did it take him to come up with that?' Simon stared ahead but no doubt stored my *lèse-majesté* for repetition to our diminutive chief. As if I cared.

Richie tore himself away from Gaby and switched on a smile – the full 100 watts. 'It's great to be here. And it's great to be out – especially after spending so many nights in.' This was obviously a reference to his magnum opus, *Richie's Night In* and we all laughed like a theatre audience acknowledging a playwright's intended joke which turns out not to be funny.

Then it was handshakes all round. Andrews introduced me with the words 'Don't trust this one – at least not with questions about *Seven Brides for Seven Brothers*.' I didn't correct him. 'Still, he's a scallywag, aren't you?' He slapped me very gently across the face and we all laughed. To someone who didn't know him, he might almost have come across as a kind, affectionate boss.

Richie looked straight into my eyes and shook my hand, really pumping it. I felt as if I was meeting a Presidential candidate out on the stump. 'I'm Richie,' he told me, somewhat unnecessarily. 'What's your name?'

'I'm David. I help to write the questions for *The Lot*.'

'Aha, you're one of the most important people in this room! I'd better make sure I keep you happy!'

It was all said with so much bonhomie that I felt mean about taking a dislike to him. His sincerity was so transparently fake. I don't know, maybe it worked with other people, but me – I'd rather he'd asked me something about the questions or even joshed me by saying, 'Get back to work, slave.' Anything but take me for a simpleton. I even found myself thinking about Kit with something approaching affection. Mind you, that was easier now that he had disappeared – literally – into thin air, fronting a programme on a satellite shopping channel.

Nor did I appreciate Richie's abrupt about-turns as soon as he'd granted me my ration of one line. Not so much as an 'excuse me' and there he was chatting to Gaby again. OK, so they'd both worked at the BBC but then so had Walter, and Richie wasn't clambering over *him* to take a bit of sleepy dust out of *his* eye.

At that moment, I was suffering from pure impotent jealousy. How dare he try it on with my girlfriend. But there was, however momentarily, a frisson of envy in me too. Why should he be so much more interested in Gaby than in me? Fortunately – because it was less corrosive – the former feeling lasted much longer than the latter.

I was pleased, therefore, that Gaby wasn't at the run-through the following day. We'd had dinner the night before and she'd reassured me that she felt nothing for Richie – although she didn't agree that he might very well be yet another one of Hughie Green's illegitimate children. I wanted to spend the night with her again but she said that even if I didn't need the sleep, she did, and besides, she didn't want us living together. In the split second before she added the word 'yet', I suffered the sort of neurotic pang of loss that had always been foreign to me.

So, even without the Richie factor, it was probably for the best that I'd had a full night's sleep, preceded by a half an hour's selective debriefing with Peter, who told me that he reckoned I'd found my 'lady'. Thus I was able to concentrate fully on the run-through which was being held in a church hall in Kensington.

This was the first time that the questions were being used properly i.e. chosen randomly by the computer from our database. The very haphazard-ness caused me low-level anxiety the whole after-noon. Not that I doubted any of my questions, but you never knew, although I *did* know that if I got something wrong, then I'd be out on my ear – irrespective of Walter's patronage.

Walter himself was a different man that day: masterful, authoritative, completely at home and totally in charge. He was unflappability personi-fied. Not so Andrews. He was running around, if not like a blue-arsed fly then like a red-marked ant, as though industriousness in itself would make a difference. He reminded me of a pre-Sven England footballer mistaking activity for action.

What made his interference in all of our jobs so *truly* annoying was that we were genuinely busy. Walter had decided not to have volunteers: as he himself had put it, 'Today is about Richie finding his feet and I don't want any civilians distracting him.' So, in the absence of hundreds of contestants, Frank, Simon, Karen, Belinda and I had to run around the hall pressing handsets in a predetermined order – the idea being to replicate a real programme.

The questions came out in the right order and we contestants were reduced accordingly until there was a winner – Simon, who hammed it up even more than I would have done.

However, the revelation was Richie Clarke. Even with the equivalent of full gallery talkback in his lughole, he was cool, fluent, *professional*: a mirror image of Walter and the perfect antidote to the ludicrous Andrews. Suddenly, I saw Richie not as a rival for Gaby but as the show's saviour: a modern gladiator taking on the immense challenge of the Saturday-night ratings war.

Who was I, a humble foot soldier, to cast aspersions on his choice of consort?

# CHAPTER TWENTY-TWO

The days between Richie's first run-through and the first show passed by in a blur of question writing and question checking. I had to buy a new Collins English Dictionary as I'd literally worn out the last one and, at night, I even found myself dreaming quiz questions.

Simon had been right to point out our preference for writing harder, more interesting questions. We now had plenty of second-half questions, but few for the first quarter of the show. So those last few days were devoted to devising questions based on what Frank called 'the curriculum' – the sort of low-level general knowledge that all averagely intelligent people should possess. Thus we were writing questions about: European capitals, currencies, flags, (Premiership) football clubs, TV presenters' catchphrases, quotations from Shakespeare, characters from the best-known Dickens books, actors in Oscar-winning films, well-known lines from classic movies, basic weights and measures, the easier chemical symbols, British Prime Ministers and current Cabinet Ministers, major storylines in TV soaps, classic number one singles and so on, and so on – until our fingers ached so much that we simply couldn't type any longer.

The worst thing about it was the sourcing. To look for one source on questions like: What is the capital of Spain? or: Who won the Best Actor Oscar for *American Beauty*? Or: How many feet are there in a yard? made me feel like an arse, let alone looking for three. You write a question like: Which British Prime Minister was known as Supermac? and the three wrong answers don't include Ramsay MacDonald – so how much scope is there for confusion?

When I mentioned this to Frank and Simon, they were so wrapped up with their own hassle, they just grunted. I understood. It was a time for pure slog: for writing the sort of questions that wouldn't be out of place at the annual village carnival's Quiz Nite. And if there wasn't time for chatting, there was also – saints be praised – little time for rowing, or for our normal trivia challenges in the office, which proved a blessing, since Frank and Simon had a tendency to use such occasions to put me down.

But if the writing was unremitting and the sourcing soul-destroying, the checking of each other's questions was piss simple. I don't know about the other two guys, but I just let everything through (almost) on the nod with the most cursory of checks. I mean, why should I bother to spend more than two seconds on questions like: In which novel by Charles Dickens does Bill Sykes appear? Or: In which Shakespeare play does the main character ask 'To be or not to be'? Or: Which TV entertainer had the catchphrase 'just like that'? The bottom line was that I was *so* certain of the answers to such questions that I would rather take the chance of a rogue answer getting through than risk my sanity in checking them.

Maybe Walter picked up on this attitude, this malaise, and judged it to be potentially hazardous to the show. All I know is that one day, the order came down – through Frank, of course – to check or rather *re*-check our checked questions and answers.

I was all for downing tools. 'Walter *knows* that each question's been sourced three times by the writer and then checked by both the other two. You know, a psychologist friend of mine once told me that you were allowed to check that you'd locked the front door/turned off the gas/switched off the telly up to four times before you were deemed to be suffering from obsessive-compulsive disorder. Does Walter want us to become obsessive-compulsives?'

'I don't know,' said Simon. 'Why don't you ask him?'

'Why don't you ask him?'

'He's not *my* bum-chum.'

'Can it, fellows,' said 'Boss' Frank. 'We'll do as we're told *because* we've been told and because it never hurts to be certain.'

I went home one evening for a rare visit (Gaby's rule was that we couldn't spend more than two nights in a row together and we had just spent three) and, if I didn't expect the red carpet – or even a fatted calf – the very least I hoped for was a warm welcome and a sympathetic ear for my problems. Apparently, Peter and Ziggy had sorted out their differences from the other week and I was really looking forward to a lads' night in but, as I found out as soon as I walked in, Peter was out 'jigging' in Worthing and as for Ziggy . . . *Ziggy had company*!

It was true. As I walked in, I heard him in the kitchen talking about *EastEnders*. 'Of course, Walford, where it's set, is supposedly in London E20 and, indeed, the show was originally going to be called *E20* and many of the characters' names were taken from gravestones in the East End.'

Nothing unusual in Ziggy's choice of conversation topic, but what was strange was the absence of someone telling him to shut up. Peter, of course, wouldn't have let him get past the first few words but Peter was out. Had Ziggy at last found a friend – possibly a deaf mute – who was interested in what he had to say? Could he be talking to himself?

I walked into the kitchen. He was facing me: scoffing a sandwich, clearly on a roll. 'Many people think that June Brown who plays Dot Cotton has been with the show since episode one. In fact, she made her debut in episode forty . . . hiya, David!'

'Hi, Ziggy.' I followed his eyes to behind the door where, sitting on a stool, was a girl. I looked back at Ziggy. 'Who's this?' I mouthed, thinking that maybe she was an opinion pollster or a new neighbour who'd popped in to introduce herself.

'No need to whisper, old boy.' He walked towards the girl. 'I have the honour to introduce you to Amelia Mears.'

I took her proffered hand. She wasn't an obvious beauty but then, judged by objective criteria, neither was Ziggy. And I'm not exactly an oil painting myself, of course. 'Hi there. I'm David Marriott.'

'Why do you call Gary "Ziggy"?'

''Cos that's his name.'

'No, it's not.'

'Yeah, all right, it's not but it's what his friends call him.'

'*Why*?' she repeated imperiously.

'He was in a play called *Zigger Zagger* at school and he used to do the chants in the playground at break.' I decided to indulge her. 'As you may know, Ziggy is something of an obsessive.'

'No, I didn't know that about *Gary* and, to be honest with you, I don't think I like it very much.'

'I'm sorry!' I was about to add words which

would prove just how unapologetic I was when Ziggy bundled me out of the room and into the sitting room.

'What is this, mate?' I asked him. 'Go ugly early?'

He pushed me into an armchair. 'Hey, David, you're way out of line.'

'Yeah, I'm sorry. But who is she?'

'She – Amelia – is my new girlfriend.'

'Oh gosh, I am sorry. I mean, I'm not sorry she's your girlfriend, I'm sorry in case I insulted you.'

He sat down as well. 'That's OK, old bean. I know she's not an obvious beauty . . .' I swallowed the retort that her looks weren't the problem, it was her attitude '. . . but she's really very intelligent and, I tell you what, I think she's gagging for it.'

I didn't know about her, but even on so short an acquaintance, *I* was gagging. However, I wasn't about to rain on Ziggy's parade. All I could do was hope that this latest fad of his wouldn't last. If only I could have escaped to Gaby's . . . Well, I couldn't but there was nothing to stop me phoning her so I braved the kitchen and grabbed the cordless. Lying on my bed, stretching out after a horribly tough day, I phoned Gaby who was as delighted to hear my voice as I was to hear hers.

We swapped the usual endearments. 'Wish I was with you, Gabe.'

'Wish I *were* with you, Dabe.' Our pet names for

each other were, I'm embarrassed to confess, predicated on the word 'babe'.

'So why can't we be together? We're both free, single and over twenty-one.'

'Because . . .'

'That's not a reason.'

'No, I know it's not, which is why I'm asking you not to go on about it.'

'That's a *non sequitur*.'

'You know I love you, David.'

'Then why don't you want to be with me?'

'Want to be with you? I *yearn* to be with you, to feel you inside me. It's just that . . .' Her voice trailed off.

'What?' I searched for an explanation out of left field. 'Is it Richie Clarke?'

'Is what Richie Clarke?'

'Are you holding yourself back for him?'

'Are you mad?'

'Well, he was all over you the other day.'

'He was even more all over me today.'

'What?'

She sighed. 'I was at the studios and he was there for a meeting with Wardrobe.'

'And?'

'And . . . he told me he was crazy about me and invited me to go to his dressing-room.'

'What?'

'I told him I have a boyfriend whom I love.'

'What did he say?'

'He told me he had a girlfriend whom he loves but that she wasn't as sexy as me.'

'What did you say?'

'I told him that, fortunately, my boyfriend was a lot sexier than him.'

'You little darling! I love you.'

'I love you too.'

I paused for dramatic effect. 'So can I come round?'

'No.'

'Why?'

'All right, David.' Her voice dropped a tone. 'I'll tell you. When I get married, it'll be for life. I don't want to make a mistake.'

'I'm with you.'

'This time last year, I was engaged to a guy named Spencer.'

'What happened?'

'He called off the engagement.'

'Why?'

'He said he didn't want to be tied down.'

'What happened to him?'

'He married his ex-girlfriend.'

'I see.'

'So that's why I want to be absolutely sure.'

'Aren't you?'

'Yes, I am, but please don't pressurise me and try to understand why I want to put the brakes on.'

'Gabsy? Do you want to know other people who were in broken engagements?'

'Go on.'

'Jimmy Connors and Chris Evert, Lauren Bacall and Frank Sinatra, Julia Roberts and Kiefer Sutherland, Naomi Campbell and Adam Clayton, Brad Pitt and Gwyneth Paltrow, Ben Stiller and Jeanne Tripplehorn, Cameron Diaz and Jared Leto, Laura Dern and Billy Bob Thornton . . .'

'Dabe?'

'Yes, Gabe?'

'I love you.'

'I love you too.'

# CHAPTER TWENTY-THREE

As the first show loomed, Gaby's workload intensified so that we became, in effect, just like the very sort of 'married' couple she was anxious to delay us becoming. She was so shattered by the end of the day that all the usual falling in love things – like romantic candlelit dinners and walking round street-markets hand in hand and, of course, marathon sex sessions – were completely out. Instead, we ate packet meals, fell asleep in front of the TV and curled up in bed together like a couple of inverted question marks, for all the world like a pair of young marrieds but without the bickering and the new crockery.

Actually, this was fine with me, especially as Gaby had amended her two nights in a row rule to five. Ostensibly, this was because of what I'd told her about Amelia but, in truth, it was because she didn't have the strength to withstand my nagging.

Having never been part of a couple, I was surprised by how easy it was. I guess when I had thought about it in the abstract, I had envisaged myself with 'a girl' rather than someone specific, doing all those awful things that only couples do: talking to each other in baby talk, feeding each other in restaurants and taking ten times longer than necessary to walk down the road because their arms are so entwined. What I hadn't reckoned on was that the girl would be Gaby and that everything would seem so *natural*.

Having said that, I'd like to think we were never as bad as my brother Clive and his lame-brained wife, Hilary, who not only bought children's cuddly toys for each other – and boasted about it – but also gave the wretched things names and celebrated their birthdays. But then that's just my perspective: *we* are in love, *you* are soppy about each other, *they* are fucking nauseating.

The fact that Gaby was also a colleague helped enormously. True, our pillow-talk made the room sound like a trendy Soho coffee bar but it meant that, at last, I had someone with whom I could share my worries (Andrews), fears (Andrews) and pet hates (Andrews). Actually, the little monster wasn't treating me too badly but that was only because, with so many different contributors to the project, he was obliged to spread his nastiness ever thinner. Fortunately, he had to be nice to Gaby because so much depended on her; unfortunately, he was incapable of being nice to a woman without coming on to her. Under pressure from me for all the gory details, Gaby revealed that he was being so lascivious that he once even dribbled down his shirt! Despite all the evidence to the contrary, maybe he thought he was flattering her.

With Gaby's support – this, after all, wasn't *her* first programme – and with the experience of the pilot and all the run-throughs, I was a lot less nervous than I'd anticipated for the first show. In fact, Gaby herself commented on how relaxed and positive everyone seemed to be – not least, in her opinion, because of Walter's charisma and Richie's professionalism. I was slightly bothered to hear her praise Randy Richie but I eventually rationalised it as a reflection of *her* professionalism.

And the first show duly turned out to be an absolute rip-roaring success.

If Murphy's Law states that 'everything that can go wrong, will go wrong' then Show One of *The Lot* totally disproved it. From the moment that Richie, in what would become part of his routine, sang Rod Stewart's 'Sailing' and kicked a number of balloons into the audience before the recording started, the show simply *worked*. Thanks to the contestant researcher with the dimples, the audience members were young, bright, exciting and excited: a whole generation and several classes removed from the traditional depressing game-show coach-party crowd. The questions thrown up by the computer were not only accurate (natch) but were also good examples for each level of the show and led to the 'right' number of people being knocked out.

Richie was utterly magnificent. When there were problems with the computer or the autocue, he stayed cool and repeated his links or questions, and during the many recording breaks, he joshed with the floor manager, the cameramen and the audience. For the first time ever, I realised that so much about being a television presenter is about what goes on when the cameras aren't recording.

After winning the contest i.e. when everyone else was knocked out, the winner, a really nice guy from Ilkley in Yorkshire named Phil, had to answer two more questions to win the £250,000 jackpot. The first was, in fact, one of mine: The fingerprints of which creatures are virtually indistinguishable from those of humans?

a)    Gorillas
b)    Marmosets
c)    Koala bears
d)    Pandas
e)    Beavers

Phil took his time to answer the question as though he were actually trying to work it out rather than merely taking a guess. Later, he told me that he answered (correctly) koala bears because he had once read something about some Aussie burglars leaving koala prints at the scene of a robbery in the hope that they would confuse the police.

He then had to answer what Frank, Simon and I called a stopper question – one to which no one could be expected to know the answer. The question was: On average, how much pizza is consumed in the USA every day?

a)    18 acres
b)    38 acres
c)    58 acres
d)    78 acres
e)    98 acres

Obviously, he had no idea but plumped for 18 acres on the basis that – or so he explained later – all the other possible answers took their figures (ending in eights) from the first option.

Whatever the reasoning, he was right and won a cool quarter of a million. He was, understandably, elated and so, no less understandably, were all the rest of us. The calibre of the winner and the result were so much better than we had ever dreamed possible, we couldn't wait until the show was aired two days later on the Saturday.

Having not been involved with the editing, Gaby and I decided to watch the show at her place as it went out. We could have taped it and gone out, but we wanted to experience it the same way as most of the rest of the population.

At 7.15, we were sat in front of her telly, on our own as Phoebe had gone out, and were already a few beers, a giant pizza and a monster pack of Maltesers each to the good. 'And now,' said the continuity announcer, 'we're going to give you *The Lot*.'

Titles – sharp, digital, innovative. Theme tune: the horrible sting drawn out to a mammoth thirty seconds. The set: cleaner, brighter, more impressive and less tacky than it had looked in real life. Richie: better, much better, now that all the gaps, breaks and pauses had been edited out.

But what I hadn't reckoned on – and what made such a huge vital difference – were the graphics. During the recording, it hadn't even occurred to me just how much information – about the rules, the questions and, most impor-tant, the contestants – could be displayed during the show to make it so much more interesting and compelling.

'We've got a hit here, Gabe,' I said more than once. Actually, I think I said it, with variations on Gaby's name (that's another thing new lovers do: have a ridiculous number of pet names for each other) more than ten times, but she was so caught up in the excitement of it all that she wasn't complaining.

And then came the moment when Nice Guy Phil from Ilkley made his pizza guess and we were hugging and kissing and . . . wait a minute . . .

why wasn't my name on the credits?

'Oi, Gabs, where the fuck is my name?'

'What do you mean?'

'Why aren't I on the credits?'

'Actually, Dabes, you'll find that the correct word is "ain't" not aren't. It's the one time that you can use the word ain't in its—'

'Never mind that! What's going on?'

'I don't know.' She sat down and thought for a second. 'Did you see Frank and Simon's names?'

I sat down next to her. 'No, I don't think I did.'

'Then I think you'll find that they've left your names off the credits to preserve your anonymity. That's why my name's not up there, either. Or didn't you notice?'

I hadn't, but now wasn't the time to confess. 'I don't want my fucking anonymity preserved.'

She pretended to berate me. 'Tut tut, such profanity, I shall have to wash your mouth out with soap.' She drew my head to her breast. 'Listen, Liebchen, don't you remember telling me that you were warned not to say anything to anyone about what you were doing?'

'What's that got to do with it? Oh, I see . . .'

'It's got nothing to do with denying you credit and everything to do with no one knowing the names of the question writers or the contestant researchers and trying to nobble them.'

'So why didn't they give us Production Team credits?'

'For the same reason. Sparkle can't take the chance that someone will get to you or me and maybe try to bribe us.'

'I wouldn't mind.'

'That's why they can't take the chance.'

From being on an absolute high five minutes before, I suddenly felt flat. Gaby sensed my mood and tried to reassure me. 'Look, Daby, it doesn't matter if your name's not on the telly so long as it's on the salary cheque.'

'Much good that does me: I'm still bloody overdrawn.'

'Have you shown *Astro Wars* to Michael yet?'

'Do you mean Andrews?'

'Yes, obviously.'

'Then say so.' I patted her hand as if to apologise for snapping. 'No, I haven't but I will.' I stood up and started to pace the room. 'Oh well, it'll still be good for me to be associated with a hit. I presume that I can put it on my CV."

'Of course you can.'

I sighed but carried on pacing. 'I don't know what to do.'

'I, on the other hand, do. David Marriott, we're going to bed. You might be anonymous as a question writer but you have the chance to make a name for yourself as a lover.'

The next morning, while Gaby slept the sleep of a well-serviced woman, I went down to the local newsagent. I leafed through all the newspapers in the hope of finding something about the show but, apart from a tiny paragraph in the *Sunday People* and the *News of the World* to the effect that a viewer had won £250,00 in the first edition of a new game show, there was nothing about *The Lot*.

Like all the other middle-class men in the shop who were poring through the red-top tabloids – for people who deplore the gutter press, we all like to spend an awful lot of time in the gutter checking that it's still dirty – I walked out with a copy of the *Sunday Times* which I took up to Gaby with a cup of tea.

'Gabs, there's not very much about the show in the papers.'

She looked at me through bleary eyes. 'That's because they'd all, or nearly all, gone to press before we'd gone on air. Wait till tomorrow.'

She was right. The Monday papers were absolutely full of it. One whole page in the *Sun*: PIZZA TOPPING GOOD SHOW!, a teaser on the front of the *Daily Star*: WE'VE GOT THE LOT. The *Daily Mirror* had PHIL'S PIZZA TAKEAWAY while the *Daily Mail* joined in with a piece headed GAME SHOW HITS THE JACKPOT. Even *The Times*'s TV reviewer wrote: *I liked it – not a little but a lot*.

In my enthusiasm, I took the papers into work but, of course, everyone else had already seen them. Besides, we had no time to rest on our laurels. *The Lot* was going out twice a week.

Saturday's show was history; Wednesday's show was being recorded that same night. There would be time for self-congratulations only when the tour of duty ended and the ratings war was won.

Meanwhile, Frank, Simon and I were like the codebreakers at Bletchley Park in World War Two: vital to the success of the whole war but forced to live in total anonymity.

# CHAPTER TWENTY-FOUR

Of course, it was all too good to last but we had a decent run.

The second show – coming as it did off the back of all those news stories – drew an audience of thirteen million. We didn't get a jackpot winner but that only served to heighten interest for the programme the following Saturday.

Once again, the jackpot wasn't won which meant that £400,000 was up for grabs on Wednesday. The press started going wild. The red-top tabloids were fascinated by the contestants and the audience being one and the same. It had the randomness that those papers valued in the Lottery – with the difference that, because it required general knowledge, the winners were more deserving.

Journalists were especially keen to find out what – if any – the audience selection criteria were. Basically, Gaby was looking for the bright, the young and the peppy with a few old-timers and eccentrics thrown in for the sake of variety. True, everyone had to apply via premium phone lines, but we didn't just use general knowledge to gauge eligibility, personality came into it as well, and Gaby's bank of telephone receptionists had been well primed to weed out the perverts and the scum and the plain moronic.

The posher papers were more interested in our stopper questions – the ones at the end of the second half designed to 'stop' know-alls – and they started providing their readers with all sorts of incredibly arcane information in a bid to second-guess us.

Frank, Simon and I were of course obliged to keep track of all these features just in case, by some incredible coincidence, a paper struck lucky but, as it turned out, we needn't have bothered. However, we did learn some extraordinary things – not least that Mongolians put salt in their tea instead of sugar, that Japan (in 1993) became the first country ever to have more than 20 per cent of their population aged over sixty-five, that the Danish flag, dating back to the thirteenth century, is the world's oldest unchanged national flag, that at any given moment, there are some 1,800 thunderstorms somewhere on earth, that ten-gallon hats only hold about six pints of water, that you could drive a car round the world four times with the amount of fuel in a jumbo jet, that snails can sleep for three years without eating and that the average person's heart beats 36 million times a year.

'It's all very well for them,' said Simon, after reading yet another newspaper crib sheet, 'but they don't have to take responsibility for their facts.'

'Yeah, right,' I said. 'I mean, how would they go about sourcing a fact like this: Sir Winston Churchill smoked three hundred thousand cigars in his lifetime.'

'S'pose they *could* make a guesstimate.'

'That's exactly what it would be, but when we say that there are three American towns named Santa Claus, we've checked it every which way.'

'That's why we don't make mistakes.'

Never mind hubris: hadn't we even heard of irony?

Programme five was when our smugness was replaced with our ultimate nightmare: the WRONG QUESTION.

Actually, it wasn't the wrong question, it was the wrong answer and it wasn't even *that* wrong but it was wrong enough to allow the newspapers the opportunity to give their newest, tallest poppy a good kicking.

The question in question came in the second-half: How many hairs does the average person have on their head? The choices were 80,000, 100,000, 120,000, 140,000 and 160,000. The correct answer – or, at least, the one that we decreed to be correct – was 100,000.

One of the newspapers, on a slow news day, begged to differ.

Apparently, according to some tame trichologist who, for the right fee, would no doubt have averred that the average person had precisely 7,548,979 hairs on their head, the number varied according to the colour of a person's hair. So whereas the average person with brown or black hair might very well have 100,000 hairs on their head, the average redhead would have fewer and the average blonde would have more.

The first I knew about it was when Walter came into the question-writers' office holding a copy of the newspaper article in question.

'What the fuck does this mean?' he demanded.

I looked blank – as did Frank and Simon.

'There's an article here that queries one of our questions.' My heart stopped beating and my colon prepared a stool. *Please don't let it be one of my questions.*

'The question was from Wednesday's show and it was the one about the numbers of hairs on the average person's head.'

Phew! It was one of Frank's!

'I want to know who was responsible for that question, or do I have to look through the database for the signature?' At the bottom of each question there was a box for our initials.

'No need,' said Frank. 'It was one of mine.'

Simon and I looked at him with a mixture of pity, horror and relief. Walter asked him for his sources. Frank scrolled down the database until he came to the relevant question. 'A book – *What You Need To Know* by A.J. Lexington, a trichologist named David Berkmann and,' he coughed as if embarrassed, 'Dudley's Barber Shop.'

Walter yelped. 'What?'

'I had to find a third source and so I—'

'. . . You went to your bloody barber. Frank! *Frank*!'

'What about Simon and David? They signed it off.'

'That's true,' said Simon, 'but I couldn't see any reason why it was wrong and, as I recall, I asked David to check it actively – that's to say, to look for a mistake – rather than passively.'

'Yes,' said Frank. 'I remember that too.'

I couldn't believe it! I was all for being sympathetic to Frank and now here he was, colluding with Simon in shifting the blame on to me. I appealed to Walter. 'This is crazy. I don't even remember the question, let alone taking responsibility for it.'

'You were probably thinking of getting inside your hamster when you should have been concentrating on your work,' sneered Simon.

I don't know whether it was the insult to Gaby, the implication that I neglected my work or just the shock of being blamed for something that so clearly *wasn't* my fault but I suddenly went berserk and hurled myself at Simon.

I rained blows down on him in the imprecise style of a twelve-year-old – which was probably the last time I ever tried to hit anyone. Simon was taken aback but not for long. I felt an exquisite pain – initially almost pleasurable in its intensity – in my nose and then he was punching my stomach as though he were a boxer working on a punchbag and I thought I was going to suffocate to death.

Fortunately, Walter, revealing surprising strength, pulled him off me and I lay on the floor, like a landed fish struggling for breath. But I wasn't letting up. 'If you *ever* say anything about Gaby again, I'll . . . I'll . . .'

Simon looked down on me contemptuously. 'You and whose army?'

And then I remembered his former occupation and realised the folly of picking a fight with an ex-soldier. Shit, he could have killed me! Shit, he might still. 'Look, Simon, surely we can be mature about this.' I got to my feet. 'I've been trying to keep my relationship with Gaby a secret but clearly it isn't. All I'm asking is for you not to slag off my girlfriend. It's not an unreasonable request, is it?'

I'd never seen Simon look embarrassed before. 'I'm sorry, I didn't realise it was um, a proper . . . er *thing*. I thought it was just . . .'

'Well, it isn't. We love each other and,' I was about to say, 'and we're engaged to be married,' but since even Gaby and I hadn't talked about it, I decided that it was probably best to discuss it with her first.

Walter inadvertently came to my rescue. 'Fellows, we still have this problem with the question.'

'Which *wasn't* my fucking fault!' I said through a haze of blood, wind and pain.

'Which is Frank's responsibility,' continued Walter. 'Michael will, no doubt, have something to say about it once he's read the papers.'

'Damage limitation,' said Frank. 'How many people were actually knocked out on this question, Walter?'

'I don't know. From memory, about eight or nine but I'll have to check. What are you thinking?'

'Well, the whole thing's a bit of a grey area. We're not necessarily wrong with our answer, but there's obviously some room for doubt.' He stood up and stretched his arms. 'Tell you what, why don't I draft a press statement apologising for any confusion and offering the people who were knocked out free entry into another show?'

Walter drummed his fingers on my desk as he thought about it. 'Not a bad idea: head 'em off at the pass and all that. But what if any of the people decided to sue us?'

'They won't,' said Frank with a lot more authority than I'd have been able to muster in his position. 'They might talk about it—'

'The newspapers certainly will,' interrupted Simon.

Frank glared at his erstwhile ally before continuing, 'But they're going to be very hard-pressed to prove loss. The onus would be on them to prove that they *knew* the answers to the rest of the questions in the show.'

'You seem very sure of yourself,' said Walter.

'I should be,' said Frank. 'I am a qualified solicitor.'

The next day, Sparkle released a cautious apology and informed the press that all the people who had been knocked out on the disputed question had happily accepted our invitation to the next show. Other newspapers tried running with the story but it wouldn't stand up: the press release had effectively killed it stone dead. Where's the story in *TV COMPANY MAKES SMALL ERROR AND ADMITS IT. NO HARM DONE*? It's not the sort of headline you could imagine newspaper vendors barking in the street.

Nevertheless, when the heat died down, Walter used the episode to remind us that we *had* to check all our questions again. 'Also, you *can't* use your friends as sources. Understand?'

We all muttered, 'Yes.' That was the price we paid for Frank's mistake and our lassitude. As Walter pointed out, 'All it takes for bad questions to slip through the net is for good question writers to be lazy.'

Once again, we all nodded our heads in agreement. Not only was Walter right, he had also absorbed all of Andrews's displeasure, though I couldn't help thinking that Simon and I might not have been so lucky if our names had been on the bottom of the question. I said as much to him later when Frank left the office to go to the loo. They were the first words I'd spoken to him since our fight the previous day and I was gratified to hear him agree with me. 'Too bloody right, mate.'

I suddenly felt an enormous sense of kinship with him. I actually discovered that I liked him. What on earth was that about? The guy beats the shit out of me and now he's my mate? What kind of masochist feels that way – or had the pummelling he'd given me cleared the air?

I would have liked to have given these questions my complete attention but I had a more important matter to deal with: Gaby. I was going to have to explain why I'd 'outed' us as lovers to the Two Mo-Ronnies and she was not going to be happy about it.

I hadn't said anything the day before because she had been down in Devon at the funeral of her friend Sally's mother. We had spoken briefly on the phone in the evening but this was surely something best said face to face. She was due home at eight o'clock and so I thought I'd be there to welcome her back. It would be a nice surprise for the girl and, besides, she wouldn't get the chance to tell me not to come over.

As I let myself into her flat with the key I had wheedled out of her the week before, I called out, 'Hi, honey, I'm home!' and a female voice called out, 'Hi, David!' Unfortunately, it wasn't Gaby but Phoebe.

I looked in 'our' bedroom but Gaby was obviously out, so I went into the sitting room and sat down in front of the television. A couple of minutes later, Phoebe walked in wearing an extremely skimpy dressing-gown which revealed her long slim legs; involuntarily, I arched an eyebrow. She smiled knowingly and sat down opposite me on the sofa. The dressing-gown fell open.

Without losing my poise, I said, 'Gaby'll be home shortly, won't she?'

'I don't know.' Phoebe shook her long blonde hair so that it cascaded over a breast that the very action of shaking had momentarily revealed. 'What's the matter with your nose?'

'I was defending a lady's honour.'

She looked at me coquettishly. 'No one has ever defended *my* honour.'

I smiled and tried discreetly to cover up my burgeoning hard-on. I, of course, had absolutely no intention of betraying my darling Gaby, especially with her flatmate; my prick, on the other hand, was taking a dissenting view. The situation couldn't be allowed to continue.

'I'm going to the pub, Phoebe,' I said hastily, and

sprang to my feet. 'Bye!' Then I scampered out of the flat like a married man leaving a brothel during a police raid.

Once I was I out in the street, I realised what a narrow escape I'd had. Phew! I couldn't believe that I had so nearly jeopardised my relationship with Gaby. For one moment I had been seriously tempted, but it was like hearing a favourite song from years ago: I knew that I had once liked it but, for the life of me, I now couldn't think why.

In the pub at the end of the road, I called Gaby on her mobile. 'Oi, Gabe, where are you?'

'I'm still in Devon.'

'What are you doing there?'

'I'm looking for a man whose parents weren't related before they were married. What do you think I'm doing here?'

'Sorry for asking.'

'Sally asked me to stay an extra night.'

'What about the show?'

'I'll be back in the office by tomorrow lunchtime. Love you, big boy.'

'Love you, too, little girl.' Pause. 'Gaby, I've got something to tell you.'

'What?'

'Simon said something insulting about you and—'

'What did he say?'

'Never you mind.'

'WHAT DID HE SAY?'

'He called you a hamster and said that I was fucking you.'

'I do look a bit like a hamster. I don't mind: I like hamsters. And you are fucking me.'

'Yeah, I know. Anyway, I hit him.'

'You did WHAT?'

'I hit him.'

'Is he all right?'

'*He's* fine but he punched me on the nose.'

'Serves you right.'

'That's not all, Gabes. I told him and Frank and Walter that, um, you and I are . . .'

'You shit!'

'Language, Gaby.'

'Well, what else can I call you? I told you I didn't want an office romance, didn't I?'

Having steeled myself for this conversation, I was annoyed by her attitude – especially as I had just demonstrated massive willpower in front of her undressing-gowned flatmate. 'Well, you should have thought of that before you went to bed with me, shouldn't you?'

# CHAPTER TWENTY-FIVE

Frank and/or Simon must have told everybody about Gaby and me because Karen said something to her the next day.

Gaby seemed philosophical enough now that there was nothing she could do about it, but warned me that I had better not start trying to get fresh at work. 'It's bad enough with His bloody Nibs.'

'What?' I said as soon as I worked out that she meant Andrews. 'What's he been doing?'

She looked uncharacteristically embarrassed. 'He's been accidentally-on-purpose brushing past me with a little boner.'

'No! Why didn't you tell me sooner?'

'And what would you have done? Hit him on the fist with your nose?'

'Well, at least I'd have known.'

She pulled me towards her and kissed me lustily – but not lustfully – on the lips. 'You're a daft pillock but I love you.'

I looked around her small office as though someone might have hidden there to spy on us. 'And I love you too, Gabe, which is why I don't like the thought of Andrews trying it on. Why don't you tell him you'll go to the police?'

'It'd be quicker to resign.'

'But there's laws against sexual harassment: you can't open the *Daily Mail* without reading about some bloke being sacked because he called a refuse collector a "dustman" in front of some dyke.'

'It's good to see that thirty years of feminism haven't been wasted.'

'Well, you know what I mean. It's bloody outrageous.'

'You're right – but who am I going to tell? There's no personnel department or shop steward, is there? And where would I get the proof?'

'We could wire you up.'

'Really? And how would you register his brushing past me? It is, like I said, such a small prick.'

Notwithstanding my anger with Andrews, her comments was music to my ears. 'Well, you just make sure that you're not alone with him.'

'What do you think – I seek out his company?'

'Tsk, you know what I mean. Stay clear.'

'Don't worry, I will. My friend Karen also looks out for me. She makes sure that I'm never alone with the creep. Besides, he's got his pudgy little hands full with Belinda.'

'Really! How do you know? Did she tell you?'

'She didn't need to: I caught him giving her one in his office the night before I went down to Devon.'

'You never!'

'I did.'

'What did you say?'

'Say? Nothing, you fool! I tiptoed away as quickly as I could.'

'I'd have watched.'

She clucked me on the chin. 'You would! And now you'd be out of a job.'

I was just about to say that it would have been a small price to pay when Walter appeared at the door of the office. 'Hello, lovebirds,' he grinned, showing us his awful teeth. 'Sorry to be a gooseberry.'

'Walter!' said Gaby, playfully chiding him in that way that ex-PAs do their former bosses.

He pulled out a newspaper from his leather briefcase. 'Have you seen this?'

'Oh no,' I said. 'Not another fuck-up.'

'Fear not, young David.'

I took the paper from him and looked at the article at the top of the page. RICHIE'S RICHES! was the headline. The story followed: *Richie Clarke, 35, is set to earn squillions as his hit show*, The Lot, *sells round the world.*

I put the paper down. 'This is complete bollocks! Richie's not on a percentage, is he?'

'No,' said Walter, 'but you have to understand

that that's how the popular press interpret it.'

'What it does mean is that Tony Bowes and Frank Stephenson are going to earn squillions. It's not fucking fair.'

'It might not be fucking fair but it's how the cookie crumbles, royalty-wise. The truth is that any young man desirous of a fortune might very well consider creating a new game show. In fact, a little birdy tells me you've done just that.'

'Blimey, there are no secrets here!'

'The only advice I would give you is to protect yourself.'

'No need. Andrews has promised me twenty per cent.'

'Ah, then you're all right.'

I wasn't sure if he was being gnomish but, in any event, I wanted to run it past him. 'It's based on astrology.'

He groaned. 'Do you know how many game-show ideas are based on astrology and bingo?'

'No.'

'Just about all of them.'

'But this one,' I said, thinking on my feet, 'is different.' I then proceeded to explain just how and why it was different. By the end of my spiel, it was clear that he was impressed.

'That's brilliant, David.'

I looked at him with a mixture of affection and curiosity. 'What's in this for you, Walter?'

He ran a hand through what remained of his

hair. 'Apart from the fact that I like you – and, of course, I've always been a fan of young Gaby here,' he blew her a kiss which she blew back, 'there's something I'm going to need from you. In the not-too-distant future.'

I was totally bemused and just a little apprehensive. 'What?'

'If I told you now, you'd be as clever as I am.'

The following afternoon, I pitched up in Andrews's office to make my pitch. Having steeled myself not to be distracted by his birthmark, I was somewhat wrongfooted to see it covered over by a plaster. I must have registered my surprise because he immediately explained what it was doing there.

'I'm being photographed in an hour's time by the *Daily Express*.' He preened himself with what he obviously thought of as his 'handsome face': we've all got one but his is just better disguised than most. 'They're doing a feature on me.' He pronounced 'feature' to rhyme with 'teacher'.

'Have you any idea how successful *The Lot* is?' he went on. 'Well, I'll tell you. We're now beating even *Coronation Street* on Wednesdays and we're so far ahead of the rest of the competition on Saturdays that they're not even at the races. You can't pick up a paper without reading about it. Every time I switch on the TV, someone's saying, "Ten seconds and that's your lot," or, "Everyone's a player," just like Richie does.'

He stared me in the face. 'Do you know what? I'm going to be in one of those Rich Lists. There was a bloke checking up on me the other day.' He then looked around his office, which was already ludicrously large for such a little man. 'I think we may have to move offices. This place is far too small for me now that Sparkle has become a major player on the world stage.'

He was, of course, tossing himself off. I knew what my job was: to sit there pulling various faces, all of them impressed, admiring and/or thrilled.

'So what do *you* want then?' he demanded suddenly.

I was just about to open my mouth and tell him but he was so full of himself that he immediately cut across me. 'We're going to have to go live, I reckon.' He was thinking aloud rather than addressing me but I was interested to know more.

'Why's that, Michael?' I addressed him by his Christian name whenever I got the chance: although it was the industry norm, I still hoped that it rankled him.

'Because, *David*,' he spat out my name, 'the results of the shows are getting leaked to the press. I wouldn't mind, but it's before they've even been fucking televised.' I forbore to mention that there wasn't much point in leaking the results *after* the shows were televised. 'At least if we go live they can't do that.'

'But what if there are mistakes?'

'We'll just have to make sure there aren't any, won't we? You can start by checking your questions a bit more carefully.'

I was about to protest that I couldn't check them any more thoroughly than I already had and that, besides, I hadn't been responsible for any mistakes, but then I realised that he wouldn't be receptive to anything I said: he was on transmit.

To prove it, he went off on another tack. 'I'm also going to up the ante for the rollover shows. I'll start doing that when we go live. At the moment, we're just adding fifty grand to the jackpot. That's not enough – especially as the phone lines are generating so much revenue. From now on, it's a quarter of a million every show. If it's won, then that's fair enough, but if it's not, it gets rolled over to the next show. That's my guarantee to the British public.' He sounded like Arthur Daley's illegitimate son.

'So you'll be giving away a million pounds every four shows?'

'That's right. The amount's not important: what *is* important is that we're seen to be on the side of the public. You see, at the moment, when the jackpot isn't won, we only roll over fifty k. Now that means that we're two hundred k better off every time it's not won. That's not right. As far as the punter at home's concerned, he thinks that we'd rather not pay out. Well, he couldn't be further from the truth. I love it when someone wins because it means we're delivering on our promise – that *our* show has a jackpot.'

I caught his drift. 'Surely someone doesn't have to win the jackpot to prove that it exists?' This seemed to me to be taking existentialism to extremes.

'Yes – no. No, you're wrong. For the punter, if he doesn't see a winner – a proper winner – he thinks we're pulling a fast one, even though we're not. So by giving away two hundred and fifty thousand every show we'll prove that we're on the level.'

He looked at me irritably. 'Now what did you want to see me about because I haven't got much time before I have to have my photograph taken. It's for the *Sunday Mail*. They're doing a feature on me.'

I took a deep breath. 'I've brought you an idea for a TV game-show.'

He laughed mirthlessly. 'Ha! Join the queue. I must have had a million ideas sent to me in the past month alone. What's your idea about then?'

'Before I tell you, can you confirm what you said before about me getting a percentage.'

'Yeah, all right. You can have ten per cent.'

'You said twenty per cent last time.'

'All right, twenty per cent. What's it about? You've got five minutes.'

I explained the basic premise of the show while he tapped his fingers against his desk-top so that his rings drummed an irritatingly inconsistent beat. At the end of the pitch, he surprised me again by jumping up from his chair and shouting, 'I like it!'

'And?'

'And so we'll do it and make a fortune. Now bugger off, I've got the *Daily Mail* coming.'

I left his office in a state of stupefaction. It couldn't be that simple. Could it?

# CHAPTER TWENTY-SIX

I was on the mobile to Tim the moment I left the office.

'Congratulations, Tim!'

'What's that? Is that you, David? Where are you? You sound as if you're at a football ground.'

'I'm sorry. I'm in Shaftesbury Avenue.' I was shouting down the phone like every other tosser in Central London.

'There's a great gay club just down the road.'

Ludicrously embarrassed in case anyone else could hear him, I dived into a coffee shop. 'Listen, Tim, I can't talk properly but it looks like we've sold the format for our little project.'

'So it's *our* project now, is it?'

Motivated by the very human desire to share my good fortune, I made the decision to hand over (potentially) millions of pounds in royalties. 'You helped me refine it: you're on ten per cent.'

'Davie baby, you're a fucking starlet.' Which is pretty well what Gaby had said to me earlier. So it was no wonder that I almost made it home by means of cloud nine rather than my trusty old moped.

Moped? Not for much longer. Since I can't be arsed to pass my driving test, I think I'll have a chauffeur for my Rolls-Royce. He'd better be on 24-hour call just in case. Will I have to put him up in my Belgravia mansion? No, I think he can have a mews cottage round the corner. He will get plenty of time off when Gaby and I are on holiday in one of our many overseas villas. French Riviera? A bit Roger Moore in *The Saint*. The Caribbean? That'll do nicely. Thinking of which, don't they do some special card that gives you VIP treatment wherever you go? What would that be? Platinum? Black? I don't know. I don't even know who would know.

I also don't know when I've enjoyed a journey more.

Back in Lisson Grove I lifted my moped into the square metre of scrub that passed for our communal front garden but, for once, I was disposed to find it a pleasure rather than a chore. These were the tough old days that I would soon be able to look back on fondly with all the nostalgia that geographical and economic distance can bestow.

I unlocked the front door and, taking even greater care than usual not to trip on the randomly placed stair-rods, made my way up to the first floor. My intention was to burst in singing 'Money

Money Money' but, as I turned the key in the lock – thinking as I did so that, as I was soon to be worth millions, it was important to get a better security system – I heard the sound of sobbing.

I rushed in to find Ziggy crying in his bedroom.

'Ziggy, mate, what's wrong?'

'Go away,' he said through his sobs.

I tried to put my arm around him to cheer him up but we just don't have a tactile relationship so I stood there helplessly like the father of an anorexic teenage daughter.

'Go away!' he said with even more conviction.

So I went away – to the kitchen where I found Peter smoking a joint.

'Hey, Peter, what's the matter with Ziggy?'

'I don't know but it's like great news, man.'

'Ziggy's in his bedroom bawling his eyes out and you say it's great news?'

'I didn't know he was crying!'

'Couldn't you hear him?'

'No. I can't.'

Now that I tried to hear him, nor could I. 'Sorry, man. Hang on, though, what's the great news? Do you know about the game show? No, how could you?'

'No, David, I don't know what you're talking about. I'm just thrilled that Ziggy's split from Amelia.'

'Oh, I see.'

'Well, she wasn't what you'd call an adornment

to the flat. It's all right for you – you're always over at Gaby's.'

'You're right, but I don't think we should be celebrating while Ziggy's blubbing like a new bug.' I returned to Ziggy's room where, fortunately, he'd composed himself. 'Hi,' I said as though this were the first time I'd seen him that day.

'Oh, hi, David. Greetings.'

'Greetings, yourself, earthling. Um, anything up?'

He sat on his bed, scratching his balls. 'It's Amelia. She's just given me the big E. She's a complete bitch!'

'I had sort of come to that conclusion myself.'

'Great tits though.'

'If you say so. But why the waterworks, big man?'

'Oh that.' Then, to my horror, he started crying again. 'It's just so unfair. How dare she terminate our relationship just as I was about to.'

'Well, it saved you the bother, didn't it?'

'That's not the point. I have my pride, you know.'

Sharing a flat with those two had one consolation: I never doubted my sanity. I also blessed my good fortune that I had chosen someone as *normal* as Gaby. In fact, I couldn't wait to see her, so I tiptoed out of Ziggy's bedroom. He had found a massive bag of liquorice allsorts and was proceeding to guzzle the lot so he couldn't have been feeling that bad.

I went to my bedroom. The bedding smelt like the ripe side of musty. I would have to change it for when I next slept at home – if, I told myself smugly as I dialled Gaby's number on my mobile, I ever slept at home again.

She answered the phone.

'Hiya, Gabe!'

'Oh, it's you, is it?'

I was a little taken aback by her coldness. 'Yes, Gaby, it's me. Who were you expecting?'

'What do you want?'

'What do you mean, "what do you want"?'

'I mean: what . . . do . . . you . . . want? Do I have to spell it out?'

'Yes. No. I don't know. You're confusing me. What I want is to know what time you want me to come over – always assuming that is, you still want me to come over?'

'Well, actually, I don't. Bye.' She put the phone down.

What the hell was the matter with the girl? Was she being held by kidnappers and being horrible so as to alert me to the fact? Sounded crazy – but no less so than the way she was treating me. Last time I'd seen her – I looked at my watch: precisely two and a quarter hours before – she'd been billing and cooing like someone trying to win a particularly competitive billing and cooing contest. What on earth had happened in the meantime?'

Had I done something wrong? Had she seen me

getting on to my mobile and assumed that I was phoning another woman? Had I forgotten her birthday? Or our seventh-week anniversary? No, even at my most paranoid, I knew that all this was nothing to do with me or what I had done. This was her problem: let her fucking own it. I'd wait for her to phone me.

Three minutes later, I dialled her number again. 'Gaby?'

'Yes.'

'David here.'

'I gathered.'

'What the fuck is your problem?'

'I don't have a problem. You do.'

'Oh, I'm sorry. And what might that be?'

'You're bloody depraved.'

'Depraved? I've been called many things but never that.'

'Well, perhaps other people didn't know you so well. By your own admission, you're not exactly the veteran of several long-term relationships.'

'I'm sorry, I really don't see what you're getting at. What am I supposed to have done?'

'You only went and tried it on with my flat-mate.'

I was stunned into silence for at least five seconds and then I let rip. 'WHAT! I did nothing of the kind. If you want to know, I went round to your place the evening you were in Devon . . .'

'. . . see? You're admitting it!'

'No, I'm fucking not. I went round to see you because in those days, I happened to love you and not hate you like I do right at this moment. I sat down in your sitting room . . .'

'What, even after you knew I wasn't coming back that evening?'

'I didn't know that till later. I was in your sitting room when Phoebe walks in with a dressing-gown slit to her fucking waist showing off acres of fucking minge and more or less asks me if I fancy getting it on.'

'I don't believe it.'

'You don't, or you don't want to?'

She paused. 'I don't know. Why didn't you say something to me?'

'Because I didn't want to upset you. I didn't want you to fall out with Phoebe. But you have to believe me when I say that I absolutely did NOT take her up on her offer. As soon as she made her intentions clear, I was out of there like a fucking flash. Why, what does she say?'

'She says that you came round here like you say, but that when you found out I wasn't coming home, you made it very clear that you would like to do it with her instead.'

'Oh yeah? And how did I make it clear?'

'She didn't say. Perhaps she was too embarrassed.'

'Perhaps her imagination had reached its limits.'

'Are you calling her a liar?'

'No, I'm saying she's very, very much mistaken.' I thought about it for a second. 'No, I *am* calling her a liar. There's no way that she could possibly have thought that I fancied her.'

'Don't you?'

Even though I should have been expecting that question, she still caught me offguard. I was so conditioned to telling her the categorical truth that I found it hard to start equivocating. Besides, given that I had nothing to feel guilty about, I had no need to lie. 'Yes, I do quite fancy her. I wouldn't climb over you to get to her, though. Wait a minute, have I got that the right way round? Yes, that's what I mean. She's quite sexy. But that doesn't mean I'd do anything to jeopardise our relationship. I mean, do you think I would do anything that stupid?'

'I don't know. Maybe you would. You wouldn't be the first man to be led by his dick. What's that saying? "An erect penis has no conscience".'

'Gaby, I love you.'

'That's what Spencer said.'

'I'm not fucking Spencer.'

'Nor am I any more.'

We both giggled. It broke the tension.

'Dabes?'

Thank goodness we were back on pet-name terms. 'Yes, Gabes.'

'Why would Phoebe lie?'

I had no idea. 'I have no idea. Maybe she

thought I was going to say something to you and was getting her retaliation in first – as rugby players say.'

'David. I think I believe you but if you're lying to me . . .'

I didn't let her finish the sentence. 'Gaby, I promise you I'm not lying to you. But then if I were lying to you, I'd promise you that I wasn't. Darling, I love you with all my heart. Yes, I do find Phoebe quite attractive – but I want you for the rest of my life and there is *nothing* I would do to hurt you or us. Please believe me.'

'I believe you. Honest I do.'

'Then shall I come over?'

'Not tonight, darling. I'm exhausted. I'm just going to crash out.'

Which is precisely what I decided to do, but not before making a silent vow: to ensure that Gaby got rid of bloody Phoebe from her flat and from our lives.

# CHAPTER TWENTY-SEVEN

I could have done without all of these domestic dramas – especially as I had enough on my hands with work problems.

Ever since *The Lot* had started airing, I'd been braced for disaster in the shape of the wrong or misleading answer: I hadn't anticipated something coming out of left field.

It happened, quite coincidentally, the very first time we went out live. It was a Wednesday morning and I was sitting in Richie's dressing-room marvelling at how incredibly spoiled the bastard was. OK, so he was a talented television presenter but it wasn't the hardest job on the planet – I mean, not compared with a *real* job like coalmining or firefighting or even just being a doctor in an inner-city – and they paid him unbelievably well: a rumoured £20,000 per show. So why did he – fuck it, a bloke no older than me – have to be so bloody mollycoddled?

All right, a TV presenter has to have a

dressing-room: somewhere he can sit and collect his thoughts before the start of a show; somewhere he can relax and have a bite to eat – though why such a self-professed 'man of the people' couldn't go to the canteen like the rest of us was never explained. But why did he need a full-sized double bed? Or an American-style fridge-freezer? Or *three* vases of flowers? Or *two* bowls of fresh fruit?

I suppose the bed was easily explained: it was where he exercised his *droit de seigneur* with production runners, secretaries and fans, although *not* (or so Gaby had promised me) with contestant researchers. But, as for the rest, it was all so *decadent*.

Or so I surmised as I lay on the couch scoffing his grapes. Richie, it has to be said, was currently on set rehearsing. Oh yeah, that's another thing: you know all his really funny off the cuff gags – the ones that have earned him plaudits for his wit even from the *Guardian*? They're all written for him by this bloke he nicknames The Squirrel who sticks to him like extra-strong glue.

Anyway, I was watching Richie on the monitor rehearsing, hugging myself with the thought that I could see him and so know that I was safe abusing his hospitality when the door opened and Walter was standing there.

I jumped to my feet. 'What the hell are you doing here?'

'I might ask you the same question.' He sat down on the sofa that I had just vacated. 'In fact, I think I will ask you the same question. What the hell are you doing here, David?'

I managed to hide my embarrassment at being caught by saying, 'No, I asked first.'

He giggled. 'I've got a headache so I thought I'd lie down and have a rest.'

'Who's looking after the store?'

'I've left Michael up there.' He's quite capable, you know. I realise you two don't get along,' I liked the way he elevated a junior employee's dislike of his boss into a disagreement between equals, 'but there's no doubting his abilities and he used to be a very good producer.' He kicked his shoes off. 'OK, not as good as the man they call Walter but still not too shabby.'

'I'll take your word for it.'

'So what the hell are you really doing here?'

'Skiving.'

'Naughty, naughty, tsk, tsk.'

'Telly Savalas as *Kojak*. Did you know his mother was once Miss Greece?'

'Yes, I did know that. Do you know why I know that? Because you told me – remember? It was in your list of celebrity pairs for *Take It Away*.'

'Oh shit! I am sorry, Walter. There's nothing worse than telling someone something you've already told them. OK, then, try this: Telly Savalas was Jennifer Aniston's godfather.'

'I didn't know that.'

'Well, now you do.' I performed a 360-degree swivel on the executive chair opposite the dressing-table. I really wanted to tell Walter how spoiled I thought Richie was but I didn't want to come across as jealous – a genuine hazard given that I was greener than Kermit the Frog in a force ten gale. 'So how's *Take It Away* doing?'

He opened his eyes and tilted his head away from the horizontal. 'So-so.'

'How did the pilot go?'

'What pilot?'

'What do you mean? What about all those questions I wrote?'

'I paid you, didn't I?'

'I didn't mean that, Walter. I meant, I thought it was a done thing.'

'Alas, not. Budgetary constraints, cutbacks, the recession, the war, the timing, the fashion: you can perm any two from six.'

I was suddenly at a loss as to know what to do. I had sold a friend something that he subsequently didn't use. Should I offer him a refund? On the other hand, if you buy a perfectly good suit and don't wear it, should you expect your money back? Against that, Walter was also my boss and it couldn't hurt to make the offer. 'Hey listen, Walter, I'm really sorry about your show. You're going to have to let me give you back the money . . .'

He sat up. 'My dear boy! That is *so* generous and gracious of you but I wouldn't *dream* of accepting.' He looked away for a second before adding, 'But there is one service you can perform for me.'

Was he going to mention this putative future favour again – whatever it might be? 'Anything that doesn't involve fluids.'

'That's a shame because I wanted you to fetch me some mineral water from Mr Clarke's fridge.'

'Sure thing, boss.' I went to the unfeasibly large fridge, selected a bottle of Perrier and handed it to him.

He shook his head to indicate that he didn't require a glass. 'As for your own game show, dear boy . . .' He shuddered as he swallowed a couple of pills and washed them down with a slug of water. 'Do you want the good news or the bad news?'

I didn't like the sound of this. 'Better give me the good news.'

'The show's being actively considered.'

'That's great!'

'But Michael is claiming it as his own idea.'

'WHAT?'

'Hey, calm down, David.'

'Calm down? Are you crazy? The bastard's stealing my idea and you're saying – calm down.'

'Snap out of it and listen.' He had switched into authoritative mode: from friend to (benevolent) boss. 'There was always the risk that this might happen and, if it's any consolation, it does have its advantages.'

'Such as?'

'I'd say it makes your position at Sparkle much stronger. He'd rather have you in the tent pissing out . . .'

'. . . than outside the tent pissing in. Yeah, but it's fucking outrageous!'

'And if I know Michael Andrews, he might find a way of making it up to you financially – just so long as he gets the credit. It's an ego thing.'

I'd pinned so much hope on my game-show idea that I wasn't prepared even to consider Walter's well-meant words of consolation. 'Yeah, well, you know what? I've got an ego too and I'm sick and fucking tired of always having to suppress it.' I stumbled out of the dressing-room, leaving Walter calling after me to, 'Cool it.' I was going to the gallery to sort the little bastard out once and for all, and if I lost my job, well then so what?

Fortunately, by the time I'd negotiated the labyrinthine television studios to reach the gallery, I had cooled down, so that instead of telling the fucking Minotaur what I thought of him, I merely said, 'Excuse me, Michael, could I please have a word with you?'

'When the rehearsal finishes.'

I looked around. Everyone seemed to be breaking for lunch. 'Hasn't it already finished?' The tone of my voice was so controlled and so *certain* that I think Andrews, like a bully getting a taste of his own medicine, was too taken aback to react typically. He followed me down the gantry to the studio floor and, from there, through the black curtain that went all the way round the studio, into one of the many scenery-loading areas.

He motioned for me to sit down on one of the stacks of audience chairs, not for my comfort but so that he wouldn't be at a height disadvantage, but I indicated that I was perfectly happy to stand. Even if it did mean being forced to look at his awesome birthmark which, since its recent veiling, had metamorphosed into what I could now only see as a red Pacman.

'What do you want?'

'To know what's happening with *Astro Wars*. I understand you're saying that you invented it?'

He smiled. If reptiles wore rings, he'd have passed for one. 'So what if I did? You brought it to me – which I appreciate – and now I'm doing my *upmost* to sell it.'

'Yes, but it's not fair . . .'

'Why not? If someone tells you a joke or gives you a good line, do you always credit them?'

'Well, no, but that's different. This is worth money . . .'

'Only if it's properly handled.'

'Yes, but even so, the idea's crucial.'

'Ideas are ten-a-penny.'

'So why nick mine?'

'Now let me see. Are you aware that you are on a contract of service?'

I nodded.

'This is opposed to a contract for services. Do you know the difference?'

I shook my head.

'Then I will tell you. With a contract of service, you are an employee, a servant, of the company: in this instance, Sparkle. Anything you do or write or create during the time that you are employed by Sparkle is owned by us. That is because we own all your work. That is what we have bought. Irrespective of whether that work is done in office hours or outside them.'

'But you *promised* me twenty per cent.'

'Did I? You must have caught me in a generous mood. Do you have it in writing?'

'No, but, you gave Frank a percentage in *The Lot*.' Suddenly I was six years old and protesting to my mother that she'd given my brother more sweets than she'd given me.

'That's different. Frank has a contract for services.'

'I didn't know that.'

'There are, it seems, many things you don't know.' That was rich coming from a man who didn't know the difference between 'upmost' and 'utmost'.

'A contract for services,' he continued, 'means that someone is simply selling their services, like a

265

plumber or a solicitor. I pay Frank by the task, not merely for showing up. Not that it's any of your business. What *is* your business – and mine too – is that you have come up with an idea, an excellent idea which, because you belong to me, belongs to me. Do I make myself clear?'

Busted, broken, defeated, I nodded. I would check it with Ziggy later but I knew – and Andrews knew that I knew – that I was well and truly fucked.

# CHAPTER TWENTY-EIGHT

To add insult to iniquity, the next day Andrews hauled Frank, Simon and me into his office to dump on us. Uncharacteristically, he started off by praising us – albeit obliquely.

'I have to say,' he said, bouncing up and down on his £200 handmade Italian cushion, 'I'm very happy indeed. *Very* happy indeed. There's a piece in today's paper all about the show and the punters who've won. The paper reckons that we're the new *Big Brother*. Can you believe it?'

In my current mood, I was determined to see the appropriate credit given. 'Yes, I can. But I think you'll find that the reason the papers are so interested in our contestants,' I couldn't bring myself to echo him by calling them 'punters', 'is because they've been so brilliantly selected.'

'Oh yeah,' said Andrews casually. 'I heard that you were giving one to Gaby.' He then had the nerve to imitate a man having sex with a woman from behind. It took an effort of will to stop myself saying, 'And I heard that you were giving one to Belinda.'

Simon – rather decently – rescued me from something between a sackable and an imprisonable offence by asking Andrews what he wanted.

'I'm glad you asked me that,' he said, putting the tips of his pudgy fingers together and looking for all the world like the baddie in a Bond film who's just dying to explain why he's going to destroy the universe as soon as he retrieves the vital cassette from his disloyal sexy assistant's bikini. 'I have the feeling that the three of you are an underused resource at this present moment in time.'

'Meaning?' asked Frank.

'Meaning that as the question database is more or less complete . . .'

'There's still some way to go,' said Simon.

'Yes, but it's well in hand and so I'm looking for other things for you to do.' He indicated a pile of folders on his desk. 'I've agreed terms for all sorts of merchandise for *The Lot*. There's going to be a computer game, a book, a video game and a board game and they're all going to need questions written for them. New questions.'

'How many?' asked Simon.

'Oh, thousands,' he said blithely. 'Apparently, you're going to have to do three thousand for the board game alone.'

Our faces all registered different degrees of horror which only served to make Andrews even happier. 'It's nothing. You can use lots of the questions you've rejected.'

'Which we've binned,' I said.

'Tough tit. The point is, you won't have to be nearly as accurate as you are with questions for the show itself.' I think he was complimenting us again. Unwittingly, of course. 'The questions will still have to be kosher but you won't have to put down all your references and all that.'

'Well, that's a relief,' said Frank as the three of us left Andrew's office. 'I mean, it's still a lot of work but it'll be a hell of a lot easier. I think it'll be fun.'

Simon waited for Frank to walk ahead to our office and then whispered to me, 'That's easy for him to say. He stands to earn even more dosh while the two of us slave away for wages.'

'Tell me about it.' I looked at him and saw, if not a friend, then a friendly colleague. I decided to confide in him: I had nothing to lose. 'It's even worse for me. I've just had my fucking programme idea nicked by Andrews.'

'What's that about?'

I told him and then repeated what Walter had said about it making my job more secure. He considered my words and then nodded. 'Yes, I can see that but I can also see how it might make Michael more antagonistic towards you. In fact, I think it's started already. For example, yesterday afternoon, he was slagging you off. I mean, really being horrible about you.'

I felt my stomach turning. Just a week ago, I'd have put Simon's words down to shit-stirring but not now. 'How? What was he saying?'

'He was saying that you had become arrogant: "too big for his fucking boots" were his precise words if I remember them accurately.'

'Was that it?'

'No. He also said that you were "a lazy tosser" and that there was no question in his mind that you were the weakest of the three writers.'

I tried looking for some consolation. 'So there was nothing about Gaby?'

'No – not unless you include the observation that "despite what he might think, he's not God's fucking gift to women".'

This was all bad news. Did I really want this increased job security that Walter and Simon reckoned I had, if it meant that I was going to be subjected to such vituperative crap? Notwithstanding our new improved relationship, I didn't want Simon to see how rattled I was so I smiled wanly and told him that, actually, Andrews was wrong: I *was* God's fucking gift to women.

Of course the one person I could whinge to was Gaby and I did. I whinged and whinged until I binged on whinge. And still I didn't let up. Not until she admitted and repeated – repeatedly – that Andrews was a bastard, a gobshite, the anti-Christ etc. etc.

We were in my bedroom lying on the bed and she was trying to jolly me out of my sour mood by offering some trivia titbits from a celebrity magazine. 'Did you know that Johnny Vaughan was born at the moment that England scored the winning goal in the 1966 World Cup Final?'

'No, I didn't. I wonder what happened on the day that Andrews was born? Hitler probably opened a concentration camp.'

'Did you know that the aeroplane Buddy Holly died in was the *American Pie* – hence the title of the Don McLean song?'

'No, I didn't. I wish Andrews could die in a plane crash.'

'Did you know that Clark Gable was listed on his birth certificate as a girl?'

'No, I didn't. Apparently, Michael Andrews was listed as a miniature pig on *his* birth certificate.'

'Did you know that my boyfriend is a monotonous, monomaniacal wanker?'

'No, I didn't,' I said automatically before realising what she'd said. 'Oi! What are you on about?'

'What am *I* on about? Since when did Willy One-Note care about anything I had to say?'

'What? What are you talking about?'

'I'm talking about you, David, and your obsession with our boss.'

'Oh, so you think of him as "our boss" then, do you?'

She got up from the bed and looked at me as

though I were mad. 'Well, he is our boss, isn't he?'

Aware that I was losing it – fast – I tried unsuccessfully to backtrack. 'Well, yes, but that doesn't mean you have to refer to him as such.' I felt vulnerable lying on the bed on my own so I sat up and, once again, attempted to articulate my distress. 'Look, Gaby, if I'm being a little Percy Paranoid . . .'

'A little?'

'All right, if I seem more than a little upset about what Andrews has done to me in stealing my idea, then don't I have good cause to be?'

'I suppose,' she sighed. 'It's just that . . .' She sat down on the bed, which I took to be an encouraging sign. 'I don't know, David, I just don't feel comfortable here. Not with Ziggy and Peter always around. I feel like *Girl About the House*.'

'Well, after what happened with Phoebe – or, rather, what *didn't* happen – I don't feel too comfortable *chez toi*. Why don't you give her her bloody marching orders?'

She stood up again. 'I don't know.'

'You do believe me, don't you?'

'Yes. Yes, of course I do.'

'Then what are you waiting for?'

'I don't know. Maybe I'm a little nervous of the next step?'

'What do you mean?'

'If Phoebe goes, then it'll just be the two of us.'

'So what's wrong with that?'

'Nothing. But . . .'

'. . . it's fucking Spencer again, isn't it?'

'I can't help being conditioned by my past.'

'And nor can I – which is why I'm so furious about Andrews.'

She blew upwards to flick a comma of hair out of her eyes. For some reason, I found it extraordinarily erotic and I mentally cursed Andrews for, effectively, estranging me from her. 'I don't understand what you're saying. What has Andrews got to do with your past?'

'I used to work for this news agency.'

'What were you, a paper boy?'

I too would have found it irresistible but, in my current mood, I couldn't tell her that. 'Please, Gaby. I worked for this *agency* – Paxton's – and I had a deal with the boss, Ron Paxton, that I got to keep ten per cent of the proceeds of any idea I initiated. Anyway, he ripped me off.'

'How?'

'It doesn't matter, nor does it matter what I did next: what *does* matter is that I don't like history repeating itself.'

She nodded. We sat there in silence. Not touching each other but not *not* touching each other either. And then I went and spoiled it all by saying something stupid. 'I was doing all that – all that work on *Astro Wars* for you, you know.'

I think if I'd said 'for us', then I might just have got away with it. 'Oh, leave it out, David.'

'What?'

'Just fuck off, all right?'

'That's pretty articulate.'

'And you're full of it.'

'Full of what?'

'You know, emotional blackmail. Laying this whole thing at my door. You came up with an idea which Andrews nicked. I'm sorry, but don't try saying that you were doing it for me as though it's now my problem.'

'That's not what I meant. Honestly. I was just trying to . . . it was all about earning . . . for us.' I'd lost it and I knew it.

Her next words so filled me with *déjà vu* that I could almost have lip-synched them. 'Listen, David, perhaps it's best we don't see each other so often.'

# CHAPTER TWENTY-NINE

'I can't believe that it's come to this: that I'm taking advice from *you*!'

'Well, you've got to take it from someone.'

'Yeah, but not from someone who's so emotionally incontinent that he cries because he gets chucked by a girl he's just about to chuck himself!'

'It was nothing: a mere workout of the lachrymal ducts.'

'Even so, you'll grant me that you're hardly in a position to give me succour.' It suddenly occurred to me that I'm a conversational chameleon: I modify my language to mirror that of the person I'm talking with. I'd never have used a word like 'succour' with anyone else.

Ziggy put down his knife and fork, a considerable sacrifice given that there was still a piece of veal escalope and a few strands of spaghetti napoletana on his plate, and looked me straight in the eyes. Once again, I was captivated by the perfection – there's no other word for it – of his big brown eyes. 'I'm not a barrister for nothing, you know.'

'Damn nearly, mate.'

'Tee hee. I know what you mean though. I'm not sure for how much longer I can carry on pretending to be Ziggy of the Old Bailey. I can't remember the last time I had a brief. Oh, I still go into chambers but it's more in hope than expectation.'

Although I'd always enjoyed teasing Ziggy, I couldn't bear to see him so vulnerable. 'Come on, mate, it's only a temporary problem, I'm sure.'

'It's kind of you to say so, old boy, but I fear that I must look for a career outside of the law. By which I don't mean a life of crime – although I don't necessarily rule that out.' He picked up his fork and then put it down again. 'However, you didn't invite me here to hear my woes.' He waved away my attempt to interrupt. 'No, what you wanted was the benefit of my wisdom. Well, I shall deliver myself of it. The fact is, David, you are emotionally immature and you were one hundred per cent in the wrong in your dealings with Miss Taylor.'

Another thing I don't like about Ziggy. In court, he whispers as though he's in a restaurant; in a restaurant, he shouts as though he's in court. 'Do you think you could speak any louder, old man? I mean, there are people on the far side of the restaurant who didn't catch every word in your last sentence.'

'You may find fault with the messenger but the message is sound.' He gave into temptation and finished his plate before mopping up the bolognese sauce on my plate with a hunk of ciabatta.

Just then, the middle-aged waitress, whose somewhat hirsute appearance had prompted Ziggy to ask in whatever the opposite of *sotto voce* is, 'Why *do* Italian girls grow moustaches? Because they want to look like their mothers?' came to our table and asked if we wanted a pudding.

Ziggy licked his lips. 'You are paying, aren't you?' I nodded. Given how little Ziggy was earning as London's least successful barrister it was a rhetorical question. 'In that case, I'll have the zabaglione and some extra amaretto biscuits to go with it.'

'And I'll just have a black filter coffee: he's eating quite enough for the two of us.'

'I told you my advice would cost you. However, I'm flattered you asked me ahead of Peter.'

I didn't tell him that I had in fact asked Peter first but that he was 'going Up West'. A Winchester education and he ends up speaking like an extra from a Guy Ritchie film.

'No, amazing as it might seem, I genuinely do value your opinion.'

'Then listen to it and act upon it. You've been using Gaby as an emotional battering ram. You've been saying things to her you'd like to say to Andrews and, not unreasonably, she's had enough.'

'OK, OK, fair enough, I've gone on a bit much but there's more to this than just my problems with Andrews: there's also the business with Phoebe.'

He leaned across the table. 'Tell me honestly, David, did you pork her?'

'No, I did not!'

'But would you have liked to?'

'In other circumstances i.e. if I hadn't met Gaby and she wasn't Gaby's flatmate, my response wouldn't necessarily have been in the negative.'

'So you reckon she's gagging for it.'

'I shouldn't wonder.' He licked his lips lasciviously. 'Ah, I catch your drift. Stand down, Ziggy. I don't think this offer is transferable. What I'm trying to say is that although she's by way of being a bit of a slapper, the reason she was offering herself to me had little to do with my charm – you can contradict me if you want – but a lot to do with wanting to put one over on her flatmate.'

'What a bitch!'

'Indeed. The thing is, what can I do about her?'

'In what sense?'

'In the sense of getting rid of her.'

He licked his fingers, put them in the sugar bowl and then sucked his sugared fingers. I decided not to have any sugar in my coffee. 'You say that Gaby doesn't believe her?'

'I don't *think* she does. I'm certain she doesn't *want* to, but there's enough doubt in her mind to let Phoebe stay – especially as that option puts off the day that I move in full-time.'

'I see.' He did the thing with the sugar bowl again.

'That is *so* disgusting.'

He took it as a compliment. 'Yes, it is, isn't it?' he sucked his fingers dry. 'I think you're going to have to adopt a threefold approach. One, you'll have to promise to Gaby that you'll stop whinging about Andrews. Two, you'll actually have to stop whinging about Andrews and, thirdly, you're going to have to do a little number on Phoebe.'

I was about to ask him for more details but his pudding arrived and he shook his hand to indicate that Phoebe's future would have to wait until after he had got outside a mound of amaretto biscuits and a tall glass of zabaglione. It smelt gorgeous – as it was entitled to for £7.95 of my hard-earned money – but if Ziggy's three-part masterplan worked, then it was worth every penny.

Stage three of Ziggy's plan – Operation Phoebe – would have to wait but I was able to implement stage one immediately by giving Gaby my word of honour that I would never again take out my problems on her. An opportunity to prove this i.e. stage two of Ziggy's plan arose very soon afterwards.

It happened like this. Belinda came into the writers' office to ask Frank for a list of the questions used in the last show. I was studiously avoiding her, as was my wont, when Shelley, her newly acquired secretary – as if a PA needs a secretary! – came rushing in to tell her that Controller One was on the phone and that, in Andrews's absence, they wanted to talk to her.

'What's it about?' I heard Belinda asking Shelley as she went back to her office.

'Something called *Astro Wars*. He says he wants it but only if he can do a deal today.'

I couldn't believe it. Sparkle – Andrews – was in the process of selling *my* show! And I wasn't going to get a penny for it. Oh sure, I'd hold on to my job, as Walter and Simon said, because my rights to royalties diminished in line with my status as an employee and, maybe, I might get a bonus – if I was lucky. But it was all so bloody unfair!

I waited till Frank left the room with his running order for the last show and then exploded to Simon. 'I don't fucking believe it! *Astro Wars* is mine – the show I was telling you about!'

'That's bad luck.'

'I don't know what to do.'

'Nothing, if I were you. There's nothing you can do.'

'There must be *something* I can do to get even with Andrews.'

'Not unless you want to tell his missus about his extra-curricular activities.'

'Such as?'

'Well, Karen, obviously but his current *inamorata* is Belinda.'

'I heard about that! Yes, he's definitely giving her one.'

'How delicately you put it.'

'And you reckon that I ought to tell the saintly Emma?'

'Me? I didn't say that. I just said that that was an avenue you might wish to explore.'

I weighed up his words. I yearned to talk to Gaby about the situation but, bearing in mind stages one and two, decided against it. I'd have to seek out Walter and get his advice instead. Thanking Simon, I left the room and went next door to see my patron/mentor. 'Right, Walter,' I said, without any conversational foreplay, 'I've had just about enough of Andrews.'

'What is it this time?'

He seemed a little weary: whether it was with me or because of something else, I couldn't be sure but I was way past caring. 'The bastard's only gone and sold *Astro Wars*!'

'How tiresome of him. To whom?'

'I don't know.'

He clucked. 'Oh dear. There was always a chance that this could happen.'

'What can I do?'

'Nothing, as far as I can tell. From what you told me about your conversation with Michael, he's made it extremely clear where you stand. I can't see any room for manoeuvre.'

'But there must be something I can do to get even with the bastard?'

'What, you mean like accepting his wages whilst plotting against him?'

'I hadn't thought of it in those terms.'

He checked himself as though he'd gone too far with me. Something was on his mind: there seemed to be a subtext, but I couldn't read it. 'Fear not, dear boy, I was merely teasing you.' He screwed up a piece of paper and chucked it into – or, rather, just to the right of – his wastepaper basket. 'So it's revenge you're after?'

'In a word, yes. I had thought of letting the saintly Emma know about Andrews and Belinda.'

'Oh, are they an item? How very tedious and predictable!'

'So what do you reckon?'

'Why would you want to upset Emma?'

'Well, I wouldn't but it would certainly get him into trouble.'

'What makes you think she doesn't know – or would care if she did?'

'Are you joking?'

'No. It's entirely possible that the two of them have what might be called an "adult relationship".'

'And it's entirely possible that she'll take the little wanker for all he's got!'

He looked at me as though he were sizing me up and, once again, I found myself wondering what favour it was that he might one day want. When he spoke again it was to change the subject. 'Are your parents still married?'

'Yes. Are yours?'

'My mother died years ago, but anyway, my parents' marriage was what you might call unusual.'

'In what way?'

'My father was a bigamist.'

I wasn't so shocked that I couldn't offer up some trivia at this point. 'Sir Michael Redgrave's father was a bigamist too.'

'You miss my point. What I was trying to say – obviously too obliquely – is that you come from a conventional upbringing: perhaps you don't understand that there are other ways of doing things.'

There's nothing I hate more than being accused of a lack of sophistication. 'What are you talking about, Walter? As soon as you said that your father was a bigamist, I was immediately able to come up with another person in the same situation.'

He smiled avuncularly. 'You still don't get it. I'm talking about experience and you're giving me celebrity trivia.' He chuckled and shook his head. It was all horribly reminiscent of Caroline and her patronising invitation to get in touch with her again 'when you've got some experiences of your own to tell me about rather than those of celebrities'.

'I think I take your point but I'm not sure what

it has to do with the price of game-show formats.'

'All right. I understand what you're saying and maybe I *was* trying to deliver a life lesson. My apologies if I've been a little too didactic.' He took a piece of string out of his top pocket and started to floss his teeth. I forced myself not to register my disgust. 'I was trying to convey to you something of the relationship between Michael and Emma.'

'Oh.'

'Did you know, by the way, that your "saintly Emma" had a long affair with Kit Connolly?'

I was genuinely lost for words. Unfortunately, the first ones I found were hopelessly wrong. 'But he's gay!'

'Oh boy, are you gauche. Of course Kitty is a woopsie – almost as much as I am – but that doesn't mean that he doesn't bat for your side too. Why, I myself have occasionally been known to pot the pink.'

'No!'

'And why not? To paraphrase James Dean, why should I go through life with one hand tied behind my back?'

'Now who's full of celebrity trivia?'

'*Touché*!'

His phone rang and it seemed like a good note on which to leave his office even if the Andrews issue was unresolved.

I went back to the writers' office and sat down to write some new questions for the board game but neither my head nor my heart was in it and so I decided to jack it in for the day.

As I walked past his desk, Frank said quietly, 'I didn't know it was Friday.'

'It's not; it's Thursday. I don't get it.'

'Friday? Poet's Day? Piss off early, tomorrow's Saturday?'

'Oh do fuck off, Frank.' I hadn't brought my moped in that morning so I started walking, vaguely in the direction of the Tube station but, when I got there, I just carried on walking and thinking.

For all his kindness, Walter seemed to be less than enthusiastic in helping me to get even with Andrews. It was as if he didn't want to rock the boat. Perhaps I was wrong to be surprised but he had been so generous to me since his arrival that I had come to rely on him.

But there was something else, something intangible that seemed to be informing his attitude. I tried to work it out but gave up – partly because I wasn't getting anywhere but mostly because it was hard enough trying to second-guess my enemies without starting on my friends.

In avoiding a party of French schoolchildren, I almost tripped over an empty Fanta can. In my annoyance, I dribbled it down the street before kicking it across the road. A taxi driver shouted at me and I gave him the finger which enraged him so much I thought for one ghastly moment that he was going to get out and throttle me. I put up a hand to placate him. What was I doing? What had I become? Why was I taking out my anger on a stranger? It wasn't he, after all, who had nicked my game-show idea.

It was Andrews. Now, how was I going to get even with him? Well, not by getting mad, that was for certain.

How could I hurt him? *Really* hurt him?

What did he care about? Himself. Sparkle. That was about it really. Whether or not Walter was right about Emma and Andrews's relationship with her, I was pretty sure that she didn't matter to him nearly as much as his business, which really defined him. And what was the cornerstone of that business? No question: it was *The Lot.*

So how could I sabotage the programme? Well, I could key in some wrong answers – obviously only on Frank and Simon's questions – no, make that just Frank's questions. But would that work? Wouldn't they be spotted at the show? Yes, but now we were live, it would be embarrassing. But then it could rebound on to me. Besides, what was in it for me? All that risk – to achieve what? Embarrassment for Andrews? No, I wanted more than that. For him and for me.

*What was in it for me?*

If I could tamper with questions – and there was no doubt that I could – was there anything else I could do? What about the contestants? Could I do anything with them? No, but I knew a contestant researcher who could. I caught up with myself. I didn't want to involve Gaby in any of this. So what did I want? I wanted to make Andrews rue the day he decided to cheat me but, just as importantly, I needed to get even, to get what was due to me. As I had done at Paxton's.

Yes, but that was only five hundred pounds. This time I wanted more – much more. How much more? Lots more. Thousands. A million. But how could I get my hands on that sort of money at Sparkle? It wasn't exactly kept in the petty cash drawer. And that was when it hit me. There was a million up for grabs: maybe even more. It was called *The Lot*.

I had reached the edge of Hyde Park. Suddenly, the enormity of what I was even beginning to think of contemplating was so breathtaking that I had to sit down on a park bench.

Was I mad, or was it just possible that I had found something that would change my life?

# CHAPTER THIRTY

By the time I reached home, I was almost high on the idea of becoming a millionaire at Andrews's expense. Unfortunately – and this is a perennial failing of mine – I was so intoxicated with the ends that I couldn't focus on the means.

It was time for a council of war.

Five-thirty was always a good time to find both Peter and Ziggy at home. Peter because, like Dracula, he never went out during the day and Ziggy because, like a complete sad sack addicted to television, he never went out in the evening. They were as different in the hours they kept as they were in everything else.

People like to distinguish between what they call 'the sexes' but I think that's too simplistic. When men live together without the opposite sex – and I'm sure the same's true for women – they divide up *all* the human characteristics between them. It's as true for flatmates as it is for other people in any single-sex institution like prisons or religious communities.

So whereas Ziggy was almost obsessively tidy, Peter was a slob. Whereas Peter forswore meat, apart from bacon butties, but gorged himself on illegal substances, Ziggy was the trencherman's trencherman but wouldn't dream of putting even a cigarette in his mouth – certainly not when there was food to cram in instead. The only thing they had in common was a crappy taste in music.

However, it was for their differences that I valued them – especially now. Much as I dreaded hearing arguments against what I was proposing, I was aware of how much I needed them. So it was with this in mind that I sat them down in the lounge and informed them I had something of vital importance to say.

'Have you brought us here for the reading of the will?' asked Peter.

'Isn't that my job?' said Ziggy.

'No.'

'What, because I'm a barrister?'

'No, because you're a crap lawyer.'

'Children!' They were only indulging in banter but I thought I'd stop it before one of them went too far.

'So what do you want, David, because I've got a joint in the oven?'

'Yeah, man, and I've got one in the ashtray.'

'Joint – joint: a play on words. I get it. A sort of a joke – without the funny bit at the end.' I sat upright in the moth-eaten armchair and tried to segue into my plan. 'This, on the other hand, is no joke. You know the game-show format I devised? Well, Andrews has just sold it.'

'Top hole!'

'Bo!'

'It would be if he hadn't ripped me off. He promised me a percentage but now he's claiming that it's his because I was his employee at the time when I devised it.'

'As I told you before, David,' said Ziggy gently, 'he's got a point.'

'Yeah, I know, but I still feel ripped off – especially as he always treats me like a complete woman's front bottom.'

'If the Dutch cap fits,' murmured Peter.

'We've been here before, haven't we?' said Ziggy. 'I mean, I don't wish to be disrespectful, David, but this isn't the first time that you've whin . . .complained to us about your boss. What's so special this time?'

'This time, I plan to get even.'

'Hang on a minute,' said Peter. 'Haven't *we* been here before? You and that agency – Patten's?'

'It was Paxton's and yes, Peter, you're right, I do intend to take what's rightfully mine. But this time, I'm not talking about petty cash. This time, with your assistance, I'm going to help myself to a million. At least.'

'You're mad!' said Ziggy.

Peter decided to give me the benefit of the doubt. 'Hear him out.'

'Look, it's very simple. On every edition of *The Lot*, there's £250,000 up for grabs, but if the winner doesn't answer enough second-half questions, the money's rolled over to the next show. All of it. And then on to the next show and the next show and the show after that. Jackpots of one and a quarter, one and a half million, will soon be common. All I propose is that we fix it that someone we know wins and then split the money.'

'You're mad,' said Peter.

'No, wait a minute,' said Ziggy. 'Let him finish.'

I didn't actually have very much more at that precise moment. So I busked it. 'OK, here's how it goes. We wait until there's a rollover of a million or more, then we get our man on to the show as a contestant. Believe me, that's not a problem. The next thing we have to do is brief him on all the questions.'

'Hang on a minute,' said Peter bewildered. 'There's thousands of possible questions. How on earth can you possibly expect yer man to remember all the answers?'

'First flaw – going down,' said Ziggy.

'I put my hands up, fellows, this is not yet the definite plan. That's why I've brought you two in to help me formulate it.'

'You're going to need a series of signals,' Peter said slowly.

'Good, I like it. But what?'

'A vibrating mobile phone?'

'There's no time – remember, it's a live show – and besides, how would it work?'

'One ring means it's the first option, two the second, three the third and so on.'

'And what if we didn't ring off at precisely the right moment? There's another thing: the security is extremely tight. Anyone who wins northwards of a million can expect to be thoroughly searched afterwards for wires and phones and any other possible aides.' Then I had a brainwave. 'Unless I made sure that I was in our man's eyeline and communicated by prearranged signals.'

'Not bad,' said Ziggy. 'Yes, I think it would work.'

'Point of order,' said Peter.

'The chair recognises you. You're Peter Franklin, porn addict.'

'No seriously, man. I've got a question. Isn't this illegal?'

'Er, yeah – just a little – but then so's smoking dope and you don't seem to have any trouble doing that. Besides, provided there's nothing to connect me to whichever person we use as our contestant, I don't see how it could go wrong.'

'I dig that, but what about the morality of it all?'

'The *what*?'

'Morality. M-O-R-A. . . '

'I understand the word, it's just your use of it in this context I don't get.'

'But you're stealing.'

'From whom? Andrews? So what, he's stolen from me. Judging by how much other game shows have made overseas, there's every reason to believe that *Astro Wars* will make him much more than I'll be taking – stealing, if you prefer – from him.'

'What about the other contestants?'

'I'm sorry, Peter, have you changed your fucking name to Jiminy Cricket? All right, for one show – and one show only – I'm conning the other contestants out of the prize. Is that so terrible?'

'Actually,' said Ziggy fussily, 'in point of fact, you're not depriving other contestant*s* but just one contestant. There would only have been *one* winner.'

'You see, Peter? I'm more decent than even I gave me credit for.'

Ziggy weighed in on my side. 'I, for one, am still interested in David's plan to make us all rich.' He turned to me. 'So tell me, old bean, have you thought whom you might use as your stooge?'

'What, you mean to be my contestant? No, I haven't but I should be able to think of someone: I've hardly got a shortage of friends.' They both pretended to suppress their giggles. 'I've got *lots* of friends!'

'How many?'

'What, including you two?'

'Yes.'

'All right.' I pretended to be counting to myself. 'Two.' They laughed. 'No, I'm only joking. I've got loads of friends: Billy Lots of Mates, that's me. However, can they be linked to me?'

'Ah,' said Ziggy, 'I see. For your *meister*plan to work, you need to find someone who won't have friends or relatives ringing the newspapers to say, "That bloke who won a million is a mate of someone who works on the show".'

'It shouldn't be too difficult, should it?' asked Peter. 'After all, you haven't actually been advertising the fact that you work on *The Lot*?'

'That's true, I haven't – although I have told a few people. The trouble is not *finding* someone, it's finding someone I can trust – one hundred per cent. That's what limits the field. I mean, just to *ask* someone is taking a huge risk.' And that was when it dawned on me. 'I've just had a thought.'

'I knew I didn't recognise the look on your face.'

'Ziggy, Peter, what is there to link you to me?'

'Are you joking?' said Peter.

'No. Think about it.'

'What about all our mutual friends and family for a start?' asked Peter.

'They'll know that you won and they'll know that we're friends but they won't know that I was working on *The Lot*.'

They sat there thinking. Eventually, Peter said, 'I see what you're getting at but, even supposing that I'd be prepared to do it – and I most emphatically am not – there are people who know me who know that I'm friends with you, that you're my flatmate, *and* that you work on *The Lot*.'

'Like who?'

'My mum, my dad, my sister Caroline, the guys in the band . . .'

'But I thought I told you not to tell anyone.'

'Not at the beginning you didn't. That came later. If you recall, when you first started, it was impossible to stop you talking about your bloody job.'

'Yes, all right. I take your point – though I never talked about *The Lot*.'

'It doesn't matter. It's enough that you talked about Sparkle.'

'OK, you're right, but what about Ziggy?'

'Who, me?'

'Is there anyone else here answering to that name? Who knows that you know me?'

'Well, a few people, I suppose.'

'But you're not close to any of those people. I mean, unlike with Peter's folks, I've never met your family and I can only vaguely remember meeting people you know, and how many of them would be aware of what I do for a living?'

'None.' He thought for a bit. 'No, none.' He warmed to the thought. 'You're right. We've always tended to socialise on our own rather than in a crowd.'

'There's nothing to connect us. Damn it, you

have all your post sent directly to chambers.'

'That's only because I'm always changing my home address.'

'And you're not even in the rent book.'

'Why on earth not?'

'Ask Peter. But *not* right now. Well, would you do it?'

Before Ziggy could answer, Peter interrupted. 'Hang on a second, David. He may not be much of a barrister but he is still a barrister. If he's caught, he'd lose his job, go to prison, everything.'

'Peter,' said Ziggy, 'if *any* of us gets caught we'd lose our job and go to prison. Besides, as I indicated to David just the other night, I am actively considering other areas of employment. My career at the Bar is, as you never cease to remind me, not entirely successful.' Peter and I looked away embarrassed – as we were entitled to be. 'However, my fine forensic mind has thought of one small problem.'

'What?'

'You mean who? Gaby.'

'I hadn't thought of her.'

'That's funny, you talk about little else.'

'I meant in connection with this.'

'Then you had better start thinking about her. Apart from anything, won't you need her help with getting me on to the show as a contestant?'

'I was planning to put you in the computer myself.'

'Isn't that difficult?'

'No, not if I put you down on the reserve list. The contestants are all checked and rechecked thoroughly but the reserves aren't – at least not until, literally, the minute they become contestants. The point is, we've never had a show when one or more reserves haven't been used.'

'I see.'

'However, Gaby's help would undoubtedly . . .' I cut myself short. 'I'm mad. There's no way she'd do it. No, the most I can hope for is that she'll turn a blind eye and not tell Andrews.'

'That's fine,' said Ziggy. 'So long as she doesn't work against us.'

'I'll get on to her immediately. What about you, Peter?'

'What about me?'

'Do you want in?'

He smiled. 'No thanks, David. As you know, bread doesn't ring my bell. But don't worry, man, you can count on me to give you advice and to watch your back.'

'Beers, mate.'

# CHAPTER THIRTY-ONE

As soon as I'd finished with the guys, I got on the phone to Gaby. We weren't meant to be seeing each other that evening but I was so full of my 'scheme' that I *had* to meet her to talk about it – and there was no way I was prepared to risk discussing the details down the phone.

'Hi, Gabes.'

'Hi, yourself.'

'I have to see you: we need to talk.'

'This isn't about "us", is it?'

'Only obliquely.'

'It's not about Michael, is it?'

'Again, only obliquely. Look, if I could tell you what it was about on the phone, I wouldn't need to see you, would I? Any chance of you coming over?'

There was a silence and then she whispered, 'No, you come here', and put the phone down.

Not trusting myself on the moped, I took a cab round. I didn't enjoy the ride because I was fretting about bloody Phoebe. Ziggy and I hadn't pursued any ideas for 'the number' we were going to do on her. Frankly, I couldn't even begin to think what we might do to pay her back and/or to send her on her way. Meanwhile, the very most I could hope for was that she would be out for the evening.

No such luck. As soon as I opened the door of the flat, I heard the bitch singing to herself. Oh well, I thought, I'll just have to ignore her. The trouble was, there was no sign of Gaby. I was tempted to go into Phoebe's bedroom and ask her where she was but, as a student of lousy sitcoms of the 1970s, I had no desire to be caught in there by Gaby.

So I phoned Gaby on her mobile but all I got was her answering machine. Shit. There was nothing else for it. I knocked on Phoebe's door. 'Phoebe?'

'Yes?'

'It's me, David.'

'Oh yes?'

'Do you know where Gaby is?'

She opened the door just enough to put her head out. 'She said she was going out.'

'What?'

'She said she was going out.'

'Where?'

'How should I know?'

'What, she was popping out to the corner shop?'

'Maybe. No, I don't think so. She was carrying her overnight bag.'

'Oh God, I don't believe it. She told me to come here. She must have changed her mind and gone to my place. What a balls-up!'

'Why don't you phone her mobile?'

'I tried. It was on the answering machine.'

'Then you're out of luck.' I was just walking back to the front door when I heard her add, 'Or maybe not.'

I turned round and there she was, totally stark bollock naked. I have to say it was a very fine sight but I was absolutely appalled. What if Gaby were to walk in now? Whatever I said, she'd give me my marching orders.

'Listen, Phoebe, don't think I'm not flattered, 'cos I am – but, you've got to know, I love Gaby.'

'What the eye doesn't see . . .'

'It's not a question of that. I told you before, I'm not interested. I only want Gaby.'

'That's bullshit!'

'It's the truth.'

'You're just scared.'

'You're dead right I am. Jesus, the last time you . . .you . . .offered yourself, I turned you down but you still told Gaby that I came on to you, so I'd be a complete cu—' with her beautifully presented binky staring me in the face, I found it impossible to use the 'c' word, 'I'd be a complete *idiot* to do anything now.' Suddenly, I found the courage to tell it to her straight. 'And you know what? You've got a good body and all that but I'd rather have Gaby any day of the week – and twice on Sundays.'

Before she could answer me, there was a noise from down the corridor and, incredibly, Gaby emerged from the airing-cupboard.

'Gabes!'

'Gaby!' said Phoebe, attempting to cover herself up in the way that women do, using two hands for three bits. 'I told him you'd gone out but he—'

'Shut up, bitch! I heard enough. You were coming on to David. Why?'

Hearing the venom in Gaby's voice, I was glad that I was between them, even though the thought of a catfight, of two girls fighting over *me*, wasn't totally unappealing. 'Hang on, Gabe.'

'This is nothing to do with you, David. Phoebe, will you answer my question: why David?'

'He's cute.'

Yes! Even in the middle of such a horrible scene, I was enormously flattered.

'There are plenty of cute men and not even you've exhausted them all. No, I'll answer my question. You wanted David because he's *my* boyfriend and because it's *my* flat. You're envious of him; you're jealous of me.'

'That's rubbish!'

'That's the truth – and you know what? In this case, I'm not just the prosecuting counsel, I'm also the judge and jury. You are guilty and you've got precisely one hour to remove yourself from *my* flat before I chuck you and all your belongings out the window. Do I make myself clear?' From the way that Phoebe hurried into her bedroom, it was clear that she did.

'What's going on, Gabes?' I asked but I knew. Obviously, after she'd invited me to come over, she'd told Phoebe she was going out and had pretended to do so. Then, she'd hidden in the airing cupboard to await my arrival and see what would happen. Suddenly, I realised the implications of what she'd done. 'Hang on, girl, why didn't you let me in on your plan?'

She smiled and I basked in her gorgeousness. 'Because I couldn't be totally sure?'

'Of what? Me?'

'No, idiot, your acting skills.'

I held her in my arms and tilted her mouth up to mine. We kissed. 'Gabes,' I said, 'I love you with all my heart.'

'That's a coincidence. I love you with all my heart.'

'Let's do it.'

'No, not until *she* goes.'

'I'm not sure I can wait.'

'Well, you'll have to and you know what else you can do?'

'No.'

'You can try a little foreplay.'

'What?'

'Just like I said. What is it with men that they go

from nought to sixty in five seconds?'

'Sounds good to me.'

'Well, it doesn't feel good to me.'

'Is that a complaint?'

'No, let's just call it a request.'

'With which I'm happy to comply. However, I would like to say one thing in my defence.'

'What's that?'

'In the two years before I lost my virginity, I did all the foreplay I was ever going to do for the rest of my life.'

'Well, if you're going to come and live with me . . .'

'Really?'

'Can you think of any good reason why we shouldn't?'

'No. Yes, actually, I can.'

'What's the matter, darling, are you married?'

'No. Seriously though, Gaby, there is something I have to tell you, to ask you, which might affect the way you feel about me. But before I tell you what it is, let me say that not only do I *not* expect you to be involved but if you don't want me to do it myself, I won't. All right?'

'I don't know: I'm intrigued.'

So, to the background noise of bags and suitcases being packed in the next room, I outlined my plan to take the lot from *The Lot*. As I spoke, I searched her face for clues as to her approval/disapproval but she was giving nothing away. I vowed never to play poker with her.

By the time I finished, I was in a classic 'you want, you'd settle for, you get' position. You know, you want a week in the Caribbean with Kelly Brook, you'd settle for a weekend in Paris with Kim Basinger, you get a night out in Nuneaton with Irene Handl. Here, I wanted her participation, I'd have settled for her acceptance but I expected to get her disapproval.

'You are aware, are you not, that you're asking me to break the law?'

'I'm not asking *you* to do anything: I'm just telling you what *I'm* proposing to do.'

'Even telling me amounts to the same thing. You're making me a what-do-you-call-it?'

'Accessory?'

'Precisely. Besides, if – and please note the word *if* – you were to go ahead with this, you would need my help.'

'I wouldn't want you to be involved.'

'Bollocks! I'd have to be – and you know it.'

'All right, so you'd be useful, I don't deny it.' I felt my spirits sinking. 'So I take it that's a no, then?'

She looked at me as though she were scrutinising me. 'What, do you think I wouldn't do something that would help the man I love? Or harm a man who only yesterday accidentally-on-purpose put his hand up my skirt?'

'He didn't!'

She surprised me with her vehemence. 'He fucking did. The scummy little shit.'

'You *must* go to the police.'

'I've got no proof and, anyway, I refuse to be a victim – especially *his* victim. So when you tell me how you're going to rip the scuzzball off, what do you think I'm going to say?'

Now it was my turn to play devil's advocate. 'Isn't there a danger we may be caught?'

'Why should we be? There's nothing to link us to Ziggy, is there?'

'No.' A thought occurred to me. 'What about Phoebe? Did you tell her about us and Sparkle?'

'Shit! I did! Hang on a second, though, she's never met Ziggy and she's only ever heard him referred to by his nickname. It's OK, we're fine.' She put my hand on her breast.

'I thought you didn't like being groped.'

'Not by midgets with fat fingers. Which doesn't get you off the hook foreplay-wise.'

'Damn.' I kneaded her breast mechanically. 'I really never knew how much you hated him.'

Her dimples disappeared as her face took on a serious look. 'Listen, David, don't think that because I don't complain about Andrews that I don't hate him every bit as much as you do.'

'Too many negatives for me.'

'What I'm trying to say, o man of small brain, is that my objection to your whining about Andrews was *you*, not him. I couldn't stand you using me as

an emotional punchbag, taking out your anger
with him on me.'

'I see. I'm sorry. No, honestly, I am. That's why I
wasn't sure about telling you this.'

'No, this is different. This isn't a problem, this is
a solution.'

We heard the front door slam. Alone at last! It
was time to make love which, after a period of
foreplay which was too long for me and too short
for her, we did. Afterwards, as we lay in each
other's arms – and I discovered that I did in fact
have an appetite for 'afterplay' – Gaby asked me
what the next step was.

'I don't know,' I said, deliberately misunderstanding her. 'A piss, probably followed by a
pizza.'

'Idiot! What's happening next with your plan?
How are we going to sort out the money?'

'What do you mean?'

'How's the money going to be shared and what
are we doing with it?'

'I don't know: I hadn't thought about it yet.'

'Well, think about it.'

'OK. It's going to be a three-way split between
you, me and Ziggy. That's only fair because
although you and I are a couple . . .'

She interrupted me. '. . . a couple that live
together but still keep two flats just in case.
Agreed?'

'Yes, under sufferance. Although we are a

couple-that-live-together-but-still-keep-two-flats-just-in-case, you and I are equal partners because we are each carrying out separate, vital functions. Talking of which, you'll be responsible for getting Ziggy on the show.'

'No problem. What about the money?'

'What about it? I told you – it's a three-way split.'

'Yes, but what are we going to do with it? Should we create a bank account for the three of us?'

'Wouldn't it just be one more thing to tie the three of us together? How would it work?'

'One account with cheques to be signed by any two of us.'

'Blimey! You done this before, girl? Hang on, though, doesn't that work against Ziggy? I mean, couldn't you and I sign a cheque?'

'Yes, but would you rip him off?'

'Obviously not!'

'Then how would it work against him?'

'OK, but I still don't like the idea of doing anything that could be traced. Since we all trust each other, why doesn't Ziggy put all the money into his account and then pay us our shares?'

'Sounds good to me.' Gaby nodded her approval. 'How? Where?'

'I don't know. In cash?'

'That's a lot of cash to walk around with, and where would we keep it? No, I think it's best if you and I open a bank account somewhere abroad and then get Ziggy to transfer our share there.'

'I like it. It's nobody's business what he does with his money and the bank would respect his confidentiality.'

She buried her head in my chest. 'So when are we going to do it?'

'Do it? We've just done it. I'm not Superman, you know.'

'*Très amusant*. When are we going to do the plan?'

'Soon as the jackpot's high enough.'

'What is it at the moment? Three quarters of a million?'

'That's right, but I think we'll wait for this one to be won and then watch the jackpot roll up again to, say, one and a quarter million and then strike.'

'What if it gets won at a million?'

'That's just the risk we take. We'd have to start again.'

'It's going to play havoc with our nerves.'

'Especially Ziggy's. We'll have to find some way of calming him down.'

She giggled deliciously. 'I can think of something that would work. Shall I show you?' And, blow me down (to coin an apt phrase), she did. The little minx.

# CHAPTER THIRTY-TWO

I didn't see Ziggy over the next few days so I didn't know how he was feeling but I found myself under a considerable strain. Everyone else was behaving so normally while I was mentally working out ways of refining the plan. But maybe they weren't so normal after all! Didn't I catch Belinda peering at me strangely? Wasn't Karen looking particularly nervous? Hadn't Frank used the word 'plan' an awful lot?

I must have betrayed my anxiety. One morning, Simon initiated a trivia test – just like the tests we used to do in the old days before I'd met Gaby and before I'd thought of perpetrating a multi-million-pound fraud – and I was struggling to concentrate and compete.

'Come on, David, you seem out of it. What's the matter? Too much bed, not enough sleep?'

I smiled. 'No, I'm just a little preoccupied at the moment.' Shit, had I given away too much? I qualified my comment. 'You know, it's pretty remorseless doing all these questions for the book and the game and the computer game and everything. The thing I find the most tiring is checking to see whether we've done a question before in a slightly different way.'

'And so? What would it matter?'

'Simon!' said Frank in only a half-mocking tone. 'What are you saying?'

'Sorry, massa,' said Simon, again only half-joking.

'OK, chaps,' said Frank, 'here's a celebrity quiz. Questions I don't think I can use anywhere else. Which actor ate a live cockroach for *Vampire's Kiss*?'

'Nicolas Cage.'

'Correct. Who invented his duck walk initially to hide the creases in his suit?'

'That has to be Chuck Berry.'

'Correct. Which actress and singer's parents married – and divorced – each other three times?'

'I don't know that there isn't more than one actress and singer whose parents did that, but I do know that Cher fits the bill.'

'Correct. Which horror writer's father went out for a packet of cigarettes and never returned?'

'Easy: name a horror writer. Stephen King.'

'Correct. Which actress's father wrote the "plop, plop, fizz, fizz" jingle for Alka-Seltzer?'

'I haven't a clue.'

'Well, I'm glad to find something you don't know, Simon. David, do you know – because you haven't even tried to answer a single question?'

'Er, no, I don't. I knew some of the others but Simon just got there before me.'

'This isn't a fucking first-on-the-buzzer competition. If you know the answer, you have to shout down your opponent. Come on, man, pull yourself together! Anyway, the answer to the last question was Julianna Margulies from *ER*. Next question: Which vocal group taught Ben Stiller how to swim? David, come on.'

'How the fuck should I know?'

'You shouldn't necessarily, but how come you're not even trying?'

I sighed. 'I don't know. The Blue Notes? The Temptations? The Shangri-fucking-Las?'

'It was the Pips as in Gladys Knight and the Pips.'

'Oh, that's interesting,' said Simon. I forced myself to mutter something similar. 'Did you know,' said Simon, 'that Mark Wahlberg has a third nipple?'

Frank pondered it. 'Yes, I think it sounds familiar. OK, last one before I finally get down to some work. Which actor was born with a partly formed twin on his shoulder?'

Part of me was interested but most of me was working out what I was going to do with my share of the loot.

Simon tried a few names before giving up.

'Don't know?' said Frank triumphantly. 'Then

I'll tell you. Andy Garcia. Extraordinary, eh?'

'Brilliant,' said Simon.

'Interesting,' was the best I could manage – which clearly left Frank feeling flat.

'What the fuck is it with you, David?' he snapped.

Well, the thing is, son, you know this show we all slave away on? I'm trying to work out what I'm going to do with the money that I'm planning to steal from it. That's why I'm so bleeding preoccupied. 'I don't know,' I answered. 'Maybe I'm losing my appetite for trivia.'

I said it, of course, to cover up my real concerns but the fact was there was some truth in it. I, of all people, was actually getting bored with trivia. Was it simply that I'd overdosed on it during the past few months or – extraordinary thought – was I outgrowing it? Yes, that was it, I decided with a mixture of pride, excitement and panic: now that I was experiencing life myself – especially with Gaby – I had no need to live through other people, through celebrities.

As I was congratulating myself on my philosophical insight, Walter put his head round the door.

'*Guten Tag, Herr Oberst,*' I said to him as we walked towards his office. '*Was ist los?*'

He, naturally, replied in fluent German which flew right over my head, although I did manage to pick out the word 'coffee'.

We went next door to the coffee bar and, while he ordered for us, I looked around as though I were doing so for the very last time and therefore needed to store up some memories. I damned myself for being sentimental and tried to concentrate on Walter since I was much more likely to give something away to a quasi-friend like him than I was to a quasi-enemy like Frank.

'David, I have a proposition for you.'

I forced myself to slip into badinage. 'But, Walter, you know I'm not that sort of girl!'

He grinned and I was reminded that it was time I booked up for my four-yearly dental check. 'As you know, I've dropped hints over the past few weeks that I might one day need to ask you a favour. Well, that day has come.'

'I'm intrigued.'

'You should be. What I'm going to say to you is quite possibly the most extraordinary thing I've ever said to anyone.' The coffee arrived and he stirred in some sugar, leaving me on tenterhooks.

'Well?'

'Listen, David, I haven't rehearsed what I'm going to say to you so it might come out any old how. The key thing is, I need your discretion.'

'You've got it.'

'OK.' He sat back in his wooden chair. 'Let me start by telling you about myself. I'm fifty-three years old. My savings – in PEPS and TESSAs and unit trusts and building society accounts – probably amount to seventy thousand. I have no debts. I live on my own in a cottage in West Acton that's worth about £450,000. That sounds a lot but unless I were to cash in and move way out of London or abroad – which I'm not prepared to do – then I've got to live somewhere. Even so, I don't have a mortgage.

'The trouble is, I also don't have a pension. By the time I started thinking about such things, I was already in my forties and, what with AIDS scares and everything, I sort of figured that the future would take care of itself. Well, it hasn't, and now that my mother's been forced to sell her flat to get into a decent nursing home, it won't.

'All of which means that I have to find some way of safeguarding my future. You see, the fact is I've probably only got another five – ten years tops – left in this business. It's a young man's game – yes, and a young woman's too. When I started in television, it was still considered rather a raffish sort of job: perhaps a little bohemian. I always say that I wound up in TV because I failed in everything else. It's true: I'm a failed actor, writer and teacher. Traditionally, people like me found a refuge in TV. But now, it's the career of choice.

'Did you know that Media Studies is the second most popular course at British universities? Every year, these places disgorge thousands of eager graduates all aching to work in "the media". And they're prepared to work for absolutely nothing, just to get a foot on the ladder. And then there's the second and even third generations of TV producers. Again, when I started – Christ, I'm sounding like an old git! – people went into television precisely because they rejected the nepotism endemic in every other career, but now you can't watch a programme without seeing the name of this person's son or that person's daughter on the credits.

'Time was, I'd have friends' children picking my brains: well, last month, I got a call from the grandson of my original boss asking for some work experience. The thing is, it's not even as though these kids are useless: most of them are extremely talented and highly motivated. They're also much more computer literate than I'll ever be and open-minded when it comes to new media and new possibilities. The truth is that I still think in terms of the BBC and ITV and terrestrial television.'

'So do I.'

'Despite your youth, dear boy, I suspect you might be a dinosaur like me.'

'I'm not sure that's fair. I'm not a Luddite. I'm happy to adapt to a changing world.'

'That's true. Sorry, I wasn't trying to undermine you. What I was trying to do was to make you see that, guys like us, we're just guns for hire in a world that, increasingly, values us less. What are you on? Twenty-three, twenty-four thousand?'

'Twenty-five.'

'I'm paid five hundred a day.'

I did the maths. 'That's one hundred and twenty-five a year. That's fabulous.'

'Not bad, but that's only when I'm working. In between assignments, I might go for five or six weeks when I'm not working and therefore not earning. The point is, David, however much I earn, it's only income: it's not capital. And, short of winning the Lottery (which is an impossibility since I don't even buy a ticket) a guy like me has no chance of accumulating any capital. Which is why I need to talk to you. Because whatever's true for me will also hold true for you. Increasingly so. I don't want to depress you, young man, but it's going to become more and more difficult for researchers and question writers and the like.'

Up to this point, I still had little inkling of the actual point of our meeting. Then he changed tack. 'How do you feel about Michael Andrews?'

'Do you really have to ask?'

'All right then. I'm not a socialist but I can't help noticing that Michael has managed to become a millionaire – potentially a multi-millionaire – in the time that he's paid you and me a measly few thousand. What's worse is that his sudden wealth doesn't just coincide with our involvement: it's predicated on it. Now, I intend to redress this imbalance.'

I could hardly breathe but I managed to croak, 'How?'

'I propose to put into effect a sort of manage-
ment buyout.'

I was so expecting him to tell me that he was
planning to do just the same as we were going to
do that I couldn't help saying, 'But that's legal!'

'Obviously, dear boy. Why, what did you
expect?'

I recovered what passed for my poise. 'Oh,
nothing. It was just all that stuff about redressing
the balance.'

'I see.' He gave me a look that made me think he
had me sussed. 'No, no, no. I have no wish to see
out my sunset years in Ford Open Prison – even if
I could think of a good enough scheme. Why, have
you got one?'

I laughed as naturally as I could – which is, of
course, the most unnatural way to laugh. 'What
can I do for you?'

'Don't get me started! No, seriously, I'd want
you to head up my question-writing team.'

'What, you mean without Frank and Simon?'

'Bloody right I mean without Frank and Simon.'

'Wow!'

'It would mean harder work and, probably, less
money.'

''S'OK with me.' For a second, in all the excitement (pace Dirty Harry), I clean forgot my own plans
for the future. I took a swig of coffee in the hope that
the caffeine would stimulate my brain into saying
the right thing. 'When would all this happen?'

'Oh, not for months. But I wanted to make sure you'd come on board.'

'Yeah, no worries.' I felt rotten but what else could I say?

'One last question. Is there anything that could prejudice your involvement in this scheme?'

I swallowed hard, feeling like a complete louse. 'Absolutely nothing.'

# CHAPTER THIRTY-THREE

'Absolutely nothing.'

'You promise?'

'On Gaby's life. I didn't tell him a thing. Honestly, Ziggy.'

'Be careful what you say on my life, Lover Boy.'

'I am careful. That's why you and Ziggy should believe me when I swear on it.'

'Is it coincidence, Dabes?'

Before I could answer, Ziggy said, 'It's what Jung would call synchronicity.'

'You've impressed the chick, Zig, but I happen to know that you don't know diddley about Jung.'

He grinned. 'I forget that you're a fellow graduate of Bullshit College, Cambridge.'

I was going to reprimand him for questioning the depth of my knowledge but I was only too relieved to see him with a smile on his face. The fact was that ever since I'd returned home (to my bachelor flat) that evening, I'd been worried about Ziggy's state of mind. He was quiet to the point of terseness, he was nibbling on raw carrots rather than stuffing his face with chocolate and when I'd asked him what was happening in *EastEnders*, he'd shrugged his shoulders. All of which was very out of character and clearly indicative of his anxiety about the plan.

Later, after he and Gaby had finally accepted that I hadn't given away anything to Walter, he actually admitted that he'd been feeling the strain.

'It shouldn't be too long, should it, Dabes?' asked Gaby.

'I don't know, I really don't. The jackpot's now up to one and three-quarter million and no one's even come close to winning it.'

'You're right,' said Gaby. 'On Wednesday's show, the winner failed to answer four correct answers in the second half – let alone five – and on Saturday's show, the winner had to be knocked back in after everyone had been knocked out on only the second question of the second half.'

'I'm mad!'

'What's that, David?'

'I'm crazy!'

'Sit him down, Gaby, I think he's blown a fuse.'

I resisted Gaby's comic attempt to guide me into a kitchen chair. 'No, seriously. It's extraordinary how hidebound I've been by what was a chance decision.'

'Are you all right, old boy?' asked Ziggy.

'Fine, mate, never finer. Listen, girls and boys, I

said that we'd wait until the jackpot had been won and then we'd wait for it to build up again. But why? To give us time. But we don't need any more time.'

'You're right!' said Ziggy. 'What are we waiting for? Let's go for it tomorrow!'

I gulped. 'No, I think tomorrow is, as they say, a little previous. What about Saturday? Assuming, of course, that it isn't won on Wednesday. What do you think, Gaby?'

'I think we're looking at two and a quarter million!'

'Yes, I know. What I mean is, do you think you can get Ziggy on to Saturday's show?'

'Sure. Why not?' She turned to my portly flat-mate. 'What about you, Ziggy?'

'The sooner the better. I know I don't let it show but all this waiting around's really getting to me: I feel like one of those Battle of Britain pilots waiting for the call to scramble.'

I decided to go to Wednesday's show. No one was surprised to see me as I probably attended roughly half the shows – even though I wasn't required to. This time, however, rather than sitting in the green room (as I usually did) or at the back of the gallery (as I sometimes did), I found a place in the wings sitting next to Richie Clarke's personal make-up assistant, Sandra, who was friendly and pretty despite wearing too much make-up. From this position, I could see – and be seen – by some ten to twelve people in the audience. I made a note of the seats in question so that I could ask Gaby, who was herself seated on the other side of the studio next to the computer boffin responsible for the scoring, if she could ensure that Ziggy sat in the right seat on Saturday.

I was so preoccupied with working out how – and when – I would do my signalling on Saturday that we were three questions into the second half when it occurred to me to start tuning into what was going on right then. After all, if one of the nine people left in answered just three questions correctly, we might have an awfully long wait until the jackpot again reached such a huge amount.

The third question was actually one of mine and so, consequently, I was simultaneously thrilled and terrified. On what date does St Swithin's Day fall? Only three people gave the correct answer of 15 July.

The next (fourth) question was: Which European country produces nearly three-quarters of the world's rose oil used for making perfume? One person, a shifty-looking bloke – probably a pervert – opted for the correct answer, Bulgaria: the other two contestants chose France and Portugal and were sent on their way with the sort of sincere consolation that only Richie can fake so brilliantly.

One man, one question: Approximately what

fraction of the 206 bones in the human body are in the feet?

a)   An eighth
b)   A seventh
c)   A sixth
d)   A fifth
e)   A quarter

I couldn't be sure but I thought the answer was an eighth. And then it occurred to me that Percy Pervert (as I'd already named him) might just be a doctor or some other medical person who'd know all about the human body.

P.P. took the full minute permitted. 'Well?' said Richie, employing the question that had become a catchphrase all on its own. 'What's it going to be?'

P.P. swallowed. 'I'm going to gave to go for a), Richie.'

Fuck! That was my guess! Was he a pal of Walter's or had Simon suddenly become ambitious?

Bugger! It was back to square bloody one and who knew if or when the jackpot was ever going to be as big again. Why hadn't we gone for it that night instead of waiting till Saturday! And then I heard Richie saying, 'I'm so sorry. Honestly I am. I really wanted you to win. The correct answer was actually e.' Never before had I been so elated to get a question wrong.

£   £   £

Albert Einstein said, 'When you sit with a nice girl for two hours, you think it's only a minute. But when you sit on a hot stove for a minute, you think it's two hours. That's relativity.' He should have tried being in my shoes between the Wednesday and the Saturday. He'd have had a whole new theory to brag about: tb = 2,250,000f – the time spent on the bog is equal to a man's natural fear equivalent in seconds to the number of sponduliks he's trying to scam off his boss.

Gaby, on the other hand, was as cool as one of Belinda's 'good mornings'. Watching and listening to her running through the plans with almost military precision, I was reminded of Dame Judi Dench as M in the Bond films. It was women like Gaby who'd held the Empire together. Unfortunately, it was men like me and Ziggy and Peter who'd lost it.

It was Thursday and the four of us were in my flat swigging non-alcoholic (on Gaby's orders) drinks.

'So what are you going to do after you've won the money?' asked Peter.

'Fucking spend it!' said Ziggy to a massive thumbs-up from me.

Gaby said, 'If we're to attract as little attention as possible then I suggest that we are discreet.'

'How do you mean, Gabes?'

'The easiest way to be found out is to give up

our jobs and go out on a great spending spree.'

'Yeah, but you can't expect me to carry on working for Andrews? Not with all that money?'

'I can and I do expect you to carry on working for Sparkle – as, of course, will I. I also expect you *not* to splash money around like a sailor on shore leave but to carry on as if, for the life of you, you haven't got a pot to piss in. It's the only way. Do you understand, David?'

'Ah, come on, Gabes.'

'She's right, man,' said Peter.

Ziggy nodded too. 'I take it that these strictures do not apply to myself.'

'Of course not. It would be strange if you *didn't* stop working and spent lots of money. You will be in the media spotlight for a week or two: you should buy a couple of Porsches and a cottage for your granny at the very least.'

'So when *will* I be able to leave bloody Sparkle?' I asked.

'Not until your contract ends.'

'But that's another two and a half months!'

'Which will give you plenty of time to plan our future.'

'Ah,' said Peter to Ziggy, 'young lovers. Doesn't it warm your heart?'

'Fuck off, hippy,' said Gaby.

'The only thing I don't understand is what we do physically with the money.'

'Tell him, Ziggy.'

'As I understand it, I run to the bank as fast as my stubby legs will take me and pay in my winner's cheque. As soon as it clears – and I'm to ask for special clearance – I arrange for your share of the spoils to be wired . . .'

'Sorry to interrupt,' I said, 'but are you sure, Peter, that you don't want a share of this?'

'Nope. I mean, yes, I am sure I don't want any.'

'You can't say we didn't offer you the choice. Go on, Ziggy.'

'As I say, I arrange for the money to be wired to the bank account that Gaby's setting up in the Dominican Republic.'

Gaby corrected him. 'Dominica.'

'Same thing, isn't it?'

'No, it's not,' said Gaby in a school-marmish tone that gave me a bit of a thrill (such are the consequences of a public-school education).

'What made you choose there, rather than somewhere else?' asked Peter.

'I went there once with my parents, on holiday. It's beautiful and the people are helpful.'

'Sounds good.'

'In fact, I've just received a fax from the notary out there to say that the account will be set up by the end of next week.'

'How did you find him?' asked Peter.

'On the net. It couldn't have been simpler. I sent him our passports and he sent us the forms. We signed them and I sent them back by return.'

I smiled. 'We also had to sign a declaration that any money we paid in was legitimately ours.'

'It is,' said Gaby, 'sort of. Anyway, the notary explained to me that they don't really care so long as he can prove due diligence.'

'What's that, Ziggy?'

He grinned and shrugged his shoulders as if to say *he* had no idea.

'Ziggy,' said Peter affectionately, 'you are the giddy limit.'

'At least I'm not a slave to self-abuse.'

It was left to Gaby as the sole voice of maturity to bring the meeting to order. 'Is there anything else we've forgotten before this meeting descends into complete farce?'

'Yes,' said Ziggy. 'You've forgotten to remind me not to scratch my balls when I'm on camera.'

# CHAPTER THIRTY-FOUR

It's funny how the memory recalls facts so much better than it does feelings. So while I have no difficulty in recalling the *fact* that I felt utterly and immobilisingly nervous the whole of Saturday, I now find it impossible to conjure up the feelings themselves. Thank God.

All I can remember is general apprehension – made worse by three days of almost zero sleep – giving way to waves of panic which I was obliged to conceal.

I couldn't resist looking for Ziggy in the crowd of people walking in but, when I saw his ghostly, haunted face, I really wished I hadn't. I told myself that he was probably shocked after finding out how we treated our punters like cattle. When that failed, I tried to persuade myself that his pallid complexion would be interpreted by other members of the production staff as simply nerves.

I took a seat in the wings next to where Sandra the make-up girl would be stationed and craned my neck to check that I could see Ziggy from that position. I couldn't. Where the fuck was he?

Trying to suppress my panic, I jumped up and scoured the audience until I found him. I looked behind me at the make-up table and realised that he was sitting in the correct seat: it was the make-up table that was wrong. No problem: I discreetly shifted the table a few key inches.

I looked at Ziggy until our eyes met. Neither of us acknowledged the other and I made a point of staring at various other members of the audience.

Gaby strolled over to me looking enviably relaxed. 'Hi, Dabes,' she said, slipping her hand in mine. 'How's it going?'

I whispered urgently, 'It's OK, I've seen him.'

Still talking in the same laidback tone – like she was Perry Como's fucking granddaughter – she said, 'Calm down, chump. Stop coming on like Secret Squirrel. Of course you've seen him: he's there,' she didn't even look over to him, 'that's why you saw him.'

'Fine. Now where are you going to be?'

'Over the other side of the studio.'

'What? Sitting down?'

'No, darling, you know that's wrong.' She might have been a mother telling off her child for flicking pizza crusts on to the floor. 'I won't be able to see him if I'm sitting down so I'll be standing just over there in his eyeline. Don't forget that he will look to you for his answers. If, for some reason, you can't signal, then he'll look at me and I'll give him the signal. Got that?'

'Yes, but you won't necessarily know the answer.'

'We discussed this yesterday. Obviously, unlike you, I don't have *all* the answers but I've been going through the printouts for the past few days and I should know some of them. The point is that I won't signal at all unless I actually do know the answer. Is that clear?' I nodded. 'One more thing. Win, draw or lose tonight, I love you with all my heart. Don't forget that.'

Her wonderful words buoyed me all the way to showtime. It was only when I saw Richie Clarke offstage punching the wall ten times – the strange ritual he does before the show starts – that the adrenaline started to flow.

I took a deep breath while I could and, for the umpteenth time, ran through the signals. Scratching my head or playing with my hair meant Ziggy should choose a), scratching my face or picking my nose denoted option b), raising my arms or stretching in any way meant option c), crossing my legs or feet was option d) and, for the second half, patting my chest or stomach indicated option e). It wasn't a foolproof system but, so long as my nerve held and I didn't become a mass of indeterminable scratches and stretches, it should work.

Richie did his pre-show spiel which varied from

all the other shows I'd seen him do by as much as half of one per cent and then the floor manager asked for 'quiet on the floor', the ghastly theme music played and we were down to business.

Maybe it was because my senses were on alert but, for the first time I noticed the ludicrousness of the floor manager exhorting the audience to cheer as loudly as possible only for Richie to plead with them to stop.

The first question was: What was the correct title of the film starring Hugh Grant and Julia Roberts? In the safe knowledge that Ziggy would know the answer, I gave an imperceptible stretch and was relieved when the entire audience gave the correct answer.

Question two was: Who wrote the Harry Potter novels? Once again, I was confident that Ziggy would know the answer but I scratched my face anyway. Incredibly, there were twelve members of the audience who thought that Roald Dahl or J.P. Donleavy were responsible and Richie – rightly – gave them a good going-over.

Question three was: What was David Bowie's surname at birth?

I wasn't sure about Ziggy on this one: right era, wrong artiste for him. So I picked my nose until the horrible sting finished and then heard Richie announce that we had lost thirty-two contestants.

The next question was: Months that begin on a Sunday will always have:

a) a Friday the 13<sup>th</sup>
b) five Thursdays
c) thirty days
d) the suffix 'ber'

It was easy if one thought about it, but the pressure of being in a TV studio can do strange things to the minds of even the most intelligent people. I twiddled some hair around my finger while I made a point of frowning at Sandra, as if I didn't understand the question. She smiled and made a face as if to say that she didn't know the answers to any of the questions. Bless.

In the event, only twelve contestants were knocked out – all of them selecting 'thirty days'.

Question five was: How many paintings did Vincent Van Gogh sell in his lifetime? This time, I scratched my head and, eventually, heard Richie say, 'It was one. From memory, I think it was *The Red Vineyard*.' From memory indeed! It was up there on the screen just below the answer. Nevertheless, we had managed to lose another twenty-seven people, leaving two hundred and seventeen, which was a tad high for five questions. Hopefully, we'd get rid of a goodly number on the next question, which was: Margaret Thatcher is a Baroness but what is her full title?

a) Baroness Thatcher of Chelsea
b) Baroness Thatcher of Kesteven

c)     Baroness Thatcher of Finchley

d)     Baroness Thatcher of Grantham

I had started to feel relaxed – too relaxed – so that instead of touching my face in some way for option b), I obeyed the demands of my body and stretched. Suddenly, the horror of what I'd done struck me. I had to do something – anything – to rectify my grotesque mistake. *But what*? Pull the cable out of the socket? OK, but which cable and, for that matter, which socket? What else? Run to the gallery and tell them that I'd stretched instead of scratched and so my mate would have been knocked out of the show? Hardly.

Perhaps he'd ignore me? Unlikely. Or look at Gaby? Why should he when I was clearly in view? Shit, shit, shit. All those hours I'd spent worrying about my fucking nerves – where were they when I needed them? If I'd been just a little more keyed up, there's no way I'd have given the wrong signal.

'. . . and, of course, the correct answer is b), Kesteven. Gosh, we lost one hundred and three people on that one – that's nearly half the audience.'

I gave a silent prayer that the light behind Ziggy's chair would stay illuminated to show that he'd answered the question correctly and was therefore still in. Who knows – perhaps he'd used his initiative and overruled me? I couldn't bear to look at his face.

One hundred and three lights duly went off. Ziggy was indeed one of the casualties.

Now I steeled myself to catch his eye. He looked absolutely flabbergasted – as well he might. I always thought that there was no worse feeling than panic but I discovered then that there was: the sickness of screwing up.

Another question was being asked but it didn't concern us: we were no longer players. I needed to consult a higher authority.

I scurried round the back of the set, tripping over cables the size of giant conger eels and bumping into the surprisingly flimsy wooden batons that supported the 'high-tech' set. There was Gaby with just the faintest trace of a scowl on her face.

'What the fuck was Ziggy playing at?' she whispered as casually as possible.

'It was my fault. I stretched. I couldn't help it. It was an automatic reaction.'

'Stupid sod.'

'I'm sorry.'

She looked away. 'All right, everything's not lost. We've still got the knock-back in question to come, as soon as there are fewer than twenty people left in.'

'Yes, but only the fastest ten get knocked back in. How can we ensure that Ziggy will be quick enough?'

'We can't. We'll just have to hope that he hasn't completely lost it. He knows the format of the show: he knows that there is the chance to get back in. Hopefully, he'll take it.'

'I won't fuck up again, I promise.'

'Let's hope you get the chance to prove it – *after* he's been knocked back in.'

I waited for the next question – something about the most recent book to win the Booker Prize – and then went back to my position by the make-up table. The fifty-seven people still in were reduced to just seventeen! Richie announced that all the people – two hundred and eighty-three of them – who had been knocked out would have the chance to get back in but only if they got the right answer and were among the ten fastest. What were the odds? 28.3 to 1? Even if Ziggy looked at me or at Gaby, he'd almost certainly lose by dint of the very time it would take him to look at us. It was crazy, especially as knockback questions had evolved in such a way that they were easy to answer but hard to answer correctly. Ziggy had as much chance of getting the right answer as I had.

On the spur of the moment, I decided *not* to signal in the hope that Ziggy would have realised that his only chance would be to go for it himself.

'OK,' said Richie, 'here's the question: How many minutes are there in three days?'

I couldn't resist having a go myself. Even if I'd written the question, which I hadn't, there was no way that I'd be able to remember the answer. It was simple, wasn't it? There are seventy-two hours in three days. So that $72 \times 60 = \ldots$ The horrible sting came to an end.

Richie smiled and said, 'Congratulations to all of you who got it right but, as you know, only ten people will be knocked back in and they are . . .' He announced the names. I didn't catch the first and the last eight also passed me by – for the fantastic reason that there at number two was none other than our plump friend Gary Manning!

We were back on track.

# CHAPTER THIRTY-FIVE

The commercial break was all that separated the first and second halves of the show. Andrews had persuaded the ITC to let him have just one extra-long eight-minute break in the programme instead of the usual number of short breaks but, even so, it was always an immense logistical effort to have everything set up on time.

All I had to do was move round the side of the studio until I was once again in Ziggy's eyeline in his new position camera right. I felt self-conscious but told myself that nothing could be more natural than that I should want to watch the rest of the show from the best vantage point.

There were sixteen contestants, the six who had answered all the questions correctly, together with the ten who had been knocked back in, and they were introduced in turn. Ziggy, who was eighth in line, said, 'Hi, Richie, I'm Gary Manning and I'm a barrister.'

Richie, who fancies himself as quick wit, said,

'Aha, so I'd better be *brief*.' And for *that* they paid him twenty thousand a show?

It was time for the first question: Who vanished on 2 July 1937?

a)   Glenn Miller
b)   Agatha Christie
c)   Amelia Earhart
d)   Charles Lindbergh
e)   Amy Johnson

I remembered writing that question. I liked it because the wrong options were all interesting and there could be no argument with the answer. It was time to have a little stretch.

Ziggy was one of only seven people to answer it correctly. Richie pretended to mop the sweat from his brow. 'One of you lucky people might be just four questions away from the biggest prize ever won on British TV. So let's have the next question.'

Once again, it was one of mine. What was Pablo Picasso's mother's maiden name?

a)   Picasso
b)   Paloma
c)   Pabla
d)   Pueblo
e)   Guernica

I scratched my head to indicate that Pablo had

used his mother's maiden name. It was meant to be a trick question but, in the event, only one person was knocked out. I felt a surge of panic. This could go on for ages: what if a question came up where I simply didn't know the answer?

Typically, my bowels decided to join in and I had to fight the urge to run to the loo. 'Just another ten minutes,' I told myself, 'then you can spend the rest of your life on the bog.'

The third question of the second half was: By what name is Bechuanaland now known?

a)  Botswana
b)  Benin
c)  Lesotho
d)  Mali
e)  Gabon

My first instinct was that I had no fucking idea but the one good thing about adrenaline is that it doesn't half slow down time so that, after what seemed like five minutes but was actually five seconds, I recalled that Bechuanaland was the former name of Botswana.

Once again – only this time more manically – I scratched my head and then, fearing that I might be spotted by other contestants or by the crew, I started playing with my hair. I couldn't have made my criminal intent any more obvious if I'd worn a mask and carried a bag marked *swag*.

Still, it worked. There were now just two contestants left in: Ziggy and a chemistry teacher from Kent named Irene. The fourth question was: To whom did Charlotte Brontë dedicate *Jane Eyre*?

a)     Mark Twain
b)     Emily Brontë
c)     Jane Austen
d)     William Makepeace Thackeray
e)     Charles Dickens

Yet another one of my questions. *Jane Eyre* is, in fact, the only nineteenth-century novel I've ever read, and I enjoyed it so much I read it twice. I crossed my feet in as desultory a manner as possible and looked forward to Ziggy being declared the winner as his opponent was, after all, a bloody science teacher who was unlikely to have read *any* novel.

'I don't believe it!' cried Richie after seeing the result. 'Both of our contestants are still in!'

*He* didn't believe it? How did he think *I* felt? How could that woman possibly know the answer? Was she also getting signals?

When the full implication of that horrendous thought sank in, I was almost poleaxed. The prospect of doing this – not for one more question, but for question after question . . . Well, it simply wasn't possible: one of us would have to stand down. By which time, we'd all be rumbled.

I carried on ruminating in that unprofitable vein until Richie called for quiet. It was time for the fifth question. In the moments before he asked the question, I discovered an essential truth about myself: for all that I had the self-image of being happy-go-lucky and adaptable, in actual fact, I like everything to be just so. The fifth question was always going to be just for Ziggy and all about winning the jackpot. I simply didn't possess the mental acuity to accept that we were still right in the middle of an unbearably tense contest to win an unbelievable amount of money. Funnily enough, even though I knew that at least half the contestants left standing were cheating, there was still a part of me that was excited by the prospect of television history being created.

'Right then,' said Richie, trying to be all understated and cool, 'are you interested in becoming two and a quarter million richer?' Irene smiled nervously; Ziggy gulped nervously. At least I was still in his eyeline though he was looking straight through me like that chap in the Roberta Flack song.

'Here it is: On average, at what speed does a drop of Heinz tomato ketchup leave the bottle?'

a)  3 miles per year
b)  5 miles per year
c)  10 miles per year
d)  15 miles per year

341

e)    25 miles per year

I hadn't written it, but once again, I had checked it. It was OK: the answer was 25 mpy. Suddenly, though, it wasn't OK. I realised, with a pang of panic that easily eclipsed all the other ones I had experienced that evening, that I had forgotten the signal for option e).

I ran through the signals in my mind. Option a) was scratching my head or playing with my hair; b) was scratching my face or picking my nose; c) was raising my arms or stretching in any way; d) was crossing my legs or feet. So what the fuck was e)?

My mind was blank: I couldn't remember. What on earth could I do? If I did a signal that wasn't a), b), c) or d), would Ziggy realise I meant e)? If I did nothing, would he look to Gaby? And would she know the answer?

With only a couple of seconds to go, I realised that doing absolutely nothing might just convey to Ziggy the fact that his mate, Sammy Shit-for-Brains, had forgotten the signal for e). In the absence of any other advice, he might as well go for it. Or was that wishful thinking?

The horrible sting came to an end and Richie asked the computer to give us the correct answer. Option e) was duly highlighted on the monitor.

Irene's hands went straight to her mouth. Did this mean that she had got it right? Ziggy, meanwhile, looked like a hedgehog which had just seen its only child get flattened by a truck.

'And which of our two contestants – if either – are still in?'

The names of the two contestants were punched up on to the screen while the studio – and, no doubt, several million people watching at home – held their breath.

Then, as if in slow motion, Irene's name went dark and Ziggy's name was lit up. He had won. HE HAD WON!

I didn't have to worry about betraying my feelings as the whole studio was going absolutely tonto.

Even Richie was whooping and hollering. Perhaps he knew that the moment would be replayed again and again on the news or maybe, just maybe, he was genuinely caught up in the excitement. After all, it would have taken him at least eight months to earn that much money.

The only person who seemed to be totally unaffected was the champion himself: Gary Manning. The truth was, of course, he was completely gobsmacked. Part of me was willing him to start screaming with joy but then, on second thoughts, I realised that he was best off reacting naturally. It was my reaction that needed controlling. So I smiled benignly and tried to look slightly amazed – as if I couldn't possibly have imagined such an extraordinary outcome but was taking it all in my stride like a true telly professional.

Which is not the easiest thing in the world to do when you've just earned three-quarters of a million pounds. Tax free.

# CHAPTER THIRTY-SIX

I was *dying* to talk to Ziggy but all I could do was shake his hand at the after-show party and make a ho-ho comment like, 'Do let me know if you want any help spending that!'

In truth, I doubt if I'd have got any sense out of him as he was practically comatose from what looked to me like a bad case of nervous fatigue. He was also going to be in for a tough time of it from the media over the next few days but he was under strict orders from Her Gabiness to base himself at his parents' house in Muswell Hill where, as far as Sparkle was concerned, he lived, and only to venture outside for essential things like doing photocalls and buying Ferraris.

The other thing he was allowed – obliged – to do was to go to the bank with his cheque. This, of course, would become just another act in the three-ring circus that was now his life.

*MANNING AND THE MANAGER!* ran the headline in one of the tabloids as Ziggy posed with some suit who wouldn't even have returned his call the week before. Still, that was better than the head-line in another rag: *COURT OUT!* All they had was an old photo, supplied by a 'friend', of Ziggy in barrister garb and they managed to stretch it into a half-page feature.

There were many other such inane and irrelevant stories. God alone knows how many rainforests were cleared in the quest to acquaint the Great British Public with my mate Ziggy. Even the broad-sheets entered into the fun. What interested them was the fact that he was a professional man taking part in what they implied was a prole activity. I recall one letter that started, '*Shouldn't Mr Manning's wealth, as derived from his practice at the Bar, have militated against his eligibility to participate in* The Lot?' I couldn't help having a chuckle over that. 'Mr Manning's wealth' indeed: any roadsweeper offered what Ziggy had earned in the twelve months before *The Lot* would have told his employer to stick his broom where the sun didn't shine. I doubt if Ziggy has ever pulled in over ten thousand pounds a year. If anyone deserved to 'win' the jackpot on a game show it was him.

I couldn't contact Ziggy directly but we had an arrangement whereby he would phone Peter (on a land line) and Peter would come round to Gaby's and let us know what was happening.

So it was that Peter turned up at three o'clock on Sunday afternoon, the day after Ziggy's big win. He plonked himself down in an armchair. I couldn't help but notice Gaby's grimace at the sight of Peter's held-together-by-dirt jeans coming into direct contact with her precious furniture.

'How are you doing, mate?' I asked as Gaby went into the kitchen to fetch some tea.

'Fine, thanks. The flat's a bit quiet with you and Ziggy not there. Quiet and peaceful and good.'

'And you're no doubt wanking yourself stupid all day long. Are you jigging at all?'

'Not much. We're in Staines tomorrow evening and then we're doing a corporate on Friday.'

'How much?'

'Share of the door in Staines and four thousand in total for the corporate.'

'That's good, Peter, but you could have more, you know that.'

'I know.'

'I mean . . . not just because we're mates. You've done your bit.'

He nodded and then shook his head. It was more eloquent than anything he could have said.

Gaby returned with a tray on which she'd placed a pot of tea and three cups and saucers and a plate of biscuits. It was wasted on Peter, of course – aye, and on me too – but somehow, I took pride in her daintiness, especially as it wasn't at the expense of her toughness or intelligence.

'Come on, Peter,' she said.

He spread himself out as if to make sure that no

part of Gaby's armchair would escape contact with his filthy clothes. 'All right,' he drawled, 'I spoke to Ziggy. He didn't make *too* much sense because he was still shattered but he told me to tell you, David, that you're an idiot.'

'Thanks, mate.'

'That's him talking, man, not me but I'm not altogether sure I disagree. What the hell did you mean by giving him the wrong answer to that Margaret Thatcher question?'

'It was a mistake. I stretched when I should have scratched. I'm sorry – honestly I am. Please tell him that it was a simple human error. If it's any consolation, it completely did my head in.'

'I'm sure that'll console him.'

'But he understood that I was leaving him to his own devices on the knock-back in question?'

'Oh yeah, he told me to tell you that, even before the question was asked, he'd decided to press a button – *any* button – as quickly as he could and take his chances that it was the right one.'

'Hang on a sec – are you telling me that this whole thing rested on him taking a random one-in-four chance? Gaby, I feel weak.'

She was as cool as ever. 'I see his point. If he'd waited for you to signal, he'd have lost anyway. If he'd tried to work it out himself, he might have got it wrong and even if he'd got it right, the chances are he wouldn't have been in the first ten. Actually, come to think of it, with over two hundred and eighty opponents and only four options, hitting a button quickly and randomly is probably the best policy.'

'I'm glad you can be so dispassionate, Gabes. I'm still shitting myself. Talking of which, Peter, how is Ziggy? I mean besides being shattered.'

'He's fine. Apparently, his mother thinks he's looking a bit peaky and so she's feeding him up with all his favourite meals.'

'I thought all meals were his favourite.'

'Peter,' said Gaby, 'David told me what he did with the tomato ketchup question. Did Ziggy realise what had happened?'

'Yeah. In that sense, David's fuckwittedness earlier stood him in good stead. Ziggy reckoned that anyone who could send the wrong signal was equally capable of forgetting a signal – especially one that was only used in the second half. So he backed a possibility against a certainty: the certainty that he himself hadn't got a clue what the right answer was.'

Before I could leap to my own defence, Gaby said, 'He's not a *total* fuckwit. At least he did nothing: he didn't start going into semaphore mode as you might have expected him to do.'

I was open-mouthed. Here were my partner and my best friend agreeing on just how much of a moron I was. It was time to reassert my authority. 'Excuse me, children, have you forgotten that I was the mastermind, the criminal genius, who put this whole caper together?'

'Is that the same mastermind who had to come running to me when he decided to take a two-million-pound stretch?'

I couldn't help giggling. After all, she was only joking. Wasn't she? Before I could say anything else, the conversation moved on to more practical matters. 'Does Ziggy know what he's got to do with the money?' asked Gaby.

'Yes, he's going to the bank first thing tomorrow.'

'He wants to ask for it to be specially presented. His bank can courier it round to the issuing bank and it'll clear by the following day. Certainly by Wednesday.'

'Coo,' I said, 'my little darling's been doing her homework, hasn't she?'

'Shut up, creep,' was 'my little darling's' pithy response. She turned back round to Peter. 'Does he know what he's got to do next?'

'Yeah. He's got to have it transferred . . .'

'. . . a telegraphic transfer.'

'Whatever. It'll be sent to your account and then, well, that's it.'

There was a silence as the three of us tried to work out if there was anything else we'd omitted to mention. Eventually, I picked up an internet access CD which had come free with the Sunday papers and chucked it at Peter. 'I really appreciate all the help you've given us with this, Peter.'

'A Chinky – menu D – will absolve you of all obligation towards me.'

'Bo!'

'Beers!'

# CHAPTER THIRTY-SEVEN

As Ziggy was paying his cheque into the bank, I was returning to the office.

Contrary to what I'd feared, over the next couple of days, work became almost a sort of refuge. At least my mind was occupied with writing quiz questions for the computer game, which required a lower standard of care than the programme, and the very fact that I couldn't talk to work colleagues about 'the plan' meant that I wasn't becoming too obsessive. Also, ever since beating me up, Simon had become almost a friend and Walter was being extra nice – presumably because of our new business relationship. True, Frank was being no less supercilious but he wasn't being any more supercilious either, while Andrews was so busy seeing overseas buyers and network chiefs that I only saw him once in the two days after Ziggy's 'win'.

Mind you, that once was enough. 'You know why I'm successful and you're not?' he said to me when he popped into the writers' office to remind me how reptilian he was.

'No,' I said, wishing that Simon – or even Frank – had been in the room so that I could have had a moan and/or a giggle with them afterwards.

'Because you work for me. And you know why that is?'

'No.'

'Because I take chances. When I started Sparkle, I took a chance; when I bought *The Lot*, I took a chance; when I hired you, I took a chance.'

I raised my eyebrows as if to thank him for his praise – however oblique it might have been.

He realised his error and immediately put the record straight. 'Yeah, well, not every chance pays off, but the point I'm making is that in order to be successful, you've got to go for it, you've got to have balls, you've got to be prepared to screw the other bastard before he screws you.'

Those were the last words he ever spoke to me, in the flesh as it were, and I can still see the little toad in my mind's eye: all puffed up with conceit. He was wanking over me, no less than he'd wanked over poor old Karen. Like Gore Vidal, it wasn't enough for him to succeed, others must fail. I found myself wishing that I could tell him what I'd done to him – just to puncture his ego.

I needn't have worried: he was going to find out much sooner than I could ever have imagined.

It happened like this. On the Wednesday, I went into work feeling on a more even keel than I had done since Saturday. Of course, looking back, that alone should have put me on my guard as I've always known that it is only constant apprehension that keeps bad news at bay. But, after a wonderful evening in which Gaby and I had discussed our plans for the future, I felt relaxed. We'd decided that, after a few more months at Sparkle, we would pursue a life of leisure, splitting our time between London, where I would write books, and the Caribbean, where Gaby would learn to dive.

It was with this in mind that I sipped a caffe latte and glanced through the newspapers. There was only one story about Ziggy – some rubbish about how his greatest wish was to visit the *EastEnders* set and how the newspaper in question was going to fix it for him. I was just thinking how unfair it was that, as soon as you win big money, newspapers can't do enough for you – at the very point in your life that you don't need them – when Gaby walked into the writers' room.

'Hello, hamster,' said Simon. He was being affectionate – not, as I'd already proved, that I'd have been able to do anything about it if he were being unaffectionate.

'Hello yourself, one-inch. David, can I have a word?'

'Don't you two get enough of each other?' asked Frank. He *wasn't* being affectionate.

'Evidently not,' I said as I followed Gaby to her office.

'Sit down, David,' she said in such a calm voice that I immediately panicked.

'What's up? Has Mum died?' I didn't know why that sprang to mind: maybe it was the degree of gravity in her voice.

'No, it's not that. Now, calm down, OK? In a sense it's good news – at least, it's good news that I took the call just now. It's the press: they know about the link between you and Ziggy.'

'WHAT?'

'Do you know someone called Amelia Mears?'

I didn't – not immediately – but the name sounded familiar. In spite of my agitation, it was almost a point of professional pride to be able to place the name. 'Is she a minor soap actress?'

'No. Apparently, she's an ex-girlfriend of Ziggy's and—'

'Fuck! She's the ugly stuck-up cow that Ziggy went out with – but what's she got to do with this?'

'Apparently, she read about Ziggy's victory and thought that the newspapers might be interested in the connection between him and you.'

'But how could she have known? It doesn't make sense. Ziggy knew that he wasn't supposed to tell anyone what I did for a living.'

'Maybe he thought it didn't matter?'

'More likely he was showing off. But why didn't he tell me that he'd told her?'

'He probably forgot, David. I expect it was a

chance throwaway remark. You know: "I bet you can't guess what my mate does for a living?" – that kind of thing. He probably said afterwards something like, "You mustn't tell anyone" and then never thought about it again. Maybe they were shagging at the time: you men don't care what you say when you're on the job.'

'This is no time for feminism, Gaby. What the fuck are we going to do?'

'OK, don't worry. No, on second thoughts, *do* worry. This is serious. Just don't panic. Like I say, it was lucky I took the call. This journalist phoned wanting to talk to Michael . . .'

'Where were Shelley and Belinda?'

'Shelley's off sick and Belinda's probably off shagging Andrews. It doesn't matter. The journalist wanted to know if we had any comment to make on the fact that the winner of Saturday's show shared a flat with someone who worked on the programme.'

'Shit! What did you say?'

'I said that we knew nothing about it but that we would make our own enquiries and get back to him.'

'Well done, Gabes!'

'Yes, but it's only a matter of hours before they track Michael down, and then—'

'Then we're fucked.

'Exactly. The thing is, has the cheque cleared and has Ziggy telegraphed the money to Dominica?

You're going to have to phone him, David.' I whistled. 'Speed is of the essence.'

I took a deep breath as though air as well as time were in short supply. 'OK, I'll phone Peter and get his number.' I dialled the flat. Thank Christ he was in. 'Peter? Listen, man, we're fucked. That girl Amelia that Ziggy went out with, she knows about him and me and the show. I've got to speak to Ziggy urgently.'

The seven or eight seconds he took to find the number might have been minutes, such was my anxiety. He gave me the number and I was about to hang up when Gaby prompted me to ask him to find my passport and to put a case of clothes together.

Not for the first time, my bowels understood the significance of her words just before my brain did. But there was no time for bog breaks. I really did have to control myself.

I dialled Ziggy's parents' number. Luckily he answered. 'Don't panic,' I said.

It was the worst thing I could have said. 'What do you mean? What's happened? What—'

'Ziggy, there isn't time for this. We've got a problem. You remember that girl Amelia? Did you ever tell her about me and *The Lot*?'

'No. I don't know.'

'Come on, man, think.'

'Oh God. Shit. I think I did. Yes, I did. I was just chatting. I'd forgotten all about it.'

'She's gone public. Has the cheque cleared? Have you had it tee-teed to our bank in Dominica?'

'Sure. I did it first thing this morning, as Gaby told me to. What's all this about Amelia?'

'Oh fuck. Look, that can't be helped. Stay by the phone.' Gaby mimed a suitcase to me. 'Yeah, listen, pack a suitcase, we're going to have to go away. Today.'

'Where?'

'Does it matter?'

'It does if we're flying. I can't fly. I'm phobic.'

Annoyingly, the names of Dennis Bergkamp, Whitney Houston and Billy Bob Thornton all flitted through my mind as celebrities who don't fly. 'What? Why the fuck didn't you tell me?'

'You never asked. It never seemed necessary to tell you.'

Gaby snatched the phone from me. 'Ziggy, it's Gaby. You've got to get on a plane.'

I stood next to Gaby so that I could hear his reply. 'I can't. Honestly, I really can't.'

Gaby looked at me helplessly. I shook my head as if to say that I was also stumped. Ziggy said, 'You two must go. Don't worry about me. I'll stay here and hold the line. I will say nothing and deny everything. Let 'em prove it.'

I detected defiance in his voice. Also relief: it was as if the potential full force of the press, the police and Michael Andrews paled into insignificance compared to getting on to an aeroplane.

'I'll phone British Airways and book us on to the next flight,' said Gaby.

'Will there be a flight to Dominica today?'

'Almost certainly not, but if we can get to one of the islands nearby – Grenada or St Lucia, perhaps – we can take a plane or a boat from there.'

I swallowed hard. I didn't like flying either, but now probably wasn't the best time to mention it. What should I do?'

'Grab anything you want to take with you from your office – oh, and call a cab. We're going to have to go from here to my flat to pick up my things, to your flat to get your stuff and then on to the airport. The number's in my address book.' She chucked a little blue book at my right ear.

I phoned the cab number and was about to go to the loo when Gaby said, 'It's all booked – even though I had to use two credit cards because I went over my limit on my Mastercard. We're going to Barbados on the 2.45 flight.'

I looked at my watch. It was a quarter to eleven. 'Have I got time to go to the bog?'

'OK, I've got to see Karen anyway. Just to check the insurance.'

'What?' Maybe I hadn't heard her properly. 'All right.' I had a thought. 'Hang on. Gaby, did you get the name and number of that journalist who phoned?' She nodded. 'Bring it with you. I'll phone from the taxi and claim to be Andrews's lawyer. I'll tell him we've got nothing to say.'

'That won't stop them publishing.'

'But it will stop them phoning Andrews again – at least until we're out of the country.'

'Dabey boy, you're a genius. Come on, let's go.'

And without a backward glance I left Sparkle for ever.

# CHAPTER THIRTY-EIGHT

We were about forty minutes into our flight and I was sitting in the aisle seat, like any self-respecting nervous traveller, fidgeting and fretting about our perilous situation.

Gaby put down her headphones. 'Will you calm down? You're ruining an enjoyable flight.'

'Enjoyable flight, huh? That's an oxymoron.' I grabbed some of her cheesy crackers – the ones they give out with the drinks – and stuffed them in my mouth. 'How can you enjoy the flight when, like as not, we'll be coming back in a few days, handcuffed to prison officers?'

'Don't be ridiculous, David. This isn't *The Lavender Hill Mob* and you're not Alec Guinness.'

'Yes, but even so, you're mad if you think that Andrews won't unleash the dogs of war.'

'Oh, I've no doubt that he'll be a little peeved . . .'

'A *little*? Jesus, I've seen him lose it completely over *nothing*. When he finds out . . .'

'Maybe he won't.'

'What, you think that call I made to the journalist will stop them printing the story?'

'They won't print it without some *sort* of comment from Sparkle.'

'You gave them that though, didn't you, Gaby, when you said that we'd be looking into it.'

'Yes, but that's nothing. They can't just print her story – not without any proof. Ziggy or Sparkle could sue the paper for millions. So long as Ziggy keeps to his policy of saying nothing and denying everything, then that's it. There's nothing to connect him to her, is there?'

'Not as far as I know, but she's been to my flat.'

'And? So?'

'Well, she could prove that possibly. She could describe me too.'

'So we say that *Peter* took her back there once and she met you. I know you're not meant to, but you must have told lots of people that you work on *The Lot*: any one of them could claim God-knows-what to get some money off a paper. And as for Ziggy, by your own admission he's not in the rent book and he doesn't get any post sent there so they'd have to do one hell of an investigation to link him to you. And why would they bother? He's a ten-minute wonder. He's already yesterday's news.'

I couldn't disagree with her but *somewhere* there was a hole in her logic. 'If all this is so, then pray tell, why are we running for our lives?'

She smiled, causing her dimples to appear. For a second, in spite of my angst, I considered making an application to join the mile-high club. 'Because we fear the wrath of Andrews.'

'My point exactly. Even if the press isn't interested in pursuing the story, he will be. He'll do *anything*: he'll employ private detectives to interview all our neighbours. Eventually, he'll find someone or something to link Ziggy and me.'

She gave me a sideways look. 'Maybe Michael will consider discretion to be the best policy.'

'Are you joking? His idea of discretion is calling someone a tosser instead of a wanker.'

'It's in his own interest – and those of the show. Think about it.'

I thought about it. She was right. If the deception had been spotted immediately, it might have been different. As it was, Ziggy had had so much publicity that for it all to come out now – as it surely would if Andrews pursued it – would be disastrous. The programme would be finished: it would lose all its credibility and integrity. As for the overseas sales . . .

Gaby interrupted my thoughts with something that had already occurred to me. 'It wasn't even as though it was his money. He'd have had to give it away to *someone*.'

'Yeah, but not to us – and that's the trouble.'

'Then maybe we'll have to help him come to terms with it.'

'What are you talking about?'

She bit her lip coquettishly. 'I told you I had insurance, didn't I?'

'Yes, you said something this morning about Karen and insurance. What were you on about?'

'Insurance, Dabes, just that.' She put her finger on my mouth to stop me interrupting. 'I might not have shown it, but I was just as worried as you. Despite our precautions, there was always the chance we'd get rumbled so I was on the lookout for insurance. When I told Karen . . .'

'*Karen*? You didn't tell her, did you?'

'I didn't tell her about the plan, no, but I did confide that I was worried about my future at Sparkle and she gave me a little dossier on Michael Andrews.'

'What was in it?'

'Nothing much about *him* but there was quite a lot on Joe Mackintosh, Andrews's sleeping partner.' She giggled. 'Rather him than me.'

'What about Joe Mackintosh?'

'It wasn't really clear but, from all the hieroglyphics and mentions of games, it looked like a record of cocaine deals.'

'Wow!'

'Wow indeed. Even if Andrews isn't directly involved, it would be damaging enough for his precious Sparkle to be linked to a drug dealer.

Besides, from the dates in the papers, it's obviously how Sparkle was financed in the first place.'

'That's fabulous! So where did Karen find all this stuff? In Andrews's office?'

She gave me a conspirational wink. 'No, she found it at Frank's flat.'

'Frank's flat? What was she doing thee?' And then I remembered his boast about taking her home and doing it to her doggy-style: 'the beast with a wheelbarrow'. 'How come Frank had it?'

'He must have taken it from Andrews. Who knows? Maybe he was blackmailing him.'

Something clicked. 'Perhaps that explains why Andrews gave him a slice of *The Lot*. It was his way of paying him off. I thought it was uncharacteristically generous of the little turd.'

'Andrews probably put together the dossier on Mackintosh just in case *he* ever needed it.'

'And Frank found the file – wherever – and took it home. I can see that. But what made Karen take it from Frank?'

'I don't know. *She* doesn't know. She just says she thought that it might come in useful one day.'

'Dead right it has! So where's the file now?'

'Karen's got the original – it's at her nan's house.'

'Karen *would* have a nan, rather than a gran or a granny.'

'Ooh, you're such a snoblet!'

'So have you brought a copy with you?'

'No, but I did put a copy in the bank.'

A thought suddenly occurred to me. 'Hang on a minute, why didn't you mention all this to me earlier?'

'It's been a busy day.'

'I didn't mean earlier today: I meant earlier. As in as soon as you knew?'

'And what would you have done with it? You'd have told Walter or you would have hinted at it to Frank or you would have confronted Michael. Do I need to go on?'

'No,' I said sheepishly.

'Good.' She picked up her headphones. 'Now can I get back to *Fawlty Towers*?'

That evening, we were lying on a desperately uncomfortable bed in a grotty hotel room just outside Bridgetown. Until we could fly to Dominica the next day, it was all we could afford, given our low credit-card limits. Frankly though, I couldn't have cared less. I was so knackered that I could have kipped down in the middle of National Heroes Square (or Trafalgar Square as most of the locals still call it).

'Dabey,' whispered Gaby as we lay in each other's arms. 'There's still something we have to do.'

'I'd love to, pet, but I'm knackered. Why don't you just give me a blow job instead?'

She pinched me. 'Idiot. We have to phone Michael Andrews.'

I sat bolt upright. 'What – now? But it's the middle of the night in Berkshire.'

'Precisely. We'll catch him on the hop.'

'All right. But first, as the Private Godfrey of this platoon . . .' I dashed to the bathroom for a dump.

When I emerged, she was sitting on the bed with her mobile telephone in one hand and her address book in the other. 'Do you want to phone or shall I?' she asked.

'You phone but I'll snuggle up so that I can hear what he says.'

'OK, but don't say anything or you'll put me off.' She dialled the number and, after three rings, a woman answered.

'Hello,' said Gaby, 'is that Emma?'

'Yes.'

'Is Michael there?'

'Yes, but he's asleep. Do you know what time this is?'

'About three in the morning?' She suppressed a giggle. 'It's extremely urgent.'

There was the sound of a phone being handed over and then Andrews himself was on the line. 'Who the fuck is this?'

'It's Gaby Taylor.'

'What the fuck do you want? It had better be important or you're out of a fucking job.'

'I'm afraid I'm going to beat you to it. I quit.'

'What?'

'I'm resigning from Sparkle. And so's David.'

'What the fuck . . .?'

'The reason I'm telling you now rather than in the morning is that there's a chance you'll be reading some rubbish in the paper about David being connected to that Manning fellow who won two and a quarter million on *The Lot*.'

'What are you talking about?'

'Listen, creep, and you'll find out.' I could hear him spluttering. No one talked like that to the boss of Sparkle, not unless they had a whip in their hand and he was paying them a hundred quid an hour to do so. 'Yesterday, a journalist phoned the office and said that some ex-girlfriend of Manning reckoned that he and David were friends.'

'Are they?'

'No. But even if they were, it wouldn't matter.'

'Are you fucking mad? Of course it would!'

'No, it wouldn't. You couldn't afford the publicity – even if anything could be proved.'

'I don't believe this! If your thieving boyfriend's ripped me off, I'll tear his fucking heart out!'

'No, you won't. Not unless you want to pick up a newspaper and read all about how Sparkle was funded by Joe Mackintosh's cocaine dealings.'

There was a silence at the other end. When Andrews spoke again, his voice was quiet and his tone was eerily even. 'Who gave it to you? Frank?'

'It doesn't matter. All that does matter is that I've got enough to make you do what I want.'

'And what's that?'

'Just leave us alone. And that guy Manning too. I'm sure he'll deny knowing this girl and if you say you've looked into it and there's nothing in the story, it will die.'

'I thought you said it would be in the papers tomorrow?'

'Paper. Singular. And I don't even know about that: there's just a chance. But, as I say, if everyone – especially you – completely denies it, it'll simply die.'

There was silence again while Andrews digested this. 'Where are you? You're abroad, aren't you?'

'That is none of your business.'

'You tell that boyfriend of yours . . .'

'You can tell him yourself.' Gaby thrust the phone into my hands.

'You fucking toe-rag!'

'Temper, temper, Michael,' I began, but Gaby indicated to me that I shouldn't wind him up. While she had been talking, I had worked out a brilliant paraphrase of that *Godfather* line, 'Tell Michael it was only personal – I always hated him.'

'I'll cut your fucking balls off! I'll have your kneecaps shot off! I've got people who can—'

'Listen, this isn't getting us anywhere,' I said crisply. 'Do I take it we have an agreement?'

'Cunt!' he shouted, and hung up.

I handed Gaby her phone. 'We have an agreement but I think it might be an idea for us to put more distance between him and us. Muddy the trail and all that.'

'What?' she said. 'Move on from Dominica?'

'Might be as well, just in case Andrews finds some way to trace the money. We must also phone Ziggy and tell him to get out of the country.'

'In case Andrews gets hold of him,' she agreed.

'Exactly.'

'But he won't fly – you heard him.'

'There are cruise ships. He could take the *QE2* across the Atlantic. I'll give him a ring. Would you mind if he joined us, or is three a crowd?'

Gaby cast her eyes down towards her belly. 'We're already three.'

'What?'

'Come on, brainbox, work it out.'

'You're pregnant?'

'Got it in one, Daddy Dabes!'

I took her in my arms and cuddled her as tightly as I could without harming the – *our* – baby.

We removed the few clothes we were wearing and got into bed. As we held each other in the hot Bajan night, my mind filled up with celebrities and their babies: the daft names they've given them, the celebrities who adopted babies and even the celebrities who put their own babies up for adoption.

I was aware that the only way that the David of old – the childish David of six months ago – could possibly have handled impending fatherhood would have been through trivia, but I was a grown-up now and it was time to act like one. So instead of offloading everything I knew, I told her the only three words she wanted to hear.

Besides, there was always tomorrow.

# POSTSCRIPT

I'm left-handed. Right-handed people live, on average, nine years longer than left-handed people do. I can't afford to waste any time. So I'll be brief.

Nothing ever appeared in any newspaper linking Ziggy to me.

After a relaxing week in Dominica, we moved on to Aruba where we're now looking for a house. After establishing that there was satellite TV on the island and that he wouldn't be eligible to practise law, Ziggy made his way here by ship via New York and Puerto Rico.

We're going to buy Walter a two-bedroom apartment on the island. He's been kind to us and we both feel a little guilty about not including him in our sting after he invited us to be in his scheme.

We've sent Karen and Peter round-trip tickets for a holiday at our expense. I offered to buy Peter a house or an apartment – here or in Britain – but he says he's happy as he is, especially as the band's getting lots of work. Nevertheless, in the next few days, he should be receiving a credit note for an original Fender Jaguar guitar which I hope he'll accept in the spirit in which it was given.

Sparkle has moved to plush new offices in Chelsea, I hear. Frank and Simon are still there. I might phone Simon one of these days – just to keep in touch. According to Karen, Andrews is still furious with us and, despite the continued success of *The Lot*, not too happy with the rest of the world either.

Gaby, who grows bigger and lovelier by the day, has had her first scan. They think it might be twins.

Which means that I'll be the father of twins – just like Jeremy Paxman, Robert De Niro, James Galway, Michael Buerk, Gary Oldman, Pele, Pat Cash, Graham Gooch, David Essex, Dr Hilary Jones, Mel Gibson, Mark Knopfler, Stan Boardman, Ed Asner, Ben Elton, Donald Sutherland, Gordon Ramsay, George W. Bush, Denzel Washington, Al Pacino . . .

# MITCHELL SYMONS

# All In

Steve Ross has had enough. Of gambling. Of losing. Of feeling bad about losing. Of lying to his wife about losing. Of worrying about what he's going to do when he's lost it all (the money, that is, followed by the wife and kids).

So naturally enough he makes a bet with himself. If his gambling account is in the black at the end of the year, he'll carry on. If it isn't, he'll top himself and leave Maggie to cop the insurance. That way, at least the kids are looked after, and he can escape the hell his life is fast becoming.

With Steve's luck it could go either way. But one thing's a dead cert. For the next twelve months he's going to experience the thrill of the ultimate high-stakes game . . .

Set in the twilight world of all-night poker games, betting shop coups and spread-betting mania, Mitchell Symons' debut novel is the darkly funny diary of one man dicing with death.

'If you've ever played poker on a Friday night, you have to buy this book . . . I couldn't put it down' Peter James

'A book about self-deception. We all deceive ourselves – but Steve would bet on it' Anna Raeburn

0 7472 7316 2

review

Now you can buy any of these other bestselling Headline books from your bookshop or *direct from the publisher*.

FREE P&P AND UK DELIVERY
(Overseas and Ireland £3.50 per book)

| | | |
|---|---|---|
| Baggage | Emily Barr | £6.99 |
| Mischief | Mark Bastable | £6.99 |
| Turning for Home | Sarah Challis | £5.99 |
| Faceless | Martina Cole | £6.99 |
| The Affair | Val Hopkirk | £6.99 |
| Homegrown | Gareth Joseph | £5.99 |
| My Sisters' Keeper | Bernardine Kennedy | £5.99 |
| Fathers, Sons and Football | Colin Shindler | £6.99 |
| Winning Through | Marcia Willett | £5.99 |

TO ORDER SIMPLY CALL THIS NUMBER

**01235 400 414**

or visit our website: www.madaboutbooks.co.uk

Prices and availability subject to change without notice.